12h2

THE
RAT
QUEEN

THE
RAT
QUEEN

PETE HAUTMAN

CANDLEWICK PRESS

Copyright © 2022 by Pete Hautman
Epigraph copyright 1923 from *Roycroft Dictionary
and Book of Epigrams* by Elbert Hubbard

First edition 2022

Library of Congress Catalog Card Number 2021953336
ISBN 978-1-5362-1858-9

22 23 24 25 26 27 LBM 10 9 8 7 6 5 4 3 2 1

Printed in Melrose Park, IL, USA

This book was typeset in Dante MT.

Candlewick Press
99 Dover Street
Somerville, Massachusetts 02144

www.candlewick.com

A JUNIOR LIBRARY GUILD SELECTION

For those of us who believed, if
even for a moment, in fairy tales

"We are not punished for our sins, but by them."
—*Elbert Hubbard*

A DREAM

The floor beneath her back felt hard and cold and gritty. She could not move, or even open her eyes.

Annie knew she was dreaming.

She had been here before. A sour, musty odor filled her nostrils. The ticking of sharp claws on concrete was closer. She could not draw a breath to call for help.

She *knew* she was dreaming. It *had* to be a dream. But the fear, the hammering of her heart, the icy dread—that was real. If only she could scream. That would break the spell.

Tiny claws tickled her leg, crept up her thighs, her hips, her belly, and settled on her chest. She sensed its eyes on her face. Tendrils of sour breath snaked into her nostrils. She heard the clack of teeth. She heard another sound as well: a feeble, terrified mewl coming from her own mouth.

Something touched her chin. A whisker. A tongue.

Raw terror shattered her paralysis. Her back arched. A ragged howl erupted from her throat.

"Mama! Mama!" Her cry broke the spell and ripped her free from the nightmare. She jerked upright, gasping, flailing her arms wildly, her heart pounding with rib-cracking ferocity.

"Mama?"

Familiar shapes appeared, faintly lit by moonlight coming in through the window: her little rolltop desk, her dolls perched on her dresser. A dim yellow stripe of hallway light spilled through the cracked door.

Her bedroom. She was in her bed.

Just a dream. The same dream.

The door opened. Papa, framed against the light. Not a dream.

"Annike? Are you all right?"

"I had a bad dream," Annie said.

Papa wrapped her in his strong arms and rocked her.

"Like you had before?" he asked.

Annie nodded. "It was trying to get me, and I was frozen, and then I was calling for Mama."

"What was trying to get you?"

"A scary animal. With teeth and claws."

"It was just a dream," he said. "We have no scary creatures here in Pond Tree Acres."

PART ONE

POND
TREE
ACRES

ARTHUR

Annie was swinging by herself when she noticed the curly-haired boy two houses down. She dragged her feet to stop the swing.

The boy was barefoot, wearing only a lime-green T-shirt and a pair of baggy yellow shorts. His right fist was pressed against his mouth. Sucking his thumb. His left hand gripped the ear of a floppy stuffed rabbit. The rabbit's hind feet dragged along the curb as the boy's feet slapped the asphalt, each step decisive. She couldn't see his eyes from that distance, but she was sure he was looking right at her.

The boy veered toward the curb and looked down at the sewer grate across the street from Mr. Wendell's house. He bent at the hips, thumb still in his mouth, bringing his face to within a few inches of the iron bars, peering into the darkness. After a few seconds he straightened, looked at Annie, and continued toward her.

As he came closer, she saw that his yellow shorts were printed with purple cartoon dinosaurs, and his hair was not exactly blond, it was more orangish. Annie had heard that color called "strawberry blond," even though it didn't look much like strawberries. The boy stepped up onto the curb and stomped across the grass to stand right in front of her.

"Hello," Annie said.

The boy did not reply. He just stood there with his rabbit clutched in his fist and his thumb in his mouth, staring at her through large, pale blue eyes. Annie slid off the swing. The chains rattled.

"What's your name?" she asked.

The boy stared up at her wordlessly.

"How old are you?" she asked.

The boy eased the thumb from his mouth. It was wrinkly from being sucked on. He held out his hand, fingers spread wide.

"Five?" Annie said doubtfully.

The boy nodded. He seemed awfully small for a five-year-old.

"I'm ten," Annie said. "I mean, I will be. Tomorrow's my birthday."

The boy was not impressed.

"Where do you live?" she asked.

The boy seemed about to say something, then changed his mind and stuck his thumb back in his mouth. Annie wondered if there was something wrong with him. Shouldn't a five-year-old be able to talk?

"I bet your mommy and daddy are looking for you." She offered him her hand. The boy looked from her face to her hand. He took his thumb out of his mouth and clasped her fingers. His wet, wrinkly thumb pressed into her palm.

"Maybe you live in the Andersons' house," she said, pointing across the two vacant lots at the next house over. The Andersons had moved away last month. A new family had just moved in, but Annie hadn't met them yet. She set off down the street slowly, so the boy could keep up. He walked alongside her, gripping her hand, bare feet slapping twice for each one of her steps. She felt very grown-up, helping a lost child find his way home.

Across the street, Mr. Wendell was weeding his flower garden. His orange cat, TomTom, had found a patch of sunlight on the front step. He was licking his paw and rubbing his face over and over again.

When they reached the sewer, the boy stopped and pulled his hand free. He got down on his hands and knees and pressed his face to the iron grate.

"What are you looking at?"

"Bunnies," the boy said. Annie bent over and looked through the grate. She saw nothing but darkness. She moved her face closer and heard something, a sound like paper rustling, and the *plop, plop, plop* of water dripping. It smelled like rotten leaves and dirty socks.

She took the boy's hand again and helped him to his feet. A streak of rust ran across his cheek where it had touched the grate. Annie wiped it off with the back of her hand.

"There are no bunnies down there," she said. "Come on."

They were almost to the house when the front door opened. A woman came out. Her hair was the same orangish color as the boy's but not so curly.

"Arthur!" she exclaimed, and ran toward them.

Annie let go of the boy's hand. His mother scooped him up.

"Where have you been?" she asked him, then looked at Annie with an expression that was both suspicious and grateful. "Where did you find him?"

"He came to my house," Annie said. She pointed at her house.

"Oh!" said the woman. "You live in the tower house?"

Annie nodded. Her house had a big brick tower set into one corner. The tower was taller than the house.

"It's the oldest house in Pond Tree Acres," Annie said.

"It's a very fine house." The woman smiled.

"My papa's uncle's uncle built it. He was a farmer. Mr. Wendell says it looks like a beer can stuck on a doll-house. Mr. Wendell lives across the street." She pointed. "He has a cat named TomTom. He's always fixing things. If you need anything fixed, Mr. Wendell can fix it."

"Good to know! We just moved to the neighborhood. I'm Emily Golden, Arthur's mom. You can call me Emily."

"My name is Annike Klimas, but you can call me Annie."

"It's very nice to meet you, Annie," said Emily Golden.

"Our street is named after my family. That's why it's called Klimas Avenue."

"Is that a fact!"

"Papa used to own all the land around here, but when I was born he sold most of it to Lucky Key Homes so they would build houses so there would be other kids around. My best friend is Fiona. Her daddy is a doctor. They live in the gray house." Annie pointed down the street. "But she's up north at summer camp. Fiona is going into fifth grade. I'd be in fifth grade, too, but I'm homeschooled now, so I don't really have a grade."

Emily Golden laughed. "My goodness, you are a fount of information!"

"Miss Mekas says I talk a lot."

"Miss Mekas?"

"She's my *aukle*."

"Your uncle?"

"My *aukle*. She's from Litvania."

"Litvania? Where is that?"

"On the other side of the world. Miss Mekas lives with us and takes care of me when Papa is working. My mama is dead."

"Oh! I see. I'm sorry."

"Do you have a cat?"

"No. Arthur would love a pet, but he keeps me busy enough all on his own."

Arthur was squirming in his mother's embrace. She put him down.

"Arthur told me he's five."

"Yes." She looked down at her son. "Arthur is small for his age, but he'll catch up. He likes to take his time about things."

"He doesn't talk much."

"Only when he has something to say." She rubbed the top of Arthur's head. "Isn't that right, honey?"

The boy had nothing to say.

"I should probably go home," Annie said. "Miss Mekas will wonder where I am." She started to back away. The boy tried to follow, but his mother grabbed his arm.

"It was nice to meet you, Annie. Thank you for bringing Arthur home."

"It was nice to meet you, too," Annie said. She couldn't bring herself to call the woman Emily.

As she walked away, she could feel the boy's eyes on her. She stopped at the sewer grate and looked back. Arthur and his mother were gone. She bent over the grate and wrinkled her nose at the dank odor. She peered through the slots and caught a glimpse of something—two shiny black eyes, a flash of yellow teeth, a blur of dark fur against the black nothingness—and it was gone.

Annie jumped back, her heart pounding. A creepy, itchy feeling scurried up her back and down her arms and tingled her fingers. She squeezed her hands into fists and backed away.

There was *something* in the sewer.

It was not a bunny.

2

MISS MEKAS

"I'm back," Annie announced.

Miss Mekas looked up from the ball of dough she was kneading. "You were gone?" Mekas's features showed no more life than the dough beneath her palms. In fact, her pale, bulbous face resembled a loaf of unbaked bread with a lump of dough for a nose, two round black eyes, and a short, flat mouth. Her gray hair was pulled back in a tight bun.

"I saw an animal in the sewer," Annie said. "It looked like a big rat."

"A rat?" Mekas's tiny eyes widened. She bit her lower lip and sucked air through her teeth. "Why you look in sewer?"

"Because Arthur was looking there."

"Who is Arthur?"

"This new boy. He just moved in where the Andersons used to live."

Miss Mekas nodded and continued to knead.

"What are you making?" Annie asked.

"*Kolduny*," Mekas said. *Kolduny* was one of her Litvanian specialties, small pockets of stuffed pastry.

"With cherry filling?" Annie asked.

"No. Some other thing."

Annie made a face. *Some other thing* could mean anything from mushrooms to sauerkraut to chopped kidneys—or all three at once.

"I make special. You like," said Mekas. The mouth on her doughy face curved into a smile.

"I'm hungry right now," Annie said. "Can I have a cookie?"

"No. You spoil appetite."

The door to the pantry was open. Annie waited until Mekas's back was turned and grabbed a box of vanilla wafers. She slipped out the back door. Mekas didn't notice.

Annie went outside to the old picnic table in the side yard, brushed the leaves off the bench, and sat down. She ate her first cookie in a circle, nibbling the tiniest amount around the outside edge until she had a cookie slightly smaller than the original. She nibbled around the edge again, and again, until it was no bigger than a nickel. She set the miniature cookie on the table and admired its roundness.

Annie took a second cookie from the box and thought about how to eat it. She had just decided to make it into a square when something caught her eye.

TomTom, Mr. Wendell's orange cat, was slinking slowly along the row of pine trees at the edge of the yard. He froze in midstep, one paw raised, tail tip twitching. Annie held her breath. She couldn't see what he was stalking.

TomTom shifted his weight to his hind legs, wiggled his butt, and pounced. A split second later came a terrible shriek. Annie jumped to her feet. TomTom erupted from beneath the pine boughs in an explosion of pine needles and dust. He hit the lawn running. The fur along his back and shoulders was puffed up and his tail was huge. Annie had never seen an animal move so fast. In an instant he was back across the street on Mr. Wendell's front steps, clawing at the screen door and yowling to be let in.

Annie looked at the dust settling in the pines. She moved closer, nervous and curious all at once. There could be wasps, or a wild animal.

She stopped about ten feet away from the trees and listened. She didn't hear any buzzing or growling. After a few seconds, she stepped closer and ducked her head beneath the trees.

She could see where TomTom had landed. There was a bare spot where the pine needles had been kicked away. In the middle of the bare spot was a hole about two inches across. The entrance to a hornet nest? Maybe it was a snake hole, or maybe a weasel lived there. She had never seen a weasel, but she had heard of them.

Annie found a stick about two feet long. She approached the hole cautiously, thrust the stick in, and jumped back.

Nothing happened. Whatever had frightened TomTom was hiding deep inside, or it had run away.

She wished Fiona was home so she could tell her what had happened. Instead, she ran to tell Miss Mekas because she had to tell *somebody*.

Mekas was still in the kitchen, her apron covered with flour, rolling out a circle of pie dough.

"Mr. Wendell's cat got attacked," Annie said. "By a wild animal!"

Miss Mekas shrugged. "I have cat in Litvania when I was little girl. He fight all the time." Mekas lifted the rolled-out crust and settled it into a pie tin. "Litvanian cats, they are strong." She looked at Annie. "You have letter."

A letter! Annie raced to the table by the front door where Miss Mekas always put the mail. It was all for Papa except for one postcard. The front of it showed two girls paddling a canoe under the words *Odyssey Adventure Camp*.

The back had Annie's name and address and was covered with Fiona's handwriting. Annie ran the postcard up to her room.

Fiona could print smaller than anybody. The letters crowded together, often touching each other, but Annie had no problem reading it. Fiona had seen some otters playing, and she got stung by a yellow jacket, and everybody made friendship bracelets out of acorns, and she went swimming every day, and she said she missed Annie and wished she was there. Annie wished she was there, too—except for getting stung by a yellow jacket. She read the postcard three times, and thought of a hundred things to say once Fiona got home from camp.

"Annike!" Mekas was calling from the bottom of the stairs. "Best you get cleaned up. Mr. Lukas be home soon."

3.
PAPA

Annie put on a fresh T-shirt, washed her face, brushed her thick black hair, and tied it back with a scrunchie.

"How do I look, Mama?" she asked, looking at the framed picture on her rolltop desk. The young woman in the photo smiled back at her. She was standing on a beach, wearing a white knee-length dress and a necklace of big green and yellow glass beads. The dress and her hair were blowing in the wind. Annie tried to remember her, but it was all a fuzzy blank—except for the necklace. She remembered the smooth feel of the beads, and the way they clacked together.

Next to the photograph was a seashell. Annie raised the shell to her ear and listened for the sound of the ocean. It was always the same, distant and mournful.

Annie hoped she would be as pretty as her mother

when she grew up. She turned to her mirror and looked closely at the scars on her chin: two perfect arcs, no larger than fingernail parings, like new moons pointing at each other. She had a similar mark on the back of her left hand, and one on her right wrist. The scars were noticeable only in the summer, when her skin darkened from the sun and the marks remained pale.

She had asked Papa where they had come from. He told her they were moon bites.

"The moon bit me?"

Papa laughed. "Yes, the moon flew down from the sky and bit you."

"How did I get them, really?"

"When you were very young, you fell down the stairs into the cellar. That is why we always keep the cellar door locked." He touched her cheek lightly. "You are lucky—not all scars are so lovely."

Annie did not mind her moon bites. Her friend Fiona had a scar, too—a tiny line on her forehead from falling off her bike.

Satisfied with her appearance, Annie went to the porch and sat on the smaller rocking chair to wait for her father. Papa had an office in the city. He was a *landlord*. He bought big buildings and fixed them up and rented apartments to people who needed a place to live.

At precisely six o'clock, his long gray car pulled in beneath the big cottonwood tree that shaded the south side of the house. The car door opened. Papa stepped out. Annie waved.

Papa was the handsomest man in the world—handsomer than any movie star. He was tall and trim with jet-black hair on top of his head and silver streaks on his temples. His posture was perfect, and he wore immaculate dark suits. All his ties were pure silk. His shoes were always polished.

He walked up the redbrick path and climbed the three steps to the porch. As he came closer, Annie saw that he looked tired. His skin clung closely to his high cheekbones. His dark, almost black eyes were slightly narrowed. His jaw was taut. His mouth was a hard, straight line.

"Annike," he said, and smiled with his mouth but not his eyes. His teeth, white as new paper, were clamped hard together.

Annie said, "Welcome home, Papa."

He touched the tips of his fingers to his lips, then pressed them to Annie's forehead.

"Never change." He went into the house and into his study and closed the door behind him. He would remain there for an hour. Papa called it his *cicenja* time. Annie couldn't play in the garden because she had just washed up.

She couldn't play music because Papa insisted on absolute quiet when he was *cicenjaing*. They didn't have a television. Miss Mekas, busy with dinner, wanted neither help nor distractions.

Annie wandered back to the library. Three whole walls were covered with shelves, floor to ceiling, all crammed full of books. The other wall was a bank of windows looking out at the cottonwood tree.

Most of the books were heavy and thick and crowded with big words in small print with no pictures. Many were written in Litvanian. One of the lower shelves held an assortment of textbooks and chapter books Papa had bought for her homeschooling. Annie was supposed to spend an hour every day reading, but the books were either too boring or too complicated. Biology? At least that book had some animal pictures, but the words were confusing.

She wished she could go to school with Fiona and the other kids, but Papa had pulled her out of school back in the third grade after her teacher, Mr. Jackson, told her there was no such place as Litvania.

"You must be thinking of Lithuania," Mr. Jackson had said.

"No! *Litvania*, where my papa is from! I'll show you!" But when Annie looked for Litvania on the classroom globe, she couldn't find it. "This globe is *stupid*!" she said.

"Annie! Return to your seat!" Mr. Jackson said in a stern voice.

"You're the teacher," Annie said. "You should know about Litvania!"

"I know that if you don't sit down and be quiet right now, Litvania will be the least of your problems."

That was when Annie picked up the globe and threw it on the floor.

Mr. Jackson sent her to the office, where she sat on a long bench for the rest of the day. Mr. Jackson gave her a note for her father. When Papa read the note, he said, "Annike, you can't go around destroying school property and calling people stupid."

"I didn't call anybody stupid. I called that stupid *globe* stupid."

The next morning as she was getting ready for school, Papa said, "Annike, I think you should stay home today. We have a whole room full of books. From now on you will be *home*schooled."

She hadn't been to school since. She missed it—even the times when the other kids were mean, or when Mr. Jackson told her there was no such place as Litvania. It was no fun to study all by herself.

Annie looked at the globe on the wooden stand in front of the windows. Their globe was bigger than the classroom globe at school, and it showed *all* the countries in the world, including Litvania.

Annie dragged a step stool over to the bookshelves and stood on her tiptoes to reach the highest shelf. Many of those books had titles that made no sense at all, like *Russia's European Agenda and the Baltic States* and *The Decline of the European Matriarchy*. She flipped through the books and, as she did so, noticed a small book that had fallen behind the others. The book was so old its corners were rounded and the edges of the pages were yellowed and powdery. On the cover were some foreign words stamped in gold. A long snake, or maybe it was a dragon, wrapped around the words like a frame.

She sat in one of the two soft leather reading chairs and paged through the book. The words were Litvanian, so she couldn't read them, but the pictures were magical: a many-winged dragon, a tree with a face, and a wolf talking to a princess. The last story in the book had a picture of a rat wearing a golden crown and holding a bright red raspberry in its tiny, human-looking hands. It was the only color picture in the book. She was sure she would like the stories if only she could read them.

Annie set the book aside. As she left the library, she stopped in the doorway and looked at the pencil marks on the doorjamb. The highest mark was from her last birthday, almost a year ago. She kicked off her shoes and stood against the jamb and put her hand flat on top of her head. She turned and looked to see where her fingers touched. She had grown two inches! She found a pencil and made a new mark.

Papa was still shut in his study. Annie knelt and put her eye to the keyhole, as she had done many times before. She could see her father's desk and his hand holding a pen. His face was out of sight. He always did the same thing during his *cicenja* time: wrote and wrote and wrote.

She stood and brushed off her knees. She went to the kitchen doorway and watched Miss Mekas slide the pie into the oven. If Mekas knew Annie was watching, she gave no sign.

Annie went outside. She walked over to the sewer grate. She looked into the dark slits but saw nothing. She leaned closer, and heard an echoey sound that reminded her of the bathtub draining. She walked a half block up to Circle Lane and followed the lane to the pond. Sometimes a row of turtles lined up on a log near the middle of the pond.

There was only one turtle. Turning toward home, Annie pretended she was in a slow-motion movie. Step. Pause. Step. Pause.

When she reached her driveway, she turned toward the house as slowly as the second hand on the grandfather clock in Papa's study.

Step. Pause. Step. Around the house, past the library windows, across the backyard, along the edge of Mr. O'Connor's cornfield. The corn, twice as tall as Annie, whispered and sighed in the breeze. The field had once belonged to Papa, but now it was Mr. O'Connor's.

She reached the tower at the corner of the house. The tower had a pointed top, like a witch's hat. When she had asked Papa why none of the other houses had a tower, he told her that they must have forgotten to build one.

The bottom level of the tower had two tall windows, set higher than Annie's head. That was Papa's study. The upper level, Papa's bedroom, had windows all along one side. From his bedroom you could see the turtle pond to the east, and to the west you could see all the way to Mr. O'Connor's barn and silos on the far side of the cornfield.

She moved past the swing set and the picnic table. The vanilla wafer box was not where she had left it. Miss Mekas must have found it. She walked over to the pine trees and ducked under the low boughs to check the hole where she had put the stick.

The stick was gone. The hole had been filled in. The vanilla wafer box lay on its side. It was empty.

4.

KOLDUNY

When Annie's father emerged from his study, he was wearing the same suit, and his hair was the same, but everything else had changed. The tightness around his eyes had disappeared, his lips seemed fuller, and the taut skin over his cheekbones had relaxed. He was *cicenjaed*.

He saw Annie standing at the other side of the dining room table. He held out his arms and smiled a real smile, warm and full, his eyes crinkling. Annie ran to him. He swept her up in his strong arms and kissed her.

"My beautiful Annike," he said.

"Guess what? I just measured myself, and I grew two whole inches since last year!"

"Why, that's terrible! Before you know it, you'll be banging your head on doorframes!"

"No, I won't."

"Maybe you should never grow up."

"But I *want* to grow up!"

"Why? You are perfect as you are!"

"I will still be perfect," Annie said. "Only more grown-up."

He set her down and looked closely at her hair. "What is this?" He plucked out a pine needle.

"Oh!" Annie said. "I was under the pine trees checking the hole."

"Hole?"

"Mr. Wendell's cat got scared by an animal that came out of a hole."

"What sort of animal?"

"I don't know, but the hole is gone."

"Probably just a gopher." He took his seat at the head of the table.

"I saw a rat in the sewer."

"A rat?" Papa frowned and shook his head. "It was probably a squirrel that fell in the sewer and got wet."

Annie was sure the creature she had seen was not a squirrel, but she didn't argue.

Miss Mekas came out of the kitchen holding a platter of steamed *kolduny*. She set it in the center of the table. "Is hot," she said, and returned to the kitchen.

"I met a little boy named Arthur," Annie said. "He lives in the Andersons' house."

"Yes, Emily Golden and her son just moved in there."

"What about Arthur's papa?"

"It's just her and her young son."

"Is his papa dead?"

"As I understand it, they are divorced. His father lives far away."

"So Arthur is the opposite of me. He doesn't have a papa and I don't have a mama."

Papa looked away. "I suppose so." He did not like to talk about Mama.

"Arthur is five," Annie said, "but he doesn't talk much."

Miss Mekas set a bowl of salad on the table. "My *brolis* not talk until he six." She sat down across from Annie. "Then he no shut up."

"*Brolis* means 'brother' in Litvanian," Papa explained to Annie.

"How old was I when I started to talk?" Annie asked.

"I believe you were talking the day you were born, or so it seemed," Papa said. "Now let's enjoy this wonderful meal, shall we?"

Annie took a single *kolduny*, because she was not sure what was in it. She cut into it with her fork. The inside was orange. She tasted it.

"Sweet potato!" she exclaimed. Annie loved sweet potatoes.

Miss Mekas smiled. Papa was already on his second *kolduny*.

Between the three of them, they ate the whole platter. Annie ate five herself, and she didn't even complain when Papa piled too much salad on her plate.

"That was delicious," Papa said when they had all finished eating.

"You say everything is delicious," Annie said.

"Only because it is true," Papa said. He pushed back his chair, stood, and bowed to Miss Mekas. "My compliments to the chef."

Miss Mekas giggled. "Mr. Lukas!"

Annie laughed. She loved it when her father was being silly.

"Pie is done," Mekas said. "But is too hot. We wait."

"Good things are worth waiting for," Papa said.

Annie knew that a pie fresh from the oven would take a long time to cool, so she said, "Papa, will you read me a story?"

"Of course! What would you like to hear?"

"A story from a book I found. I'll show you." She took Papa's hand and led him to the library. "This book." She handed him the book with the pictures.

"Why, I haven't seen this book in many, many years!" Papa said.

"I found it on the shelf."

He flipped slowly through the yellowing pages. "So many memories," he said quietly. He looked up. "But Annike, darling, these stories are all written in Litvanian."

"You can tell me what they mean." She took the book from him and found the picture of the rat holding the raspberry. "Can you tell me this one?"

Papa frowned. "'Matas and the Rat Queen'?" He shook his head. "That is not a nice story. How about I tell you the story called 'The Changeling and the Girl'?"

"Which one is that?"

He turned back toward the beginning of the book and showed her.

"The princess talking to the wolf?" Annie said.

"That is no wolf, and she is not a princess."

"But she is very pretty!"

"No prettier than you."

"I might be a princess when I grow up!" Annie said.

Papa looked startled, then laughed. "Perhaps so!"

Annie ran over to the globe and spun it. "Show me Litvania!"

Papa smiled. "I have shown you many times."

"Show me again!"

Papa rotated the globe, stopped it, and pointed. "This is the Baltic Sea. And here we have the country of Latvia. Below that is Lithuania. And squeezed in between them . . . you see this green country shaped like a mouse? See the pointy nose and long tail? That is Litvania."

"It's so small!"

"The Queendom of Litvania is the eighth smallest country in the world."

"Queendom? Don't they have a king?"

"Litvania is ruled by Queen Zurka, who is, in fact, related to you. So you are almost royalty."

"I would like to meet Queen Zurka," Annie said.

"Perhaps one day you will. Now let's sit, and I will tell you a story about a girl very much like you."

5

THE CHANGELING
AND THE GIRL

Papa sat in one of the chairs and opened the book. He turned to the picture of the wolf-that-was-no-wolf and the girl-who-was-not-a-princess.

"Once upon a time," he began.

"What time?" Annie asked.

"A very long time ago."

"Before I was born?"

"Before even *I* was born. Now hush and let me read, or we will be here all night."

Annie pretended to zip her lips shut. Papa smiled and settled back in his chair.

"Once upon a time, there was a changeling—"

"What is a changeling?" Annie interrupted.

"You talk a great deal for a little girl who has just zipped her lips," he observed.

"Sorry!"

"If you listen, all will be revealed. Okay?"

Annie *double*-zipped her mouth shut.

"The changeling was very, very old, and he had learned to change his shape. That is why he was called a changeling. He could be an elephant, a fish, a tree, or anything else."

"Why would he want to be a tree?" Annie asked.

Papa sighed. "I don't know that he *did* want to be a tree, but he could turn into one if he wanted. You see, the changeling was a silly-looking creature no taller than a goose. His head was bald, but the rest of him was covered with hair the color of straw. He had little round green eyes, a long pointy nose, ears as big as soup bowls, and only three fingers on each hand. And his feet looked like dog paws."

Annie giggled.

"You laugh, and that is exactly why no one ever saw him in his natural form. He knew people would make fun of the way he looked, so he was always changing into other things.

"One day the changeling was eating blackberries in his favorite berry patch when an old woman came along carrying a basket. He ducked down so she would not see him. The woman began to pick the berries. The changeling wanted the berries for himself, so he turned himself into a bear and rose up onto his hind feet and *ROARED!*"

Papa *roared* that last word. Annie screamed, then laughed. Papa chuckled.

"You are a very scary bear," she said.

"Thank you. The old woman screamed even louder than you. She dropped her basket and ran away, and the changeling ate all the berries she had picked. Then he ate every last berry in the patch because he was a bear now, and bears are always hungry.

"When all the berries were gone, he curled up in the middle of the berry patch and fell asleep, because bears are also always sleepy.

"Sometime later, the changeling was awakened by a tinkling sound. He sat up. While he slept, he had returned to his usual shape, so he had to stand up on his dog paw feet to see over the berry bushes. A little boy was leading a goat down the forest path. The goat had a bell around its neck. The changeling was angry at being awakened, so he turned himself into a tiger and jumped onto the path right in front of the boy. The boy yelled and ran off into the woods, leaving the goat behind.

"Because the changeling was a tiger, and tigers are even hungrier than bears, he ate the boy's goat."

"The whole thing?" Annie asked.

"Everything except the bell," Papa said.

"That seems very rude."

"Changelings are not known for their manners. Now, after eating all those berries and an entire goat, the change-ling decided to go for a stroll. He kept his shape as a tiger, just in case he came across something else he could eat, and sure enough, down by the brook, he spotted a little girl sit-ting on a stump eating a jam sandwich."

"What kind of jam?"

"Strawberry, of course. Your favorite! And do you know what else? The little girl's name was the same as yours: Annike."

"You're making that up!"

"I am not! Annike was exactly your age, and she was extremely perturbed when the giant tiger came padding out from the woods—but not for the reason you might think! Do you know what Annike said to the tiger who was really a changeling?"

Annie shook her head.

"She said, 'You're not a real tiger!'

"The changeling growled, 'If I am not a tiger, then what am I?'

"'There are no tigers hereabouts,' the girl said. 'Besides, real tigers can't talk. You're just a silly changeling!'

"'I am a changeling, it is true.' The changeling bared

his ferocious tiger teeth. 'But you will not think me so silly when I *eat* you!'

"Now, you and I know that the changeling was embarrassed by his real appearance, which is why he was always making himself into other things. Annike knew it as well, because her father had warned her about such creatures.

"'I would prefer not to be eaten by a tiger that is not really a tiger,' she said. 'But I suppose it would be too hard for you to change into something else.'

"'Not at all,' said the changeling. 'Observe!' And with that he transformed himself into a big gray wolf with long fangs and hungry yellow eyes. 'You see? I am a wolf now, and I am going to eat you and the rest of your jam sandwich!'

"'Changing into a wolf is easy,' the girl said with a toss of her long black hair.

"'Then how about *this!*' The wolf changed into a gorilla.

"'Gorillas eat only fruits and leaves,' the girl said.

"The changeling was frustrated. It was no fun to eat a girl who wasn't even afraid. He made himself into a rhinoceros. The girl laughed at his nose. He tried being a crocodile. She told him she could easily outrun a crocodile. He transformed into a snorting bull with long, sharp horns. 'I had beef for supper last night,' she said. 'Maybe I will eat you!'

"The changeling snorted and stamped his hooves in frustration, then turned himself into the same bear that had frightened away the old woman.

"'That's pretty good,' the girl admitted, 'but do you know what would really impress me?'

"'What?' asked the changeling, who was becoming even more impatient.

"'If you could turn into a bug.'

"'Ha! Bugs are easy. What sort of bug?'

"'I bet you can't turn yourself into a little beetle!' the girl said.

"The changeling could not resist a challenge, so he turned himself into a beetle. Not just any beetle, but a beautiful golden scarab beetle, which he was certain would impress her.

"The little girl looked at the tiny golden beetle by her feet, then STOMPED on it. And she STOMPED and STOMPED and STOMPED until it was completely gone."

Annie waited for more, but Papa simply sat with the open book in his lap and smiled up at the wall of books.

6.
BAD MOUTH

Annie waited as long as she could for her father to continue, but he seemed lost in his thoughts. Finally, she asked, "Did Annike kill the changeling?"

Papa jerked, as if she had poked him in the ribs, then looked at her. "Even magical creatures die."

"Then what happened?"

"I imagine the girl finished eating her jam sandwich and went home."

"She was lucky she didn't get eaten."

"It was not luck. Annike was clever. And the changeling was foolish. He let her talk him into becoming something less than he could be."

Annie thought for a few seconds, then said, "I think I like the picture better than the story."

"That is often the case with fairy tales."

"Why are they called fairy tales if there aren't any fairies?"

"Ha! Good question!"

"Are all made-up stories fairy tales?"

"No . . . but Annike, what makes you think they are made up?"

"Because there's no such thing as a changeling!"

"Are you sure? In Litvania, many impossible things are true."

"Like what?" she asked.

"Well, for example, in Litvania, magic is real. I knew a woman, she had a curse put on her. Her memory was stolen."

"Like Fiona's grandma?"

"No. Fiona's grandmother is old, and she has Alzheimer's disease. The woman I knew was young. Her memory was taken by a . . . by a spell. To this day she does not remember who she was. Oh, and in Litvania, there used to be dragons."

"*Real* dragons?"

"I never saw one, but my great-grandmother did."

"But we don't have dragons here, right?"

"Not that I have noticed."

"Do we have magic?"

"Yes, but not so much as in Litvania." He closed the book and looked at her with a curious expression. "One day I will take you there, and you will see."

"When?"

"Not right now, but you *are* getting older. Tomorrow is your tenth birthday. You know, in Litvania, ten is a magical age. It is the age of the conscience, when bad things begin to eat at your soul. Tomorrow I will show you some ancient Litvanian magic. I will introduce you to the *nuodeema burna*."

Annie did not know what those words meant, but a chill rose from the soles of her feet, ran up through her legs and her spine, and prickled her scalp.

Papa must have sensed her alarm, because he reached over and squeezed her hand. "It is nothing to be afraid of, Annike. I should not have mentioned it. Forget I said anything."

Annie smiled back at him, but it was not her best smile. The words he had spoken echoed through her. She would not forget them. The *nuodeema burna*, he had said. *"It is nothing to be afraid of."*

Miss Mekas was in the kitchen cleaning the counters. Annie watched silently until Mekas noticed her standing there.

"Yes, Annike?"

"Do you believe in magic?"

"In old country, yes. Here, maybe, maybe not. One night I make six cherry tarts, and in the morning, there are five. Magic? I do not know."

Annie remembered that night. The tart had been delicious, but she still felt bad for stealing it.

"What does *nuodeema burna* mean?" she asked.

Miss Mekas frowned. "Where you hear that?"

"From Papa."

"What he say is?"

"I forgot to ask him."

"I see. In Litvania, *burna* is 'mouth.'" She pointed at her lips. "And *nuodeema* is 'bad thing.' So, in English . . . I am not sure. I never hear those words put together. Bad mouth? Maybe is to say bad thing? You ask your father. He know."

Annie did not ask her father about the *nuodeema burna*. She was afraid he would refuse to tell her, and that would make her even more afraid.

7.
THE SIN EATER

For Annie's birthday breakfast, Miss Mekas made waffles and bacon and fresh fruit salad. A present wrapped in gold foil sat next to her plate. It was shaped like a book, only bigger. Annie lifted it and shook it. Something inside rattled faintly.

"Mr. Lukas say you wait to open," Mekas said. "When he come home."

After that, the day passed very, very slowly. Fiona was still at camp. Mr. Wendell was busy doing something in his garage. There were no turtles on the turtle log. The new boy, Arthur, did not appear. So far, being ten years old was not much fun.

That afternoon Annie looked through her closet and changed into her yellow dress. She hadn't worn that dress since her last birthday, and it was a little tight, but yellow was her favorite color so she wore it anyway. She took one of her homeschool books to the porch and sat on the small rocker and read while she waited for Papa to get home.

She had been sitting there a long time when Miss Mekas poked her head out and said, "Mr. Lukas call. He say he be little late."

Annie's shoulders slumped.

Mekas said, "We eat if you want, or we wait." She was making Annie's favorite: fried chicken, mashed potatoes, sugar-glazed carrots, and honey biscuits. With angel food cake for dessert, of course.

"We have to wait for Papa."

Mekas nodded and went back inside.

Annie squeezed her eyes closed. She refused to cry. She was ten years old now. But it wasn't fair. She looked down at the book she had been reading. The words skittered around on the page like crazy ants. Mr. Wendell was trimming his bushes. Annie glanced down the street and noticed a funny-looking lump at the sewer grate. It took her a second to realize it was Arthur. He was hunched over the grate, reaching through the opening.

Annie got up and walked across the lawn and down the street.

"Arthur, what are you doing?" she asked.

Arthur turned his head to look up at her. "Stuck!" He looked scared.

Annie sighed and rolled her eyes. She was hungry and cranky. She didn't want to deal with Arthur; she just wanted her father to come home so they could eat her birthday dinner and have cake and open her present. But she couldn't leave him like that. She knelt down and examined his arm. Arthur had reached through the back opening of the sewer grate, all the way past his elbow, and he couldn't get it out.

"Turn your arm," she suggested.

"I can't."

"Here." She grasped his arm and twisted it to the right. Arthur let out a yelp. He was still stuck. Annie tried to slide his arm toward the wider end of the opening, but Arthur resisted.

"Stop it!" Annie said. "Do you want me to help or not?"

Arthur whimpered.

"We have to push your arm over here, where it's wider. Okay?"

Arthur was crying.

Annie dragged his arm across the rough, rusted iron. Arthur howled, but his arm slipped free from the grate.

Arthur clutched his arm. Annie stood up and brushed off her knees. Now she was dirty and it was all his fault. She looked at his arm. There was a small scrape, but otherwise it looked okay. Annie grabbed his other arm and helped the boy to his feet.

"Stop crying!" she said. "You're fine. Now come on, I'm taking you home."

"Everything okay?" Mr. Wendell was standing at the end of his driveway, clipper in hand, looking at them.

"He was stuck, but I got him out," Annie said.

Mr. Wendell nodded and went back to his bushes.

By the time they reached Arthur's house, the boy had stopped crying except for an occasional snuffle. When his mother opened the door, Annie told her what had happened.

"Oh, Arthur," Emily Golden said, kneeling down and examining the scrape on his arm. "Whatever am I going to do with you?"

"You should keep better track of him," Annie said.

Emily Golden looked up and frowned. "Yes, thank you, Annie. I'll keep that in mind."

Just then, Papa's car drove past them and turned into their driveway.

"I have to go," Annie said. "It's my birthday." She turned and ran home, but not in time to greet her father. She ran into the house and yelled, "Papa!"

"He is in study," Miss Mekas said.

Annie knew better than to interrupt Papa during his

cicenja time, but it was her birthday and she hadn't been on the porch to greet him. She opened the door to the study. Papa was sitting at his desk writing on his pad of pink paper. He glanced up, startled.

"Annike," he said in a hoarse voice.

He looked terrible! The skin around his eyes was dark and bruised-looking, his forehead was deathly pale, and the lines around his mouth were etched deep.

"Papa! I just wanted to say hi."

He held up a hand. "I need my time alone, Annike." His voice sounded scratchy and hollow.

"I'm sorry," she said. "I just wanted—"

"Please . . . not now. I had to evict another tenant this morning. I need a few moments to myself." He smiled as if it hurt to do so. "I'll be out as soon as I can." He flicked his fingers, shooing her away. "Now go."

Annie backed out of the room. She went up to her bedroom and closed the door and sat on her bed. Her face felt numb, and she thought she might cry. What was wrong with Papa? He always seemed a little tired when he got home, but she had never seen him like that, and it scared her. She felt bad that she hadn't been waiting for him when he got home.

It was Arthur's fault. Then she thought of how scared Arthur had been. How long had he been stuck in the sewer grate? She remembered how she'd yelled at him and how rough she had been. He was just a little kid. And then she'd been sort of nasty to his mother. She felt horrible. She didn't deserve birthday cake, or a present, or *anything*. Tomorrow she would go tell Arthur how sorry she was, and apologize to his mother for being rude.

It was almost dark out when Annie heard Miss Mekas call her for dinner. She ran down the stairs and got there just as Mekas set a platter of crispy fried chicken on the table. Papa was sitting with his back to Annie.

"Papa?" Annie was a little nervous because he had looked so bad before. He pushed back his chair, stood up, and turned. A wave of relief washed over her. He looked so much better. His eyes were shining and his smile was warm. Annie ran to him. He lifted her and kissed her cheek and hugged her.

"My beautiful Annike," he said. "Happy birthday!" He set her down and winced.

"Papa? Are you okay?"

"Just a twinge in my back." He pressed a hand against the small of his back and forced a smile. "You're bigger than you used to be!"

The three of them sat down. Annie ate two whole drumsticks and a big serving of mashed potatoes. Papa and Miss Mekas put gravy on their potatoes, but Annie preferred butter—a *lot* of butter, because it was her birthday. Finally, it was time for the angel food cake with ten candles. Annie blew them all out in one try. Papa cut the cake and gave her the biggest slice. Miss Mekas had made strawberry preserves to go on top.

By the time she licked the last bit of strawberry from her fork, Annie was full.

"That was the best meal *ever*," she declared. Miss Mekas smiled.

"I completely agree," Papa said. He stretched out his arms and yawned. "It must be time for bed!"

"Nooo!" Annie cried. "Present!"

"Oh yes, of course! Let's see . . . did I remember to get you a present?" He looked around. "Now, where did it go?"

"I put in library," Miss Mekas said.

Papa stood up. "You go get your present, Annike, and bring it to my study."

Papa's study was a big round room that took up the whole bottom level of the tower. Two tall-backed wooden chairs faced a fireplace on one side. Papa's desk was on the opposite side. On his desk was a pad of pink paper, a fountain pen, and several manila folders. Behind the desk stood a grandfather clock, taller even than Papa, with a slowly swinging brass pendulum behind a leaded glass panel. The time on the clock was seven hours later than the actual time. Papa said it showed the time in Litvania.

Most of the floor was covered by an enormous rug woven with images of peacocks and foxes, soldiers on horses, lions attacking antelopes, and sinewy, many-winged dragons. Papa had brought the rug all the way from Litvania. It made Annie dizzy to look at it. Perched on the mantel above the fireplace was a brass candelabra with five white candles, and a black-and-white photo of a stern-looking man wearing an old-fashioned army uniform and holding a rifle. Papa said it was his granduncle Valdemaras, who had served in the army before coming to America to be a farmer. Even with the uniform and the photo's grainy texture, the resemblance to her father was striking.

Papa touched a long wooden match to the kindling under the logs in the fireplace. The flame caught.

"I know it's still summer," he said. "But autumn will be here soon, and what would a birthday be without a little fire?" He tossed the match into the flames and sat down in one of the tall-backed chairs. Moments later the fire cast a warm glow throughout the room.

Annie hopped up on the other chair. "Now?" she said.

Papa nodded. Annie tore through the wrapping paper.

Inside was a wooden box decorated with painted flowers and birds. She slid back the top of the box. There was a thick pad of yellow paper. Underneath was a set of colored pencils.

"The colors are very pretty," she said, trying to sound enthusiastic.

"That is only a small part of my gift to you, Annike. Ten is a portentous age. It is the age at which you must begin to take care of yourself. It is time for me to share with you the Klimas family secret."

"Secret?" Annie loved secrets . . . but Papa looked so serious.

"Yes. The *nuodeema burna*."

As before, hearing those words sent a shiver through Annie's body.

"The *bad mouth*," she said in a whisper.

He looked startled. "Where did you hear that?"

"I asked Miss Mekas."

He shook his head. "Mekas knows nothing. The *nuodeema burna* is . . . it means the eater of sins. You see, it is our sins that destroy us. Do you know what a sin is?"

"When you do a bad thing?"

"Yes. We are all sinners. Sometimes, even when we are trying to be good, we do bad things."

"Not me," Annie said. "I would never—" She remembered how mean she had been to Arthur.

Papa saw her hesitate. "Have you done something you regret, Annike? Told an untruth? Committed an unkindness?"

Annie said, "Today, I—"

"Do not tell me! Here is what I want you to do. Take one of your new pencils and write down what you did. Can you do that?"

Annie looked at the colored pencils and the yellow paper. She nodded.

"Write it down. But do not show it to me!"

Annie chose a brown pencil. She did not like this game. She did not like having to think about hurting Arthur. But Papa was watching her, so she wrote carefully.

I was mean to Arthur.

"Okay," she said.

"Good. Now tear out the page and roll it up tight."

Annie did so.

"Tighter, the *nuodeema burna* is small."

Annie rolled it tighter.

"Now bring it over here." Papa folded back the corner

of the rug where it was closest to the fire, revealing a nickel-size hole in the wooden floor. Its edges were worn and dark.

"This is the *nuodeema burna*. Now put the paper inside."

"In there?" Annie did not like that hole.

"Yes."

Annie stuck the rolled-up paper into the hole.

"Push it all the way in."

"What will happen?"

"It will go away."

Annie shoved the paper all the way into the hole and jerked her finger out quickly.

Papa peered into the hole.

"Good," he said, and kissed her forehead. "You are a good girl." He folded the rug back over the hole and returned to his chair. "Do you feel different?" he asked.

Annie considered his question. Mostly, she felt relieved that the *nuodeema burna* was out of sight, beneath the rug. What else did she feel? She thought about the thing that had happened with Arthur. It had been only a few hours ago, but now the memory was fuzzy and soft, like something that had happened to somebody else, or like a dream.

"I feel fine," she said.

Papa sat back, the tension going out of his shoulders.

He smiled and looked at the fire. "From now on you must feed all your bad things to the *nuodeema burna*. Anytime you do anything that makes you feel guilty. Anything you regret."

"Why?"

"So you can be happy."

"Is that what you do when you *cicenja*?"

"Yes." He breathed out the word so quietly she could hardly hear him.

"Does Miss Mekas?"

"No! The *nuodeema burna* is our secret. You must tell no one." He leaned forward and looked at her intensely with eyes dark and hard. "Promise me!"

"I promise."

That night Annie didn't fall asleep right away. Instead, she thought about the colored pencils and the *nuodeema burna*. She thought about Arthur. She remembered pulling Arthur's arm out of the sewer grate—she remembered every detail. She remembered feeling bad about how she'd treated him . . . but she didn't feel bad about it anymore. Arthur had gotten himself stuck, and she had saved him!

Still, beneath the triumph lurked something rotten, something soiled. It was as if she had caught a whiff of something bad, and that smell had left its ghost in her nostrils.

She sat up and turned on her lamp. Her clock said it was almost midnight. She opened the box from Papa and counted the pencils. There were twenty-four. She riffled through the pages of the tablet. She didn't count them, but it was a big number. Each blank sheet waiting for her to write down something bad that she had done. Annie did not think she would need them all.

8.
FIONA

The next week, Fiona Bray returned from summer camp.

The Brays had been one of the first new families to move to the neighborhood, six years ago. Back then, many of the houses were still being built. Annie's earliest memories were of big machines roaring and carpenters pounding and the smell of new construction. Lucky Key Homes put in curvy streets and more than thirty houses on what had once been woods and fields. They named the new neighborhood Pond Tree Acres because there was a pond, and lots of trees.

Fiona was Annie's first and best friend. They both had long black hair, and they both liked to talk, and their birthdays were only a few weeks apart, so they were almost like twins. Sometimes they both talked at the same time—there was so much to say! Especially now, because Fiona had just

gotten back from camp and she had to tell Annie everything that had happened.

Fiona told Annie she had hiked to the top of a waterfall,
and one day it rained so hard, they stayed in their cabins
and played games.

"And I saw a moose!" she said. "It was as big as an
elephant!"

"What was it doing?" Annie asked.

"Standing in the water looking at us. We were in the
canoe. I thought it was going to charge at us!"

"Did it?"

"No! I'd be *dead!*"

"Mr. Wendell's cat got attacked by an animal. It came
out of a hole in the ground."

"Maybe it was a groundhog," Fiona said. "I saw a
groundhog once. It ran across the road when we were
driving."

"I think maybe one lives under our pine trees."

"Eww! I hope not! Oh, I almost forgot. I have a present
for you." Fiona dug in her bag—she still hadn't unpacked
from camp—and pulled out a braided cord with two acorns
strung on it. "It's a friendship bracelet!"

Annie took the bracelet and slipped it over her wrist.
"It's beautiful," she said, her eyes watering. "But I didn't get
you anything!"

"That's because you didn't go anywhere," Fiona said.

They were talking so much that Fiona's mom told them to go outside, so the two girls walked over to the pond, talking the whole way. Annie kept shaking her wrist because she liked the way it sounded when the acorns clacked together. When they got to the pond, there was only one turtle on the log.

"We had a pet turtle in our classroom last year," Fiona said.

It made Annie feel bad when Fiona talked about fun things from school. "Yesterday I saw five turtles here," she said.

"My mom's taking me and my sister to the mall for school clothes tonight. Is your dad going to let you come to school this year?"

"I don't know. I hope so." Every time she asked Papa, he said, "We shall see."

"I hope so, too. You don't want to get left behind. Fifth grade is *so* important! It's our last year before middle school. We get to be the biggest kids . . . Hey! Who's that?"

Annie turned to see where Fiona was looking. "Oh. That's Arthur."

The boy was on the street, thumb in mouth, walking toward them. He was wearing pajama bottoms, a light blue T-shirt, and no shoes. "He's five years old. He moved in where the Andersons used to live. We should probably take him home."

Arthur stopped a few feet away.

"Why is he *staring* at us?" Fiona asked.

"That's just what he does," Annie said. "Arthur, this is my friend Fiona."

"Hello," Fiona said.

Arthur looked away. He took his thumb out of his mouth and pointed at the turtle. He started toward the edge of the pond.

"He seems sort of *immature*," Fiona said in a whisper.

"He just likes to take his time about things," Annie said. "Hey, Arthur!"

Arthur ignored her and kept going. It looked as if he was going to walk right into the water. Annie ran after him and grabbed his arm at the last second.

The turtle slid off the log and plopped into the water. Arthur put his thumb back in his mouth and let Annie pull him away.

"Does he talk?" Fiona whispered to Annie.

"Only when he has something to say."

"He's looking at me weird."

"You get used to it," Annie said. "Come on, Arthur." She took his hand. "Let's go home."

On the way back, Arthur insisted on stopping at the

sewer grate. He got down on his hands and knees and pressed his face to the iron bars.

"What is he *doing*?" Fiona whispered.

"He thinks there are bunnies in there. But I saw a rat."

"No way!"

"It had yellow teeth."

"Yuck! I hope it doesn't bite him!"

Annie was thinking the same thing. She pulled Arthur to his feet.

"Hey, Mr. Wendell!" Fiona yelled, and waved to Mr. Wendell, who was standing in front of his garage holding a small, oblong cage.

"Well, if it isn't the neighborhood gang," he said. "How are you all on this lovely day?"

"We're fine," Annie said. She looked back at Arthur, whose face was striped with rust and grime. "Arthur was just looking in the sewer."

"What's that?" Fiona asked, pointing at the cage Mr. Wendell was holding.

"It's a live trap," he said.

"What are you trying to catch?"

"Varmints."

"What's a varmint?"

"Critters you don't want. Squirrels, most likely. Ate up

all my birdseed, tore up a box full of magazines, and made some sort of nest in the corner."

"Can we see?"

"It's not much to look at, but you may." He led them into his garage. In one corner there was a mass of chewed-up paper mixed with sunflower seed hulls and bits of dry grass. The pile was taller than it was wide and had a man-like shape.

"That's a nest?" Annie asked.

"I don't know what else it could be."

"Doesn't your cat chase the animals away?" Fiona asked.

"TomTom has been kind of nervous lately. He doesn't want anything to do with strange critters."

Arthur was crouching down, examining the thing in the corner. "They like your seeds," he said.

Mr. Wendell chuckled. "Yes, I imagine they do."

Arthur looked up at Mr. Wendell, then back at the thing.

"They made it look like you," he said.

The man-shaped clump of sunflower seed hulls and paper scraps did, in fact, resemble Mr. Wendell. There was even a shiny piece of paper on top of the lumpy head, just like Mr. Wendell's bald spot.

. . . . .

The next day, Annie went over to Fiona's to see her new clothes. Fiona was happy to model everything: a pair of jeans with fancy embroidery on the pockets, two pairs of leggings, one with pink polka dots and one all black, a black-and-blue-striped pullover dress, and several tops, including a T-shirt with Wonder Woman on the front. She also got some pink tennis shoes to match the polka-dot leggings, and a pair of suede boots with fur on the tops for winter.

"We had a fashion show at camp," Fiona said as she twirled around her bedroom in her striped dress, the polka-dot leggings, and her new boots. "Only all we had was our camp clothes, so we had to improvise. I made a hat out of leaves. Some girls just showed pictures of themselves on their phones. I hope I get a phone for Christmas. You should ask your dad for one. We could talk all the time!"

"I guess," Annie said. She was pretty sure Papa would say no. "Where are all your dolls?" she asked.

Before, the shelves in Fiona's bedroom had been lined with dolls and stuffed animals: Barbies, baby dolls, several teddy bears, a floppy gray poodle, and more. The only one left was a single, forlorn Raggedy Ann.

"I got rid of them. Rachel says we're too old for dolls. She says they're *immature*."

"Who's Rachel?"

"My friend from camp. Rachel's a year ahead of us.

She's going to be a sixth-grader at Wellstone."

Wellstone was the name of the local middle school. Annie felt left out.

"Rachel's been everywhere. Her parents took her to France last year, and she's been to the Grand Canyon, too. She's so cool. You'd like her."

Annie already didn't like this Rachel, but she didn't want to argue with her best friend. Her eyes landed on the Raggedy Ann doll. "You're keeping Raggedy Ann?"

"Raggedy Ann is a classic," Fiona said. "That's what my mom says."

Annie ran home and threw herself down on her bed. She landed on Muffles, the stuffed lion she'd had ever since she could remember. She grabbed him by his mane and threw him across the room. She set her jaw and glared at the ceiling. A few seconds later, she sighed, rolled off the bed, and retrieved Muffles.

"Sorry," she said, and set him in his place next to her pillow. She looked at the three teddy bears—Papa, Mama, and Baby Bear—lined up on top of her dresser. She didn't have as many dolls and animals as Fiona used to, but she couldn't imagine getting rid of any of them, even if that made her *immature*.

. . . . .

That night at dinner, Annie asked her father to take her shopping for new clothes.

Papa looked up from his plate and raised his eyebrows. "Do your clothes not fit you?"

"No. And everything's old."

"Well, I suppose we will have to see about some new ones if your clothes are aging."

"Fiona got all new clothes for school," Annie said.

Papa cut a piece of chicken.

"Fiona says fifth grade is really important. I don't want to get left behind."

Papa ate his bite of chicken. "Left behind? Have you not been doing your reading?"

"Reading all by myself is boring. I miss my friends! Besides, Fiona said they had a pet turtle in their class last year."

"You don't need to go to school to see a turtle. You have turtles in the pond."

"Papa!"

"Okay!" He threw up his hands. "You are right. It is all well and good to read the many fine books with which I have provided you, but I have been remiss. What you need, my dear Annike, is a *mokytojas*."

"A what?"

"A teacher who will guide you in your reading, and answer any questions you might have."

"But I want to go to *school*! I want to be with my friends! I want a *real* teacher!"

"I will find a real teacher for you when I travel to Litvania in a few weeks."

"You're going to Litvania? Can I come?"

"Not this time, Annike. But one day."

Annie wasn't ready to give in. "You never take me anywhere. Not even to the mall. All my clothes are boring!"

"What do I know about little girls' clothes? I'll tell you what—tomorrow afternoon I will have Miss Mekas take you shopping. How would that be?"

"Okay, I guess." She was disappointed that she wouldn't get to go to school, but going to the mall would be fun.

9

FASHION ADVICE

The next morning, Annie sat around and moped and pretended to do her homeschool work. She was sitting in the library paging listlessly through a book about the American Revolution when the doorbell rang.

"Annike," Miss Mekas called out. "Your friend is here!"

Annie shoved the book aside and jumped up, eager to see Fiona so she could tell her that she was going shopping for new clothes. She ran down the hall to the front door.

It wasn't Fiona. It was Arthur, standing in the entryway looking at her with his usual attentive, inscrutable gaze.

"Oh," Annie said. "Hi, Arthur."

"Turtles," said Arthur. His mom had forbidden him to go to the pond alone, but said he could if Annie was with him.

"Arthur, we just looked at the turtles yesterday."

Arthur said nothing.

Annie sighed. Even looking at turtles with Arthur was better than reading about George Washington and thinking about missing out on the fifth grade.

Of course, Arthur had to stop at the sewer grate and drop in the cookie Miss Mekas had given him. Annie waited patiently as he peered into the damp darkness.

"You know there are no bunnies in there, don't you?"

Arthur shrugged and stood up.

On the way to the pond, they ran into Mr. Dennison walking his wiener dog.

"Good morning, Annie," said Mr. Dennison.

"Good morning."

Arthur dropped to his knees and reached out to pet the dog. The dog backed away and hid behind Mr. Dennison's legs.

"Daisy has been nervous lately," said Mr. Dennison.

"Why?" Annie asked.

"Something has been stealing her food from her bowl on our porch."

"A wild animal scared Mr. Wendell's cat. We think it was a groundhog."

"Really! Well, I don't think a groundhog would be interested in dog food."

"I saw a rat in the sewer!"

"A rat? In Pond Tree Acres? I certainly hope not!"

Arthur was on his stomach, getting down to the little dog's level. Daisy approached him cautiously and gave his forehead a lick. Arthur grinned. Daisy backed away. Arthur climbed to his feet.

"Doggie," he said.

Mr. Dennison laughed. "You two have a nice day," he said, and walked on.

There were three turtles sunning on the log in the pond—one big one and two babies. As always, Arthur charged up to the pond. The turtles plopped into the water and sank out of sight. Arthur stood with his toes touching the edge of the water and stared at the empty log. For a moment, Annie thought he might wade right in.

Arthur was a weird little kid, but at least she had one friend who didn't think she was immature.

When Annie got home, she found Miss Mekas sitting on the porch with her hat on her head and her purse in her lap.

"I have call taxi," she said.

"Taxi?" Annie was confused.

"For mall," Mekas said.

"Oh!" Annie brightened. She had almost forgotten. Miss Mekas was taking her clothes shopping.

.....

The mall was amazing. Annie insisted on visiting every store that had kids' clothes. Mekas grumbled and complained the whole time. "When I was girl I have one dress, one pair shoes," she said. She tut-tutted at the prices, and kept reminding Annie that they had to get home to make dinner.

Annie tried on everything. She ended up buying a pair of jeans with embroidery on the pockets, two pairs of leggings—one with polka dots and one all black—and three T-shirts. She found a pair of pink high-top tennis shoes and a pair of winter boots with fur around the tops, just like Fiona's. With each purchase she imagined what Fiona would say. She would be so impressed!

Fiona came over the next day. Annie modeled her new clothes, twirling around like Fiona had, waiting for her friend to love what she had done. Fiona just stared—and not in a good way. Her lips were pressed tight together, and her eyes were narrowed the way they got when she was mad about something.

"Don't you like it?" Annie asked, holding up her Supergirl T-shirt.

"You *copied* me," Fiona said.

Annie was shocked. "No, I didn't! This is Supergirl—you have Wonder Woman!"

"Yeah, but everything else is the same. You can't just go around copying me!"

"I thought you'd like it!"

"We're not twins, you know."

"I'm sorry!" Annie's face was hot and she could feel her eyes tearing up. Of *course* they weren't twins, but she'd always thought, in a way, that they kind of were.

"You should find your *own* style," Fiona said.

"I don't know what my style *is*!" It wasn't fair. Fiona had a big sister, and a mom, and she got to go to school with all the other kids.

"I'm going home," Fiona said.

Annie was too embarrassed and mad to say anything. After her friend left, Annie looked at the new clothes laid out on her bed. A few minutes ago, she had loved them, but now she hated them.

Miss Mekas looked up when Annie clomped into the kitchen.

"Why you walk like angry bull?" Mekas asked.

"Because Fiona is stupid and mean and I hate her."

"You want cookie?"

"I don't want a stupid cookie!"

Mekas frowned. "You should no talk that way."

"Why?" Annie stomped her foot.

Mekas's small mouth got smaller. "You go outside."

"I don't want to."

"You go."

Annie went. She wished her mother were here to tell her what she was supposed to do. All she had was Miss Mekas. Having just Mekas was worse than having nobody at all.

Annie looked up and down the street. No one was outside. Not even Arthur. Not even Mr. Wendell. She circled the house and walked along the edge of the cornfield. It was like a green, tassel-topped wall, much higher than her head. Some of the leaves were beginning to turn yellow, and the ears were fat on the stalks. Mr. O'Connor would be harvesting them soon. She went over to the pine trees, ducked underneath the boughs, and let out a little yelp.

The hole was back, surrounded by the chewed-up remains of the vanilla wafer box.

10

THE CELLAR

"I'll be gone for several days, perhaps a week," Papa said. He was packing for his trip to Litvania.

"Can I come?" Annie asked again.

"Not this time, Annike. One day I will take you there."

"Will you see Queen Zurka?"

"It is unlikely," Papa said. "I will be devoting my time there to finding you a *mokytojas*. A teacher. In the meantime, you be sure to keep putting your papers in the *burna*."

Every night while Papa was gone, Annie wrote things on her yellow tablet and dutifully put the rolled-up papers in the *burna*. There was always something—like when she picked all the petunias in Miss Mekas's window box and tried to make a necklace out of them. The necklace hadn't worked out, and when Miss Mekas asked what had happened to her flowers, Annie lied and told her a squirrel must have eaten them. There were other things, too. She wrote them all down and fed them to the hole in Papa's study, and she always felt that same fuzzy feeling as the guilt faded and the memories lost their sting.

Both Fiona and Arthur had started school. Since there was nobody to play with during the day, Annie became an explorer.

She began with the house. She already knew many of its secrets. Next to the stairs was a closet. Annie called it the skinny room, because it was only three feet wide and ten feet deep. An old-fashioned light bulb hung from the ceiling. Annie pulled the cord and looked around. Over the years, the closet had accumulated an odd collection of objects: a broken broom, a bucket filled with gray stones, some old window screens that they never used, a metal box filled with screws and bolts, a wooden chair, a pile of rusty and dusty tools, and several other items. Annie had looked in the skinny room before, but now she went all the way to the back, and examined everything to make sure she hadn't overlooked a treasure.

There were no treasures. It was a closet for useless things that would never be missed.

The extra bedroom was not as dirty as the closet. Once

a month or so, Miss Mekas would go in and dust. There was an old iron bed that screeched when Annie jumped on it, a table with a beautiful stained-glass lamp, and framed black-and-white photographs on the walls. The photos were all of men in suits and women in long, dark dresses standing in front of buildings. They all looked unhappy. The room had a big walk-in closet with dresses on hangers and other clothing folded and packed into yellowing cardboard boxes. There were ladies' shoes of all sorts, from lace-up boots to delicate dress shoes with spiky heels. They were her mother's. She tried on the best ones, clomping around with her feet wedged into the toes.

Miss Mekas's bedroom was at the other end of the hall. Annie wasn't supposed to go in there, but she sneaked in and looked in Mekas's dresser drawers. There wasn't much—just old-lady underclothes and so forth—but she did find a small medallion on a chain. The medallion had a picture of a bearded man embossed on it. Under the man's feet were the words *Svetais Kristofers*. She put it in her pocket.

Annie knew it was wrong to take the medallion, but she wanted to keep it, so she wrote down what she had done and put the paper in the *burna*, and the bad feeling faded away.

There was only one place left in the house to explore: the cellar.

The cellar door was in the kitchen. It was always locked. Annie waited until Mekas was outside hanging sheets on the clothesline, then inspected the lock. It was an old-fashioned keyhole, the kind you can peek through. Annie poked the tip of a butter knife into the hole and wiggled it around. That didn't work. She looked in the kitchen junk drawer, where they kept everything that didn't belong someplace else. She found a paper clip. That didn't work, either. She tried a screwdriver. After a couple of minutes of twisting and turning, she heard a click. She turned the knob. The door opened with a loud creak.

Annie had been in the cellar only once that she knew of—the time she fell down the steps. She didn't remember that at all. But it still scared her, especially now, looking at the cobwebs filling the dark stairwell and smelling the damp, musty air. She almost closed the door and abandoned her plan—but she'd worked so hard to get the door open, she had to at least take a quick look.

She clicked the light switch at the top of the steps. A dim glow from below filtered up through the cobwebs.

Using the screwdriver to push aside the spiderwebs, Annie descended, pausing with each step to look for spiders. She didn't see any. When she reached the bottom, she saw that the light came from a single yellow bulb hanging from a cord.

The cellar was one big room, as big as the house above, with wooden pillars the size of telephone poles holding up the ceiling. The floor was dusty, gritty concrete. The furnace looked like a giant octopus made of iron and rust.

The walls were large, irregular stones fitted carefully together, except for one corner where the wall was redbrick and bulged out in a curve. That must be the wall beneath the tower, Annie decided. At the base of the wall was a small wooden door, big enough for her to walk through if she ducked her head. The door was fastened shut with a hasp and a brass padlock. She went to take a closer look, and heard something—a faint scratching or rubbing sound: *scrish-scritch, scritch-scrish*. Over and over again.

She put her hand on the door. It was warm, as warm as her skin. The scratching sound stopped. Annie held her breath and stood perfectly still. She leaned forward and put her ear to the door.

Scrish-scritch! Scritch-scrish! So close it sounded as if it was right inside her ear.

She yelped and ran up the stairs, into the kitchen, and full-on into Miss Mekas's soft belly. Mekas let out a screech and fell backward onto her butt.

"There's something down there!" Annie could feel her heart pounding.

Miss Mekas rolled onto her hands and knees and, with some grunts and groans, climbed to her feet.

"Child, you stop this nonsense," she said. "What you doing down there?"

Annie said, "I *heard* something!"

Mekas shook her head and rubbed her butt. "This is old house. You chase after all creaks and rattles, you make us both *pamises*." She glared at Annie. "That mean 'crazy.'"

"It wasn't a creak or rattle. It was this scritchy scratching, like something was trying to get in."

Mekas closed the cellar door. "Foolish girl," she muttered.

"I heard it!"

"You hear nothing. Go outside. Play."

"There's nobody to play with!"

"Then go outside and *don't* play." Mekas turned her back. *"Pamises!"*

Annie pushed through the back door and slammed it behind her.

II.

MATILDA

The weather was warm for September, and dry. Annie stood in the backyard, looking around for something to do. There wasn't much left of the flower garden—just a few clumps of pink and purple asters, and the tall coneflowers with all their petals gone.

Mr. O'Connor had not yet harvested his corn. The brown stalks were like an eight-foot-tall wall, making a raspy, whispery sound in the slight breeze. Annie had to turn sideways to fit between the plants. The edges of the leaves dragged against her shirt and made a hissing sound as she moved along the row.

Annie had been in the cornfield before, but never very far. She took a few more steps, until she could no longer see the house or her yard. She imagined she was lost in an endless ocean of corn. That sent a shiver up her spine.

Of course, she knew she wouldn't get *too* lost. The cornfield was big, but not so big that she couldn't reach the edge if she kept walking in a straight line. She kept on, and soon came to an open space. The cornstalks had been flattened in an area about twenty feet across, and a large number of corncobs were scattered about. Annie puzzled over that.

Could some deer have done it? She had seen deer in the neighborhood, and had once heard Mr. O'Connor complain that they were eating his corn. She examined the trampled ground and saw what looked like several two-toed hoofprints.

While looking at the prints, Annie lost track of which direction she had come from. Now she really *was* lost. That made it an adventure.

She heard a grunt, like the sound Miss Mekas made when she was lifting something. She heard it again, but from a different direction. Annie stood perfectly still, her heart pounding.

More grunts, and snuffling. She saw something down one of the rows. At first she thought it was a little dog, but as it approached the clearing, it became obvious that it was something else. A raccoon? No, it looked nothing like a raccoon. The creature did not notice Annie. It entered the clearing not fifteen feet away from her, snorted, and began snuffling through the corncobs. Once she got a look at its nose, Annie knew what it was: a baby pig!

Not a pink, curly-tailed pig like in storybooks, though. This piglet had gray-and-brown-striped hair.

Annie heard more grunts and snorts, and soon the first little pig was joined by five more identical piglets. None of them paid any attention to Annie, who stood as still as a statue until she was startled by the crackling of cornstalks breaking and a much louder, deeper grunt.

An enormous version of the little pigs came crashing into the clearing. In an instant Annie went from enchanted to terrified. She screamed. The giant pig turned its tiny eyes and its quivering pinkish nose toward her. Two long, sharp teeth curved up on either side of its snout. It let out a loud snort. The piglets melted into the corn. The big pig tilted its head, as if trying to figure out what sort of creature Annie might be, then shook its entire body like a wet dog drying itself, and galloped off after the piglets.

Annie ran in the opposite direction, crashing through the corn, heedless of the scratches to her arms and face. She ran until, suddenly, she was out of the cornfield and standing on a grassy lawn in front of a small white house. Behind the house was a barn and a silo. Next to it stood a chicken coop, a tractor, and a corncrib.

A man wearing bib overalls and a green cap was standing next to the corncrib. It was Mr. O'Connor. He was bending over, looking at something on the ground next to the corncrib.

Annie ran to him, gasping for breath. Mr. O'Connor heard her and stood up quickly.

"Where did you come from?" he asked.

Annie, still panting, pointed back at the cornfield.

He leaned forward and looked at her closely. "Aren't you Lukas Klimas's girl?"

Annie nodded. Mr. O'Connor had long arms, big hands, a red face, and a toothy smile. Annie had met him only a couple of times before. She liked him.

"Your arms are scratched up, girl. Are you okay?"

"I saw a giant scary pig!" she said.

"Ugly gray thing, 'bout yay high?" He held his palm at thigh level.

"It had teeth," Annie said.

"Tusks, yeah, she sure does. You're lucky she didn't use them on you. That's Matilda—least that's what I call her. She's a mean old gal."

"There were some baby pigs, too."

Mr. O'Connor compressed his lips. "I was afraid of that. We'll have a whole new pack of wild boars come spring. I'd

best get to harvesting my corn before they gobble it all up."
He shook his head. "Those hogs would like to eat me out
of house and home. Them and the rats."

"Rats?"

"They been raiding my corncribs. You see those little
brown pellets on the ground?" He pointed at the base of
the corncrib. "That's rat scat."

"What's rat scat?"

"Turds," Mr. O'Connor said. "Wherever there are rats,
there is rat scat. These are no ordinary rats, though. My
cat's scared of them." He looked back at Annie. "What
were you doing out in the corn, anyway?"

"Exploring," Annie said.

The door to the house opened and an old woman
stepped out onto the porch.

"Hal? Who is that?" the woman asked.

"Just a neighbor, Mama."

The old woman descended the three wooden steps.
She was holding an aluminum cane, but she didn't really
seem to need it. She crossed the lawn, the breeze stirring
her long, wispy white hair. She peered at Annie through
enormous, thick-lensed eyeglasses. She was the wrinkliest
woman Annie had ever seen.

"I'm Annie. Annie Klimas."

"Lukas and Kundze's girl? I remember your mother.

Kundze used to take me to get my hair done."

"She died," Annie said.

"Yes, it was very sad. She caught a fever, I heard. Your papa took her to the hospital and she never returned. Do you remember your mama, child?"

"Not really, but I have a picture."

"Well, you were only three when she passed. Lovely girl. I knew your father's uncle Petras as well. And *his* uncle Valdemaras. We called him Mr. Valdo. I was only about eight years old when he came to a tragic end. His car went into the river and he was never found."

"Mama, you are being morbid," said Mr. O'Connor.

"My years give me the right to dwell upon the tragic," the old woman said.

"How old are you?" Annie asked her.

"Mama Dara will turn ninety-nine in January," Mr. O'Connor said.

"Mr. Valdo was the handsomest man in the county," said Mama Dara. "And when his nephew Petras came into the land back in the Depression, why, he was just the same. Handsome as a hatchet to the day he died."

"My papa is handsome, too," Annie said.

"Yes, he looks just like Petras. Runs in your family, it does. But I've not been able to see as well the past few years, what with these cataracts in my eyes."

Annie tried to see her eyes through her glasses but could make out only pale blue smudges.

"How's your daddy doing?" asked Mr. O'Connor. "Haven't seen him in an age."

"He's in Litvania," Annie said.

"Ah, the country of his birth. Mama still talks about going back to Ireland."

"And I will someday," said Mama Dara.

"I should probably get you home, Annie," said Mr. O'Connor. "Have you ever ridden on a tractor?"

Annie loved the tractor. They sat way up high, and as they drove down the long dirt driveway, she could see out over the tops of the corn plants. The brown tassels wiggled in waves; it looked as though you could swim across them.

Mr. O'Connor turned left on Highway 9 and stayed on the shoulder. A dozen cars whooshed by. He raised his voice over the rumble of the tractor engine and said, "Time was, I'd see two, maybe three cars drive by all day."

"Did you always live here?"

"Yep. Born and raised. Except for four years in the army."

"Did you know Papa's uncle?"

"Sure I did. I used to lease the field from his uncle Petras. When your papa inherited the land, he sold it to me." He shook his head. "Strange what happened. I come back from the war and they tell me Petras is dead. Next thing I know, your daddy moves in and takes over like nothing had changed. If nobody had told me different, I might've thought they were the same person. Course, your daddy's a lot younger. Petras's hair was white as snow."

They turned on Tustison Street, then again on Klimas Avenue. They drove past Fiona's house, then Arthur's house.

"Papa's home!" Annie yelled when she saw his car in the driveway.

Mr. O'Connor pulled into the driveway behind the Cadillac. He shut down the tractor engine, climbed off, and helped Annie down. She ran to the door. Just as she reached it, the door opened and Miss Mekas came out.

"Where have you been?" she asked.

"I was visiting Mr. O'Connor. Where's Papa?"

"He is in study. Very tired from trip."

"I bet he is," Mr. O'Connor said. "That Litvania is a long ways off." He looked behind Mekas and said, "Speak of the devil."

"I thought I heard a tractor out here," Papa said. The lines framing his mouth looked deeper, and his skin was pale.

"How are you, Lukas?"

"Happy to be home," Papa said. "Happy to see my Annike." He lifted her into his arms. "Wherever did you find this waif?" he asked Mr. O'Connor.

"Marching out of the cornfield just as proud as you please. Thought she could use a lift home."

"Well, we appreciate it, Hal." He set Annie down. "What were you doing in the corn, Annike?"

"Exploring," Annie said. "I met Mama Dara. She's almost a hundred years old!"

"Why, I haven't seen Dara in ages!" Papa turned to Mr. O'Connor. "How's her health?"

"Feisty as ever," said Mr. O'Connor.

"Glad to hear it. She was quite the woman in her day."

Mr. O'Connor tipped his head. "So they tell me, but—*in her day*? She was in her seventies when you met her."

Papa looked startled, then recovered and said, "She was a handsome woman, is all I meant."

"Indeed. Say, Lukas, you been having any rat problems lately?"

"Rats? No. Why?"

"Caught one in my corncrib. Biggest rat I ever saw. Black as coal."

"You don't say! Hmm. Maybe if you put some food out for them, they'll stay away from your corn."

"You want me to feed the rats?" Mr. O'Connor raised

his bushy eyebrows. "No offense, Lukas, but that's the craziest thing I've heard since Mama Dara claimed she saw a leprechaun!"

Papa laughed. "I guess so! Anyway, I wish you luck with them, Hal."

"Gonna take more than luck." Mr. O'Connor looked up at the cottonwood tree looming over them. "That's a big tree you got there," he said.

"My uncle's uncle, Valdemaras, planted it back in the 1880s," Papa said.

"That's mighty old for a cottonwood. When she comes down, you'll have yourself a heck of a mess. Probably knock out the power line and the back end of your house."

"Oh, I think it's got a few years left on it," Papa said with a chuckle.

"Suit yourself. It was me, I'd take it down right now." He pointed at a crack running up the trunk to the lower branches. "You got a split happening right there. Only a matter of time."

"I'll keep that in mind, Hal. Thanks again for bringing Annie home."

After Mr. O'Connor rode off on his tractor, Annie started telling Papa all about the pigs, but he stopped her and said, "Annike, there is someone I want you to meet." He put his hands on her shoulders and turned her toward the house. Standing in the doorway was a young woman with wavy blond hair and a spray of freckles across her nose and cheeks. She was wearing blue jeans, a pink sweater, and red cowboy boots. The woman smiled, and her smile spread almost across her whole face.

"Hello, Annike," she said with a slight accent. "My name is Ona Smetona. I will be your *mokytojas*."

12

STORY PROBLEMS

If John has ten apples, and he gives one apple to Alice, and two apples to Kevin, and one apple to Mary, how many apples does John have left?

Annie scowled at the problem. She asked, "Ona Smetona, did John eat any of his apples?"

Ona Smetona looked up from her phone. "You may assume that he did not," she said.

"Did he lose any?"

"No."

"Why did Kevin get two apples?"

Ona Smetona sighed. "Annie . . ."

"Because I don't think it's fair. And besides, I already did arithmetic yesterday."

"We do arithmetic every day. You know that."

"I don't like it."

"Yes, I understand that. But if you want to avoid doing *more* problems, you must show me that you are able to solve the problems at hand."

"Where did he get all the apples?"

"From his apple tree."

"Why is he giving them away?" Annie knew she was being difficult, but it was more interesting than arithmetic.

"You have only four more problems to solve, Annie. If you do that, I will read you a story from that old fairy-tale book you showed me."

Annie refocused on the apple problem. If John gave one apple to Alice, then he would have nine. And if he gave two to Kevin, ten minus two was eight. And ten minus the apple he gave to Mary would be nine. She wrote 9+8+9 on the paper. Nine plus eight was seventeen, and seventeen plus nine was . . . twenty-six. That seemed like a lot of apples, but Ona Smetona said John had an apple tree, so maybe it was right. In any case, she was bored with that problem, so she wrote down 26, and started on the next one.

Homeschooling with Ona Smetona was better than homeschooling by herself, but Annie still missed her friends. She saw Fiona some days after school, but it wasn't as fun as it used to be. Fiona just wanted to talk about school and new friends that Annie had never met.

At least Ona Smetona was nice. She taught Annie all kinds of things about history and reading and how the world worked. She learned that the South Pole had penguins, and that the North Pole had polar bears, and that kings and queens had once ruled all the countries, but now most countries had presidents instead.

Ona Smetona had been born in Litvania, but she had gone to college in Boston. She had been teaching English in Litvania when Papa hired her to be Annie's *mokytojas*. She told Annie that she had always wanted to visit America again.

"In Litvania we do not have so much freedom. We must do as Queen Zurka says."

"I am related to Queen Zurka," Annie told her.

Ona Smetona laughed. "Everyone in Litvania is related to Queen Zurka."

"My arithmetic is done," Annie announced.

Ona Smetona looked up from her phone. "Show me your work."

Annie's answers to the story problems made Ona Smetona frown, then laugh.

"You have a curious way of thinking," she said. "If you are to learn arithmetic, you must learn to control your imagination."

"I would rather imagine things than do arithmetic."

"Clearly. In any case, I can see you worked hard on these, so I will read you a story."

"Can you read the one with the two girls and the dragon?" Annie held open the book of Litvanian fairy tales.

Ona Smetona smiled and took the book. "I remember this story from when I was a little girl," she said. "It is called 'The Sisters and the *Slibinas*.'"

"It looks more like a dragon," Annie said.

"In Litvania, *slibinas* means 'dragon.'"

"Are there really dragons in Litvania?"

"Of course! Do you not have them here?"

"We have wild pigs," Annie said.

"Those are scary, too. Now listen, and I will read you this story."

13.

THE SISTERS
AND THE
SLIBINAS

✤One day a very long time ago, in the tiny
Litvanian village of Kusk, there lived twin sisters named Freka and Rayka. The only difference between them was that Freka's right eye
was green, and her left eye was brown. Her sister,
Rayka, had opposite eyes—brown on the right
and green on the left. When Freka and Rayka
looked at each other, it was as if they were looking in a mirror.

None of the villagers could tell the two girls
apart. They were not clever enough to see how
their eyes were different, so they simply called
them the twins.

Back in those long-ago days, Kusk was ruled

by a great dragon named Vlang, who visited once a year on Midsummer Eve and demanded a tribute of three bulls, six sheep, two piglets, and one villager. If the villagers refused, Vlang would burn their village to the ground with his fiery breath. Of course, he had never done so, but no one questioned that he could, for Vlang was as big as a house, and smoke came from his nostrils as he spoke.

Most years, the villagers chose to sacrifice the oldest person in the village, reasoning that he or she would die soon anyway. Sometimes they chose someone who had committed a crime, such as the baker who, ten years ago, had been caught adding sawdust to his bread dough. Or, a few years before that, Vlang was offered the woman Helgira, who was suspected of being a witch. But most years it was the eldest among them who was sacrificed to the dragon Vlang.

On this particular year, the villagers had a problem. Their three eldest citizens were all exactly the same age! Not only that, but they were all elders on the village council—the group responsible for gathering the annual tribute to the dragon. And since there were only five members of the council, it was quickly voted that in this case, the three eldest would have to be excused from the duty of becoming a meal for Vlang.

Who then should make the ultimate sacrifice? The farmer who beat his wife? The apothecary whose drugs were not always effective? The blacksmith's apprentice, who drank too much ale?

"What about the twins?" suggested Einar Ghent, the tallest and the baldest of the three elder councilmen. "They are impossible to tell apart! No one would miss one of them."

"Except, perhaps, the other twin," said Kline Damion, the youngest member of the council.

"Henceforth, she must rely upon a mirror to keep her company," Ghent replied. "It is all the same."

Ghent's logic was irrefutable, and so the council voted to offer either Freka or Rayka to the dragon Vlang.

"But which one?" asked Kline Damion.

"Does it matter?" said Ghent. "Let the dragon choose."

And so it was that on Midsummer Eve, the dragon came sailing over the trees on his twelve tiny wings and alighted upon the village square, where three bulls, six sheep, and two squealing piglets waited nervously in a willow withe pen.

"What is this?" the dragon roared. A plume of rancid smoke gushed from his fearsome maw. "Only eleven? I require one morsel for each of my beautiful wings! I will burn your village to the ground!"

"Wait!" cried Einar Ghent. "We have your twelfth tribute."

Freka and Rayka were brought out to face the great dragon.

"You may have whichever of them you choose," said Ghent. "Freka or Rayka."

"Which is which?" asked Vlang.

"I do not know," said Ghent. He bowed and backed away.

Vlang lowered his head and examined the two girls with his golden eyes. Wisps of smoke trailed from his nostrils, and his wings twitched in frustration.

"I cannot tell one from the other," he grumbled smokily.

"This is our conundrum as well," said Ghent, scratching his hairless scalp.

"We are not the same," said Freka to the dragon. "Can you not tell?"

Vlang brought his smoldering snout close to the girls and sniffed each of them. "You smell the same."

He licked the girls' cheeks, one with each tip of his long, forked tongue. "You taste the same."

"We are not the same," said Freka and Rayka together.

"You sound the same."

Vlang drew his head back and regarded the twins with puzzlement.

"I can detect no difference," he said after a moment.

"The difference is obvious," said Freka.

"If you cannot tell us apart, then you are unworthy of a tribute," said Rayka.

Vlang blinked his great golden eyes and sat back on his haunches so that his head towered far above them. His voice boomed and sparks flew from his mouth. "You dare speak to me thus?"

Freka and Rayka spoke as one: "We have nothing to lose."

The dragon's head shot down, and for a moment it looked as though he was going to devour the two girls then and there, but he stopped mere inches from their frightened faces.

"You have courage!" he said. "Unlike your elders." Vlang looked past the girls at Einar Ghent, who was trying to hide himself among the crowd of wide-eyed villagers. Vlang's tongue shot out like the tongue of a frog and snatched Ghent from the crowd.

It was over in an instant. The last they saw of Einar Ghent was the shiny top of his hairless head disappearing into the dragon's mouth.

Vlang, of course, was still hungry, so he roasted the bulls and the sheep with his fiery breath and ate them right there in the village square. The two piglets he spared, giving one piglet to each of the girls.

"A gift, for your courage," he told them. "I will return next Midsummer Eve and have another look at you, and if I can tell you apart, I will eat one of you then."

With that, the great dragon rose into the sky on his twelve tiny wings. He was quickly gone from sight, and the villagers of Kusk returned to their homes.❖

. . . . .

Ona Smetona closed the book.

"Then what happened?" Annie asked.

"They lived happily ever after," said Ona Smetona. "Vlang was never able to tell the sisters apart because as everyone knows, dragons cannot tell left from right."

"I didn't know that."

"Now you do." Ona Smetona set down the book. "At least one thing you have learned today, Annike Klimas—a thing you would not have learned at school."

"Ona Smetona, what does *Svetais Kristofers* mean?"

She wrinkled her forehead. "*Svetais Kristofers?*" She pronounced it differently than Annie had. "Where did you see that?"

"I think in a book."

"It is the Litvanian name for Saint Christopher, who keeps travelers safe. There, now you have learned two things."

PART TWO

ZELTY
MARAS

14.

A CARPET
OF RATS

The days and weeks and months passed. Annie continued to feed the *nuodeema burna*. Usually, it was some little thing, like telling a lie to Miss Mekas or Ona Smetona. Lying was easy. When she told Ona Smetona she had read a whole book that she hadn't read—even if Ona Smetona caught her in the lie—she felt bad only until she wrote it down on her yellow tablet and pushed the paper into the little hole in Papa's study.

Christmas came and went. Papa was not much interested in holidays. In Litvania, he said, every day was a holiday. But he gave her a bright yellow fleece hoodie. "So I can always find you," he said. Annie wasn't sure it was her style—whatever her style was—but she told him she loved it. Ona Smetona gave her a set of velvet scrunchies in all the colors of the rainbow, and Miss Mekas cooked a gigantic turkey that took them a week to eat.

Ona Smetona was a good teacher. Over the winter Annie learned the history of Litvania, how to multiply and divide big numbers, how frogs and turtles hibernate in the mud during the winter, and how to look up words in the dictionary.

Annie's lessons were in the morning. In the afternoon, Ona Smetona got in the little red car Papa had bought for her and drove back to her apartment in the city. Papa was always at work, Miss Mekas was not much fun to talk to, Annie had explored every room in the house a hundred times, and it was too cold outside to play. Sometimes Annie drew pictures and sometimes she read books.

She didn't see Fiona very much anymore.

At ten minutes after three o'clock every day, Fiona's school bus would drop her off at the corner. As soon as Annie heard the bus, she would look out the window and watch as Fiona ran home. Some days Annie would put on her hat and coat and go over there, but more often she walked past Fiona's house without stopping because she was afraid Fiona would be mean to her.

She missed her friend—her *old* friend. Every time they talked, Fiona made some kind of comment about kids

Annie didn't know, or clothes Annie didn't care about, or bands she hadn't heard of, or some TV show she hadn't seen. Fiona knew Annie didn't have a TV. The only time she ever watched TV was with Fiona.

She didn't see much of Arthur, either. His mom mostly kept him inside over the winter, but one day in March, Annie noticed him bent over a snowbank, poking at it with a stick. He was wearing rubber boots and a puffy down jacket with the hood up, even though it was not that cold. Annie put on her yellow hoodie and went out to see what he was up to.

"Hi," Annie said, coming up behind him.

Arthur straightened up and looked at her with his unnervingly direct gaze. Annie was surprised at how tall he had gotten over the past few months.

"What are you doing?" she asked.

"Making holes," Arthur said.

"Why?"

"To see what's inside." Arthur walked a few steps and made another hole in the snowbank.

"What do you expect to find?" Annie asked.

"Stuff," he said. A few steps later they arrived at the sewer grate where Arthur had gotten his arm stuck. Arthur bent over and peered into the grate. Water from the melting snowbanks was trickling in from both sides.

"Do you still think there are bunnies down there?" Annie asked.

"They're not really bunnies." He pushed his stick into the grate and let go. It fell into the darkness and landed with a faint splash.

"I don't think you're supposed to put sticks in there," Annie said.

"They like sticks."

When she got home, thinking about how much Arthur had grown, Annie went to the library doorway and measured herself. She stared at the new mark in shock. She was exactly as tall as she had been on her birthday, and that was many months ago. She hadn't grown even a fraction of an inch.

Papa was in a bad mood when he got home. He said one of his tenants had refused to pay his rent.

"He will be sorry," he said.

"Why?" Annie asked.

"Because I will make them pay." He went into his study and closed the door.

At dinner that night, he asked Annie what she had done that day.

"I measured myself," she said.

"Oh?"

"I think I'm stuck. I'm the same height as I was on my birthday."

"That is not unusual."

"Arthur is getting taller. And so is Fiona."

"Children grow in spurts. I wouldn't worry about it. Besides, what's your hurry?"

"I don't want to be littler than everyone else."

"You'll catch up. Now, if you'll excuse me, I have work to do." Papa stood up and went back to his study.

Annie tried to help Miss Mekas clean up, but Mekas shooed her away.

"Is harder when you help," Mekas said.

In the library, Annie sorted through the stack of books Ona Smetona had brought for her. Some of them were for little kids. Others were big and fat and looked too hard to read. Annie found an in-between book with a picture of a boy and a girl in a canoe, and some sort of animal swimming alongside. Annie read the description on the back. It was about a brother and a sister who had a pet otter named Otto.

She settled in to read, but after a couple of chapters she lost interest in Otto the otter. She went out to the porch and sat on her rocking chair. A thin crescent moon hovered over Mr. Wendell's house, barely showing through wisps of cloud. The neighborhood was cloaked in shadow. She looked down the street. The sun had worked hard all afternoon; the remains of the snowbanks were pale smudges.

A motion caught her eye. Something was moving by the sewer grate. Annie tried to make it out. It looked like a dark stain spreading from the sewer onto the street. Was water coming up from the sewer? It didn't move like water; it was more as if a dark, lumpy carpet was crawling out from the grating. The edges of the carpet started to break up into individual lumps. Not lumps. Animals. Hundreds of them scurrying up the street toward her, then over the curb and across the vacant lot toward the cornfield.

Annie screamed, "Papa!" She ran to the door and yelled into the house, "Papa, come quick!"

A few seconds later, her father came running out onto the porch, looking back and forth for whatever had frightened her.

"What is it?" he said.

"Over there!" Annie pointed—but there was nothing. They had all disappeared.

"Where?" he asked. "I don't see anything."

"They were there!"

"Annike . . ." He knelt down and put his hands on her shoulders. "What is it you think you saw?"

"They came out of the sewer and ran toward the corn-field! Hundreds and hundreds of them!"

"Hundreds of what?"

"I think they were rats! The rats that eat Mr. O'Connor's corn!"

"Annike, you were seeing things."

"I wasn't!"

He took her hand and led her back into the house, saying, "Sometimes when it is dark, we imagine things, Annike."

"I saw them!"

Papa frowned. "Annike, have you written to the *nuo-deema burna* today?"

"I didn't do anything bad."

"I want you to get your pencil box and think. I'm sure you'll come up with something."

Annie was furious. He didn't believe her! She stomped up to her room and took out her tablet and pencils and wrote in big letters,

I SAW RATS!!!

She rolled up the page tightly and took it downstairs and put it in the *burna* without saying a word to Papa, who watched her from behind his desk.

"You will feel better now," he said.

Annie left the study. As she walked back up the stairs to her room, she muttered, "No, I won't."

15

THE SEVENTH PRINCE

The sewer grate looked completely normal when Annie checked it the next morning. She put her face as close to the grate as she dared. She wrinkled her nose at the smell: sour milk, stinky socks, and wet leaves.

"Did you see them?"

Annie let out a little screech and jumped to her feet.

"Where did you come from?" she asked.

Arthur pointed down the street at his house.

"Don't sneak up on me like that!" she said.

"Not sneaking," Arthur said.

"You scared me!"

Arthur shrugged, as if scaring her had been a necessary thing. He was not at all sorry. "They come out when the moon is little," he said.

Annie remembered how last night the moon had been hardly there at all, just a little curved sliver of light.

"How do you know?" she asked.

"I can see from my window." Arthur pointed toward the cornfield. "They get hungry."

When Ona Smetona showed up for lessons that day, Annie told her about the rats.

"Are you sure they were rats?" Ona asked.

"Yes. But Papa doesn't believe me."

"In Litvania, rats are very important," Ona said. "When the Golden Horde invaded Litvania eight hundred years ago, it was the rats who saved us."

"Really?"

"Yes. The rats spread a plague among the invaders. Many Litvanians got sick, too, but the invaders were much worse off. Thousands died, and the rest fled back to China. That is why a bronze statue of a rat guards the gates of the queen's castle. There is even a rumor that Queen Zurka keeps a rat as a pet. They say it sleeps with her in a golden cage."

"Queen Zurka sleeps in a cage?"

Ona Smetona laughed. "No, just the rat. It may not even be true, but Queen Zurka is peculiar, so who knows?"

"Is Queen Zurka beautiful?"

"Ha! She looks like a dried-up apple. She was a wrinkly old lady when I was a little girl, and my mother claims Zurka was old when *she* was a child. They say that she is kept alive by ancient magic. The story is that when the queen's artisans cast the bronze rat statue, the rats created their own statue of Queen Zurka deep in the cellars of the palace. It is that statue that keeps the queen alive."

"Is it true?"

Ona Smetona smiled and shook her head. "In Litvania, people love to tell stories."

"Like fairy tales?"

"Yes. Some of the stories are made up, but some are true—or partly true. It is very difficult to tell which is which."

"But you believe me? About the rats?"

Ona Smetona shrugged. "Rats are mysterious creatures. Why, just yesterday, one of the other tenants in the building where I live came home and found several rats going through his cupboards."

"Really?"

"That's what he claimed, but nobody else saw any rats. Your father, who owns the building, said he was making it up. But when I talked to the man this morning, he seemed really scared. He wouldn't go into his apartment. He said he was moving. I don't blame him. In any case, your father will be glad the man is leaving, because he hasn't been paying his rent."

"Do you have rats?"

"What? Of course not—there are no rats in *my* apartment! If there were, I'd move, too."

"But what if they're hiding in the walls?"

"So long as they stay there, I'll not be bothered. Would you like to hear a story about a castle full of rats?"

"A fairy tale?"

"Yes, but this one is not from your book. It is called 'The Seventh Prince.'"

✤In the Olden Days, a queen bore seven sons. The eldest son became the Crown Prince. He sat at his father's side and learned the skills necessary to one day become king. The second son was trained in the art of war, and was named the Royal Defender. The third son studied to become the Exchequer, responsible for collecting taxes and managing the king's fortune. The fourth son mastered the ways of high society, and was placed in charge of parades, galas, costumes, and decorum. The fifth son traveled the lands in a gilded coach as the Royal Diplomat. The sixth son was named Prince of Ways, and presided over the building of roads, bridges, and ships.

The seventh son, whose name was Zogg, had no job, as all the important positions had been taken by his brothers.

One day, as Zogg was moping about the castle, the queen observed that he seemed unhappy. "Zogg," she said, "what do you do with yourself?"

Zogg thought for a moment, then said, "I do nothing. I have no purpose, as you have borne too many children, and I was the last."

The queen could not argue with that. As she was considering her response, a rat scurried out from a crack in the wall and ran over her royal slipper. The queen let out a screech and leaped back. The rat ran down the hall and disappeared into another hole.

"Perhaps," she said after she had recovered, "you could do something about these pestilent vermin!"

"I know nothing of rats," said Zogg, who had grown accustomed to the army of rodents infesting the castle. Like lice, fleas, grain weevils, mold, bats, and pigeons, the rats were simply a fact of life.

"Nor do I!" said the queen. "Nor do I want

to! I hereby create a new Highly Important Royal Office. Henceforth, you shall be known as the Queen's Ratter."

Although Queen's Ratter did not have the prestige of Crown Prince, it was something to do. Zogg took on his new job with enthusiasm. He began by catching the rats in clever little snares, but the rats quickly learned to avoid his traps. He tried poison, but the rats would not eat the tainted food. He tried drowning them by piping water into their holes, but managed only to flood the servants' chambers. Finally, after weeks of failed efforts, he thought to wonder why he never saw a rat when he was carrying a torch, or even a candle. Only when he blew out his candles at night did he hear their scurrying and scratching. Could it be that the rats were afraid of fire?

Zogg set up an experiment. In one room he placed a platter of cheeses and bread. In the next room he did the same, but set a burning candle on the table with the food.

The next morning the platter in the first room was clean. In the candlelit room, the food was untouched.

Aha! he thought. *Rats fear fire!*

Zogg sought out the Royal Chandler, whose job it was to make all the candles and torches for the castle, and ordered him to make one thousand beeswax candles.

"M'lord, that is too many!" exclaimed the chandler. "There are not bees enough in the land to produce so much wax!"

Zogg thought for a moment, then asked, "How is our supply of pigs?"

"We have many pigs."

"Then make me a thousand lard lamps, and use the fat of the pigs for fuel."

And so the chandler made one thousand small lamps of hardened clay, filled them with lard, and placed a wick in each. Zogg recruited all the pages and maids and castle guards to place the lamps in every room, every nook, every cranny of the castle. When all was in readiness one moonless night, the lamps were set ablaze.

Zogg stood high upon the parapet while beneath his feet the castle glowed with the light of a thousand lamps. The air smelled of burning lard. Zogg watched from above as the rats fled the castle. A first there were only a few, scurrying across the drawbridge, but soon a few became hundreds, then thousands, crowding the bridge, swimming across the moat, and leaping from windows. Soon, all the rats had left the castle.

What Zogg did not realize was that the last rat to leave dared to approach the lamp burning in the Royal Granary, where the wheat and corn and flours were stored. The rat tipped the lamp onto its side. The molten fat spilled across the floor and was set ablaze by the burning wick. The rat fled, and the granary burst into flames.

Now, castles have walls of stone, and stone will not burn. But the wooden rafters and shelves, the tables and chairs and beds, the tapestries and carpets and curtains and rugs—all these things will burn. Within minutes the entire castle became an inferno, and all those within it perished. ✦

That night, Annie brought a candle to her room and set it on her bedside table. She lit it, turned out the lights, and watched the orange flickers dance across the ceiling until she fell asleep. By morning, the wax had melted away and the flame had gone out.

16.
THE PARTY

When the public schools let out in June, Ona Smetona went back to Litvania.

"You must still do your lessons," Papa told Annie.

"Even arithmetic?"

"Are you able to multiply and divide?"

"Yes. If the numbers aren't too big."

"Do you know your fractions?"

"Some of them."

Papa chuckled. "All right, then, you may take a break from arithmetic."

"Can I go back to regular school in the fall?"

"Keep up with your reading and writing, and we'll see."

By that time, Annie had half convinced herself that the sewer rats had been a dream. She still looked suspiciously at the sewer grate when she walked past it, but most of the time she didn't think about rats at all.

A letter arrived for Annie. It was an invitation to a party for Fiona's eleventh birthday. At the bottom of the invitation was a phone number followed by the letters *RSVP*. When Papa got home, Annie asked him what those letters meant.

"RSVP stands for *répondez s'il vous plaît*." The words sounded like gobbledygook. "It's French," Papa explained.

"But what does it mean?"

"It means you should tell them if you're coming."

Annie called the number on the invitation. Fiona answered.

"Happy almost birthday," Annie said.

"Annie?" Fiona seemed surprised.

"I'm RSVPing for your party," Annie said.

"Okay . . . um . . . it's on Saturday."

"That's what it says on the invitation."

"So . . . you are coming?" Fiona did not sound very enthusiastic.

Annie suspected that Fiona didn't send her the invitation at all. It must have been her mom. That made Annie mad.

"Of course I'll come," Annie said as she thought, *Whether you want me to or not!*

. . . . .

The day of the party, Annie wore her best dress—the green one—and brought a Wonder Woman comic to give to Fiona because she had a Wonder Woman T-shirt. When she got to Fiona's, the other kids were already there—about twenty of them milling around in the backyard. Next to the gate was a card table piled with gifts. Annie added her present to the pile. None of the other girls were wearing dresses—they all had on shorts or jeans. Why hadn't Fiona told her not to wear a dress?

Another thing that bothered Annie was that she was the littlest kid there. Before, she'd never worried much about how big she was because they were all about the same size. Now it seemed that everybody had gotten a growth spurt except her. She recognized several of the girls from school. The Choi twins, Jessie and Jamie, were talking with Keisha Johnson. Hannah Trager was eating chips and looking at another girl's bracelet. Most of the kids were new to Annie. She didn't see any boys, and that was fine with her.

On the picnic table was a big birthday cake with eleven candles. Annie looked around for Fiona, and found her talking with a tall girl she didn't know. The tall girl had long blond hair and a rainbow-patterned shoulder bag resting on her hip.

Fiona waved Annie over.

"Annie, this is Rachel. Remember I told you about her? From summer camp?"

"Hi," Annie said. "I like your purse."

"It's not a *purse*," Rachel said with a smirk. "It's a *cross-body bag*."

"What's the difference?" Annie said.

Rachel frowned at Annie. "Oh. Right. You're the *home-school* girl."

Fiona laughed uncomfortably and walked away. Annie just stood there in front of Rachel, not sure what to say.

"My dad says your dad is a slumlord," Rachel said.

"What's a slumlord?" Annie asked.

"He rents dirty old buildings to poor people. My dad is in real estate, and he says your dad is *notorious*. His buildings are full of rats."

"No, they aren't!" Annie said, but she was remembering what Ona Smetona had told her about the man with rats in his apartment.

Rachel shrugged. "Whatever." She went across the yard to where Jessie and Jamie and Keisha were standing. She said something. They all looked at Annie and laughed.

Annie felt her face get hot. She turned away. Why would Rachel be so nasty to her, and why didn't Fiona stop her? Determined not to cry, Annie pressed her lips tight together and looked around for a friendly face.

She found one—on a boy sitting in the corner of the yard, his back against the fence, eating cheese curls out of a bowl.

"Hi, Arthur," she said. She wasn't the shortest person there after all.

Arthur gave her an orange grin and offered her a cheese curl.

"No, thank you." Annie sat down on the grass beside him. "Why are you sitting way over here?"

"Fiona said to."

"Oh."

"I found a hole." He pointed. Annie leaned over him and looked. There was definitely a hole, about the same size as the hole under her pine trees. "Everybody has holes in their yard," Arthur said.

"You shouldn't sit so close. Something might come out and bite you."

Arthur dropped a cheese curl into the hole. "No, they won't. I'm nice to them."

The girls were gathering at the picnic table, taking their seats. It didn't look like there was any more room, and Annie didn't much want to join them anyway. She and Arthur watched as Rachel took charge and cut the cake, passing out slices on paper plates. Fiona looked over at

Annie and Arthur. She grabbed two plates and brought them over to them.

"It's chocolate," she said. She did not ask them to come to the table. Arthur immediately started eating, pausing only to drop a few crumbs into the hole.

Annie tasted the cake. The frosting was too thick and gooey, and her appetite had deserted her. She stood up and crossed the lawn to the gate. On the grass next to the table with all the presents was a rainbow-patterned bag—Rachel's *crossbody bag*. Annie glanced back at the picnic table. Nobody was looking at her. She opened the bag, shoved her gooey cake inside, and smooshed the sides of the bag together. Nobody saw her.

She slipped out through the gate and headed for home.

17

NAILED

"You have nice time at party?" Miss Mekas asked when Annie came in through the kitchen door.

"We had cake," Annie said.

"I suppose your appetite is ruin for dinner."

"What are you making?"

"Soup. Is okay?"

Annie nodded.

"Is not for two hours yet," Mekas said.

Annie went to the library and measured herself against the doorframe. It had been almost a year since her last birthday, but she hadn't grown at all! She was a home-schooled shrimp, she didn't know how to dress right, and everybody hated her. She tried to make herself feel better by imagining Rachel's face when she looked in her purse.

At first Annie felt a thrill of triumph, but moments later she felt kind of queasy. How would she feel if someone did that to her? Rachel was mean. Annie had never done anything *that* mean. She went up to her room. The yellow tablet was waiting on her bedside table. She wrote down what she had done. She rolled the page into a thin tube and carried it downstairs to Papa's study and pushed it into the *burna*.

She sat back and closed her eyes. Her scalp prickled, then grew warm, and a softness settled over her. The cake in Rachel's purse was not so bad. It was just a little joke. Besides, Rachel deserved it. Rachel was mean. Annie was never *mean*.

Annie was a good girl.

She folded the rug back over the *burna* and went out to the front porch. Arthur was sitting on the steps, crying.

"Arthur?" She sat down next to him. "What's the matter?"

"Fiona said I put cake in that girl's bag," he said. "But I didn't."

Annie felt a sharp pang in her chest.

"You did it," Arthur said. "I saw you."

"I'm sorry."

"I didn't tell. Fiona was really mad at me. She made me go home."

Annie didn't say anything. She didn't feel bad about

putting the cake in Rachel's bag because she'd already fed that to the *burna*, but now she felt bad for Arthur. There was nothing she could say that wouldn't make both of them feel worse, so she put her arm around his thin shoulders and said nothing.

"I guess everybody's mean sometimes," Arthur said.

A moment later she heard a shout, and then a loud screech from Mr. Wendell's garage. Annie had never heard a scream like that—a *man* scream. She jumped up and ran across the street, followed by Arthur. Something dark and fast scurried from the open garage door into the bushes. Mr. Wendell was in the garage, slumped over the hood of his car, clutching his wrist. TomTom was on the roof of the car, his fur all puffed up.

"Mr. Wendell? What happened?"

Blood was running down his hand, dripping on the garage floor. Next to the drops of blood was the live trap, upside down, its doors hanging open. Mr. Wendell looked up. His face was red.

"Little devil nailed me!" he said.

"What devil?"

He stood up straighter and looked at his wrist. "I finally caught him," Mr. Wendell said. "That same varmint that's been making a mess in here."

"Was it a squirrel?"

"Wasn't a squirrel. I heard it banging around and came out to see what I'd caught, and it managed to tip the trap over. I tried to grab it, but—" He scowled at the wound on his wrist. "Probably not a good idea."

"What was it?" Annie asked.

Mr. Wendell took a breath and regarded her thoughtfully.

"Looked like a big black rat," he said. He examined his wrist. "Got me good."

"I saw rats coming out of the sewer," Annie said.

"Rats are like cockroaches—if you see one, you know there are plenty more. Anyway, this one took off. TomTom almost got the little devil."

"He has blood on his foot," Arthur said.

TomTom was licking his paw.

"I hope it's not his blood!"

TomTom allowed Mr. Wendell to examine his paw. "Looks like that rat took a little nip out of TomTom, too. I just hope we scared him bad enough he won't be back. Now, if you'll excuse me, TomTom and I need to attend to our battle wounds." He lifted TomTom and carried him into the house.

"He shouldn't have made them mad," Arthur said.

18

THE CULVERT

The next day the doorbell rang. Annie opened the door. It was Arthur's mom.

"Hello, Annie," she said. "Is Arthur here by any chance?"

Annie shook her head.

"Have you seen him this morning?"

"No."

"Well, I'm a little bit concerned. He's been gone for two hours. Would you help me look for him?"

"He likes the turtles."

"Oh dear. That blasted pond!" She turned and ran across the street and down Circle Lane. Annie followed. When they got to the pond, five turtles slid off the log and sank beneath the pond scum.

"I don't think he was here," Annie said.

Emily Golden gave Annie a panicky look.

Annie said, "If he'd been here, the turtles wouldn't be on the log. When you get close, they go in the water, and Arthur always scares them."

"Where could he be?"

"He might have gone to visit the Dennisons' dog," Annie said.

"Where do they live?"

"Across the pond, in the green house. They have a wiener dog."

Emily Golden headed quickly around the pond. Annie started to follow her, then stopped. Arthur was fascinated by sewers, and there was a big culvert spilling into the ditch along Tustison Street on the other side of Fiona's house. Would Arthur go that far away from home? If he knew the culvert was there, he wouldn't be able to resist.

Annie ran down the street past Fiona's, then up Tustison. The ditch along the side of the street was full of muddy water and cattails and weeds. Annie climbed down the bank to where the culvert emptied onto a pile of rocks.

The culvert was big, almost big enough for her to stand up in. It was dry inside, because it hadn't rained lately. She shouted Arthur's name. The culvert swallowed her voice without an echo. She leaned in and saw a small, brown, person-shaped object standing motionless a few feet inside the culvert. For one brief heart-stopping moment, she thought it was alive, but it wasn't. She stepped into the culvert, bending over so she would fit, and examined the object. It was about the size of a Barbie doll, but chubbier, and was made out of sticks and twigs and held together by what looked like a paste made of soggy leaves. It reminded her of the nest in Mr. Wendell's garage. It also reminded her of Arthur—something about the shape of it, and the way it was standing.

She heard something—a rustling sound—deeper in the culvert.

"Arthur? Is that you?"

"Hi."

Annie stood up straight and banged her head.

Arthur was standing outside the culvert looking in at her.

"Arthur!" She climbed out of the culvert and felt the top of her head. She would have a bump. "Where *were* you?"

"Looking at frogs." He was covered with mud from the knees down. His hands were dirty, too.

"You were in the ditch?"

Arthur nodded.

"I was afraid you went in the sewer," she said.

"I'm not supposed to."

"But *did* you?"

Arthur shrugged and pointed into the culvert. "Just to look at the stick man. Don't tell."

"I won't, but we should get back." Annie grabbed his muddy hand. "Your mom is looking all over for you."

They climbed out of the ditch and walked back up Tustison Street. As they turned onto Klimas Avenue, Annie saw a police car parked in front of Arthur's house. His mother was talking to the policeman through the car window. She saw them and came running. She swept Arthur into her arms, heedless of his muddy condition, and hugged him.

"Where did you find him?" she asked Annie.

"He was looking at frogs in the ditch." Annie didn't say anything about the culvert, or the little stick man.

19

ZELTY MARAS

Annie stopped at Mr. Wendell's on her way home to ask him if he'd caught any more rats. She rang the doorbell and waited what seemed like forever. When Mr. Wendell finally opened the door, he was wearing his bathrobe and carrying TomTom in his arms.

"Hello, Miss Klimas," he said. Mr. Wendell did not look good. His eyes were red and his face was flushed.

"Hi, Mr. Wendell . . . um . . . are you okay?"

"A little under the weather, I'm afraid." He turned his head and coughed. "I would invite you in, but I may have a cold. I wouldn't want to pass it on to you."

"Oh." Annie took a step back. "I was just wondering . . . did you catch any more rats?"

"No, but I found out where it was getting in—a little

hole in the side of the garage. Plugged it up with steel wool and plaster." He coughed. TomTom jumped from his arms and ran back into the house. "I think I'd best go back to bed now. Thank you for stopping by, Miss Klimas."

Back at home Miss Mekas was in the kitchen as usual. Annie asked her what she was making.

"*Titeni,*" Mekas said. "Cabbage roll."

"Oh." Annie was not a big fan of cabbage rolls. "Mr. Wendell is sick."

"What he have?"

"He says a cold. He was coughing."

Miss Mekas frowned. "Cough not good. I make him chicken soup. With Litvanian dumpling."

"What is Litvanian dumpling?" Annie asked.

"Just dumpling. All dumpling are same," Miss Mekas said.

"Are we still having cabbage rolls for dinner?"

"Yes. And chicken soup."

Papa arrived home at his usual time and shut himself in his study to *cicenja*. Miss Mekas carried a small pot of chicken and dumpling soup over to Mr. Wendell. Annie took out her yellow tablet and pencils and tried to think of something bad she had done that day. She couldn't think of anything, so she drew a picture of TomTom chasing a rat, then a picture of the rat chasing TomTom. She drew a golden crown on the rat's head. That didn't look fair, so she gave TomTom a crown, too.

Miss Mekas was at Mr. Wendell's house for a long time. When she returned she did not look happy. Papa, who had just come out of his study, asked her what was wrong.

"Mr. Wendell, he is very sick," she said. "I think he maybe have *zelty maras*."

"What's that?" Annie asked.

"Litvanian plague," Mekas said.

"I'm sure it's not that," Papa said. "I'll call Dr. Bray." Dr. Bray was Fiona's father.

A few minutes later, Dr. Bray came walking up the street carrying a shoulder bag. Papa went out to meet him. Annie followed, but Papa said, "Annike, you wait outside. I don't want you to get sick, too."

The two men entered Mr. Wendell's house together. Annie went back to her house and watched from the porch. After a while, Papa returned.

"Mr. Wendell is in good hands now," he said as he stepped up onto the porch. "I'm sure he'll be fine." He smiled, but Annie could tell he was worried.

Mr. Wendell was not fine. The next morning, Dr. Bray visited him again. Annie was eating breakfast when an ambulance pulled up in front of Mr. Wendell's house. Papa told her to stay put, and he ran across the street to see what he could do. A few minutes later, Papa came out of the house, looking grave; he was followed by Mr. Wendell, who was being helped along by two paramedics. Papa and Dr. Bray watched the ambulance leave, then stood on the street talking. Annie went over to hear what they had to say.

"Could be any number of things, Lukas," Dr. Bray was saying. "Anything from a bad cold to COVID, but he has a peculiar rash on his palms. I've never seen that before. The thing is to keep him breathing until we can figure it out."

Papa shook his head. "I hope you do."

"The human body is amazingly resilient," Dr. Bray said. "But you just never know. He's an old man."

"Maybe it was the rat," Annie said.

Both men looked at her.

"Mr. Wendell caught a rat in his trap and it got out and bit him on the wrist," she said.

"When was this?" Dr. Bray asked.

"Two days ago, I think."

Dr. Bray frowned. He took out his phone and made a note. Papa seemed about to say something, then gave his head a little shake and remained silent.

"What about TomTom?" Annie asked.

"TomTom?" Dr. Bray looked up.

"His cat."

"TomTom can stay with us," Papa said.

That night after dinner, Papa shut himself in his study. Miss Mekas went over to Mr. Wendell's and came back with TomTom in his crate, along with his litter box and a bag of cat food. She put the litter box in the mudroom by the back door, and filled two bowls, one with cat food, the other with water. She let TomTom out of his crate.

"You live here for a while," she told him.

TomTom sniffed the cat food, sniffed the litter box, then began to explore the house. Annie followed him.

TomTom was very methodical. He examined the stove, the refrigerator, and every cabinet in the kitchen. When he got to the cellar door, he put his nose up against the crack, hissed, and backed away.

In the dining room, he jumped up on the table.

"TomTom! No!" Annie said.

TomTom gave her a reproving look.

"Down!" Annie said in her most stern voice.

TomTom hopped off the table. He walked down the short hall to Papa's study. The door was closed. TomTom meowed and scratched at the door, but it did not open. He moved on, checking out every room on the first floor, then bounded up the stairs to check out the bedrooms. After exploring each room, he decided to plant himself on Annie's bed. Annie sat next to him. She stroked his back and scratched his ears until she heard Papa's phone ringing. She ran downstairs and pressed her ear to the study door. She could hear talking, but not what he was saying. A minute later he came out of his study. Annie was waiting for him.

"TomTom is on my bed."

"Is that so?" He smiled. "I guess it's as good a place as any, if you don't mind sharing."

"Have you heard anything about Mr. Wendell?"

"Yes, I just spoke with Dr. Bray. Apparently, Mr. Wendell has something called Haverhill fever."

Miss Mekas came out from the kitchen wiping her hands on a dish towel.

"Is *zelty maras*," she said.

20

PEST CONTROL

Mr. Wendell did not return the next day, or the day after that. TomTom settled into his new home, sleeping with Annie every night. The news about Mr. Wendell traveled quickly through the neighborhood. Hal O'Connor, Dr. Bray, and Mr. Dennison showed up one evening to talk to Papa. They sat on the porch. Annie listened from inside the house.

"We have a rat problem, Lukas," Dr. Bray said. "Aside from the rat that attacked Wendell, Hal here says they've been raiding his corncribs."

"I've seen 'em," Mr. O'Connor said. "Big black devils, not your normal rat at all. My guess, the way my corn's being eaten up, there are dozens. Maybe more."

"I've seen them, too," Mr. Dennison said. "I used to feed my dogs out on the back steps, but their food kept disappearing. I put out a security camera to see what was stealing it. Thought it might be a raccoon, but it was a naked-tailed rat, big as you please."

"We'd like to hire an extermination company," Dr. Bray said. "These rodents are carrying Haverhill bacteria. Rat-bite fever, it's sometimes called. We would be wise to take care of it at the source."

"You think rats are spreading the disease?" Papa asked. "I mean, it could be anything, right?"

"Wendell said it was a rat that bit him. Besides, who wants to live in a neighborhood full of rats? I've been in touch with West Exterminating. A tech came out this morning and found dozens of holes he said were rat holes. He thinks we have hundreds of rats—but he couldn't figure out where the main colony is. They may be spread across the entire neighborhood. The cost will be minimal if we all chip in. What do you say?"

The next day, a white van with a cartoon of a dead mouse on the side rolled into the neighborhood. A thin young man wearing gray coveralls and a red cap got out and began distributing black plastic boxes around the houses. When he reached Annie's house, he took three of the black boxes from the back of his van. She went outside and asked him what was in the boxes.

"These here are bait stations," the man told her, holding out one of the boxes for her to look at. The box was about the size of the big dictionary in the library. There were round holes in each end. "These will take care of your little rat problem."

"But what's in them?" Annie asked.

"Well, now, I'll show you just this once so you don't get curious and try looking yourself." He pressed the tabs on the sides of the box and folded the top back. Inside was a squarish green bar about three inches long held in place by a metal rod. "This green thing here is a bait block," he told her. "Peanut butter, grain, and rat poison. They gobble it up like candy." He closed the box. "Rats can fit through these here holes in the side, but the holes are too small for cats or dogs, so it's pet safe."

"What about chipmunks?" Annie asked.

"It's just for rats."

"But what if a chipmunk got in?"

"Chipmunks don't like rat bait. Now, let's have a look around." He walked across the front of the house, stopped, and set the bait station under the lip of the porch next to the steps. "See? You won't hardly notice it's there. But them rats, they'll find it."

"Are you putting them in the sewer, too?"

"That's a common misconception, little lady."

Annie did not like being called *little lady*.

"Rats don't live in sewers. They like to stay close to your garbage, your garden, and your house. Where the food is."

"These rats come out of the sewer," Annie said.

"Is that a fact?" He laughed. He didn't believe her.

"You're stupid," Annie said. It just came out of her mouth, like a burp. "You don't know anything!"

"I know you're a little brat," the man said with a scowl. "Now go away and let me do my work."

Annie crossed her arms and glared at him, but he ignored her. He placed a second bait station behind the bushes at the base of the tower, and a third one under the picnic table.

"There ya go, Miss Smart-mouth," he said. He went back to his van and drove down the street to the next house.

Annie went up to her room and sat on her bed and *seethed*. Maybe she was a kid, but she sure didn't like being treated like a baby. The exterminator would put poison all over the neighborhood and kill the chipmunks and the field mice and maybe some rats. She did not regret what she said: he *was* stupid, and he *didn't* know anything. But she knew she shouldn't have talked back to him, so she wrote down what she had done in her tablet.

I talked back to the rat man.

Then she added,

But he was stupid.

She rolled up the sheet of yellow paper and went down to Papa's study. TomTom followed and watched as she shoved the paper in the *burna*. He padded over, sniffed the hole, and hissed.

"What's the matter, TomTom?"

TomTom backed away and hissed again, his eyes fixed on the *burna*.

"You don't like it?" She flopped the rug back over the hole. "Come on, I'll find you a treat."

She bent over to pick him up, and as she was lifting him, TomTom twisted and flailed. He leaped out of her arms and ran out of the room.

"TomTom!" Annie yelled after him. She looked at her arm. TomTom had left a scratch three inches long. Little beads of blood welled up, like shiny round rubies on a red chain.

21.
RAT FOOD

That night Annie woke up feeling thirsty. TomTom was perched on her legs, purring. She pushed him aside and went downstairs to get a glass of water. Light from a full moon was flooding in through the windows. She didn't even have to turn on the lights.

As she was drinking her water, she saw a movement outside the kitchen window. Someone was in their yard, with a flashlight. She pressed her face to the glass. A man. He turned his face so that the moonlight caught it. It was Papa!

What was he doing out there? She watched him follow the flashlight beam over to the base of the tower and bend over. He was doing something with the bait station. He walked around the tower. Annie ran to the mudroom and watched through the window as he picked up the bait station from under the picnic table. He opened it, closed it, put it back under the table, and walked around to the side of the house. She heard the lid to the garbage bin clunk shut. She had the feeling he was doing something he didn't want anybody to know about. Why else would he be sneaking around in the middle of the night?

She ran upstairs when she heard Papa's footsteps on the front porch. The front door opened and closed. From the top of the stairs, she heard the distinctive creak of the cellar door opening, then echoey footsteps. Annie crept downstairs and sat on the bottom step, listening.

Click.

It sounded like metal touching metal.

Creeeeak.

The sound of a rusty-hinged door opening. She thought of the locked door in the tower wall.

After that, just some faint shuffling noises, then silence. She couldn't imagine what he was doing down there. She listened until she heard Papa coming back up the stairs. She heard the cellar door close. A few seconds later, the back screen door creaked. Annie peeked into the kitchen. She heard the top of the garbage bin clunk down, and Papa came back in through the mudroom.

"Annike! What are you doing up?"

"I heard you."

"I'm sorry, I didn't mean to wake you."

"That's okay. Were you in the cellar?"

"Yes . . . um . . . I was checking the furnace."

"Why?" Annie could tell he was lying.

"I just wanted to make sure it was okay. You go back to bed now, all right?"

The next morning after breakfast, Annie went outside to look at the bait stations. She tried to open the one under the picnic table, but the plastic clips were too hard for her to undo. She got the screwdriver from the junk drawer and tried again. The box popped open. The poison green bar was gone.

She slid the box back under the table and walked over to the garbage bin. It was too tall for her to see inside, so she dragged one of the picnic benches over, stood on it, and opened the top. Several flies came buzzing out, startling her—she almost fell off the bench. She waved away the flies and looked inside. There were two white plastic bags full of garbage, and an empty bag with a picture of a mouse on the front. She lifted out the empty bag. Beneath it were three green bait blocks.

Papa must have taken the bait out of the black boxes and thrown it in the trash. But why? She read what it said on the bag with the mouse picture:

NUTRIRODENT

COMPLETE RAT & MOUSE FOOD

40 POUNDS

"What are you doing?"

Annie dropped the bag and whirled around. Arthur was standing right behind her.

"Nothing," she said.

"Sometimes I look in our garbage cans, too," Arthur said.

"Why?"

Arthur shrugged. "I like to look at things."

Annie closed the lid of the bin and climbed down.

"Did the rat man put boxes by your house?" she asked.

"Three."

"Same here. Dr. Bray says it was rats that made Mr. Wendell sick," Annie said. "Now the boxes are supposed to make the rats sick."

"I just hope it doesn't make them mad," Arthur said.

. . . . .

Over the next few days, the people of Pond Tree Acres noticed a nasty odor in the air.

The smell seemed to come from everywhere, an invisible cloud around the foundations of the houses. The man from West Exterminating came to check the bait stations. Annie went outside to watch as he refilled the bait station under the picnic table.

"You must have had a lot of rats here," he said. "They ate every last crumb of that bait bar!" He took a deep breath through his nose. "You smell that?"

"Everything stinks," Annie said.

"That's dead rats. We'll keep baiting them for another week or two, even though judging from the smell in this neighborhood, we may have gotten them all."

Not all, Annie thought. For some reason her papa didn't want the rats by their house to eat the poison.

Late that night, she watched through the windows as Papa emptied the bait stations again. She watched him open the trunk of his car and lift out another sack of rat and mouse food. She listened as he carried the bag into the house and down the cellar stairs.

22.
NOT SICK

Annie woke up with the morning sun blasting in through her window. TomTom was curled next to her head, purring.

Merp? he said. That was his way of telling her it was time for breakfast. She sat up. Her throat was scratchy. She got dressed and put on her new pink shoes—the ones just like Fiona's.

Miss Mekas was in the kitchen cutting up a chicken. "You sleep long time," she said. "How you feel?"

"Thirsty." Annie poured herself a glass of water from the pitcher in the refrigerator. The cold water felt nice on her throat.

"You pink in face," Mekas said.

Annie did feel warm, but otherwise she felt fine.

"I'm okay," she said.

Mekas frowned at her. "I make chicken soup for later," she said.

TomTom was swiping his body against her legs. She filled his bowl and watched him eat.

"You want waffles?" Mekas asked.

"No, thank you."

Mekas frowned. "You no feel good?"

"I'm fine," Annie said. She went out onto the front porch. What day was it? Had Fiona started school yet? No, it was still summer. She walked over to the Brays' house. Mrs. Bray opened the door.

"Hello, Annie." Mrs. Bray looked at her closely. "Are you feeling all right?"

"I'm fine," Annie said, although her cheeks did feel sort of hot. "Is Fiona home?"

"Yes, but . . . I don't think you should play with her right now."

"Why?" Annie asked.

"You know . . . with this sickness . . . I just don't think it would be a good idea. Just to be on the safe side, let's see how you're feeling tomorrow, okay?"

Annie walked back toward home, then stopped in front of Arthur's house. She went up to the front door and pressed the doorbell. Emily Golden answered.

"Hi! I was wondering if Arthur wanted to go look at the turtles."

"Well, Arthur is resting right now, and—"

"I'm right here," Arthur said. He was standing behind his mom.

"Yes, but you *should* be resting."

"I'm not sleepy," Arthur said.

"Yes, you are, honey," she told him. "Go back to bed." She turned back to Annie. "You look a bit flushed. Are you feeling okay?"

"I'm not sick."

"Are you sure? You don't look well."

"I feel fine!" Annie turned and walked away to hide the angry tears in her eyes.

She wanted to smash something. She walked up the street toward Tustison, and soon reached the mouth of the big culvert. The little stick man was still there. Annie ducked her head and entered the culvert and kicked and stomped until the little man was nothing but scattered sticks and leaves. She backed out of the culvert, tears running down her cheeks.

She didn't feel any better. She felt worse. The walk back seemed to take forever, and now her feet itched.

By the time she got home, her feet were itching so bad she couldn't stand it. She ran up to her room and took off her shoes and socks. The soles of her feet were covered with tiny red bubbles, like poison ivy, only worse.

"Miss Mekas!" she screamed.

Mekas came clomping up the stairs, took one look at the bottoms of Annie's feet, gasped, and clapped her hand to her heart.

"*Zelty maras!*" She traced a cross on her chest and backed away. "I call your papa."

23.
THE HOSPITAL

At first, Annie liked the hospital.

Dr. Bray was there to meet them when Papa carried her in through the big glass doors, and everybody was really nice. The nurse put some ointment on her feet that stopped the itching, and gave her some ice cream that felt nice going down her throat.

But she did not like the needles, and she didn't like the IV tube taped to her arm.

"What's that for?" she said, looking at the plastic bag of fluid hanging from the rack above her.

"That's saline solution," Dr. Bray said. "You're a little dehydrated, so we're giving you some water."

"Miss Mekas says it's the *zelty maras*," Annie said.

Dr. Bray furrowed his brow. "The what?"

"It's a Litvanian term," Papa explained. "It means 'golden plague.'"

"And what is that?" Dr. Bray asked.

"It's an old story, going back seven hundred years. When the Mongols invaded the Baltic states, they were supposedly driven off by a plague."

"Interesting." Dr. Bray looked at Annie. "I'm sorry about all the poking with needles. The tests will tell us what we're dealing with. We'll know more in the morning. For now we just want to keep you comfortable."

"Can I have more ice cream?"

"I think that can be arranged."

"Am I going to die?"

"Absolutely not!"

"What about Mr. Wendell?"

"He's doing just fine. Right now he's resting in his room down the hall. Maybe later you can visit with him."

The two men left the room. Annie could hear them speaking in low voices. It scared her that they didn't want her to hear what they were saying. They moved off down the hall. A few minutes later, one of the nurses came in and gave her another small bowl of vanilla ice cream. The nurse showed her the remote control next to the bed.

"You can make the bed go up and down," she explained.

"And if you need anything, just press this big red button and someone will come."

Annie woke up with a start. It was the middle of the night. Both her legs were throbbing. It felt as if someone had pounded her shins with a hammer. The pain ran up her legs all the way to the base of her skull. Annie tried to sit up, but that made everything hurt worse. The room lights were out, but the door was open and light filtered in from the hallway. She fumbled for the remote next to her bed and pressed the red button. A minute later a nurse she didn't recognize came into the room.

"Can I help you?" the nurse asked.

"My legs," Annie sobbed. "They hurt a lot!"

"Which leg?"

"Both of them!"

By the time Dr. Bray got to the hospital, Annie was feeling a little better. The nurse, Ms. Farah, had massaged her legs gently, tucked a warm towel around them, and brought her a cup of hot chocolate.

Dr. Bray examined her. He looked closely at her feet. He shone a light in her eyes, and looked down her throat, and took her temperature, and listened to her heart.

"You're doing very well, Annie, but your fever is worse,

so rather than wait for the blood test results, I think we'll start you on some amoxicillin right away."

"Will that make me feel better?"

"I believe so. Ms. Farah will be setting up an antibiotic drip, along with something to help you rest." He turned to the nurse and rattled off some instructions. After she left he sat down beside the bed. "How do those legs feel now?"

"They still hurt, but not so much."

"Good. By the way, I spoke with Miss Mekas, and she mentioned that you've been taking care of Mr. Wendell's cat?"

"TomTom?"

"Yes, TomTom. Did he ever scratch or bite you?"

"Once." She held up her arm to show him the faint pink line where TomTom had scratched her. "But it was an accident. He didn't mean it."

"I see." Dr. Bray nodded thoughtfully. The nurse returned with a liquid-filled plastic bag. As she attached it to Annie's IV tube, Dr. Bray continued.

"If you have what we suspect, it's possible you got it from TomTom."

"But TomTom's not sick!"

"I know, but Mr. Wendell told us that TomTom was bitten at the same time he was. Rodents—especially rats—are known to carry a bacteria called *Streptobacillus moniliformis.*

That's what made Mr. Wendell sick, and why we had all those exterminators in the neighborhood."

Annie didn't say anything. She was thinking about her father emptying the bait stations and buying rat food.

"Cats don't get sick from it, but they can pass the infection on to humans. Mr. Wendell was bitten, but you don't need a rat bite to get sick. And now you are displaying similar symptoms. If your tests come back positive, we'll have to take TomTom over to the veterinarian and have him tested as well."

Dr. Bray kept on talking, but his words were swirling confusingly in Annie's head. She opened her mouth to ask him something but couldn't catch her breath. Her throat felt thick and clogged.

Dr. Bray frowned. "Annie? Are you all right?"

She couldn't answer him. All she could do was wheeze. Dr. Bray's face filled her vision and he was shouting something, and her chest hurt and people were moving around fast and the light went out of the room.

24

GROWTH SPURT

When Annie woke up, she had a plastic mask over her mouth and nose. Papa was looking down at her. The last thing she remembered was not being able to breathe.

"Welcome back, Annike," Papa said.

"Papa?" The mask muffled her voice. The silver streak in his hair looked wider—or maybe it was just the bright hospital lights that made it appear so.

Dr. Bray came into view. He lifted away the mask. "Are we breathing better now?"

Annie nodded.

"Good," said Dr. Bray. "I'm afraid amoxicillin does not agree with you. You had an anaphylactic reaction."

"What's that?"

"It's rare," Dr. Bray said. "Usually, if someone is allergic to an antibiotic, they develop a rash or get itchy. I'm afraid your reaction was rather more severe."

"I thought it was supposed to make me better."

"It was. We'll have to try a different medicine. But don't worry, we'll figure this out together."

Annie was in the hospital for five days. Every day Papa came to visit her. After that first horrible day, she started feeling better. The new medicine worked. Her legs still ached at night, but the rash on her feet faded, the headaches stopped, and her fever went away.

On the fifth day, Papa showed up with a big smile on his face.

"Do you know what today is?" he asked.

"Is it the day I get to go home?"

"Yes! Dr. Bray says you are cured. But even more important, it is your birthday! Did you forget?"

Annie was completely surprised. She had lost track of the days while she was in the hospital.

Papa handed her a small, gold-wrapped package. She tore through the wrapping. Inside was a felted, hinged box. She opened the box. Resting on a bed of white satin was a shiny black rat with a long tail and a sparkly green eye. Annie lifted the object and examined it. The back side was gold, with a pin and a clasp.

"A rat pin?" she said.

"It is a brooch in the shape of Litvania," Papa said. "It is made from polished obsidian—in Litvania it is called *slibliakom*, or dragonstone. The green gem is a peridot. It represents Zük, the capital city of Litvania."

"It's very pretty," Annie said. It still looked like a green-eyed rat. She closed the box. "Thank you, Papa."

"You are most welcome. I'll go get Dr. Bray, and then we can go home."

Papa left, and a minute later, Dr. Bray came into the room. "Has your father told you the good news?" he asked.

"It's my birthday and I'm cured! But why do I still get leg aches?"

"I don't think that's related to your illness, Annie," Dr. Bray said. "Leg aches are common for kids your age. Some people call them *growing pains*, because kids usually get them during their growing years."

"You mean my legs are stretching?"

He laughed. "Something like that. How do they feel right now?"

"They just hurt at night."

"I'm sure it will pass. Your father is bringing his car around to pick you up. I'll let you get dressed now. Your clothes are hanging in the closet here." He pointed out the shallow closet near the foot of her bed.

After Dr. Bray left, Annie got dressed. Her jeans had shrunk. They must have washed them and left them in the dryer too long. Her shoes were tight, too. Maybe her feet were still swollen. She left them unlaced, sat on the bed, and waited for Papa to come and get her.

The first thing Annie did when she got home was to measure herself against the library door. She had grown a whole inch!

She ran to tell her father. He was in the kitchen.

"Papa! I grew an inch!"

"Is that so?" He seemed neither surprised nor pleased. "Well, don't grow too much or your clothes won't fit."

"I think I had a growth spurt!"

"That's wonderful." It didn't sound as if he thought it was wonderful.

"What are you doing?" she asked.

"Making peanut butter sandwiches. Are you hungry?"

"Yes, but . . . where is Miss Mekas?"

"Miss Mekas has gone back to Litvania."

"Why?"

"She is a silly, superstitious old woman. Do you want jelly on your sandwich?"

"When is she coming back?"

"I don't know. Possibly never."

"But who will take care of me?"

"At the moment, *I* am taking care of you. Look, I'm making you a sandwich! Do you want jelly, or not?"

"Yes. What about when you're at work?"

"I will find you a new *aukle*." He handed her a small plate with a sandwich on it. "Until then we will make do."

Annie looked at the sandwich. "Miss Mekas always cuts my sandwiches in triangles."

"I am not Miss Mekas," Papa said.

"Are you mad at me?"

"Mad at you?" His expression softened. "Why would you think that?"

"Are you mad because I got sick?"

"No! That was not your fault."

"You always tell me not to grow up. Are you mad that I got taller?"

"I'm not mad at you at all." He picked up his plate from the counter and set it on the kitchen table. "I'm sorry, I have been worried about you is all." He looked at her closely. "Have you fed the *burna* today?"

"I just got home! Besides, I haven't done anything bad."

"Are you sure? No bad thoughts while you were in the hospital?"

Annie thought back over the past few days. "Mostly I just felt sick," she said.

They ate. The bread was dry, and Papa hadn't used enough jelly.

"Are you going to cook dinner tonight?" she asked.

Papa looked at the stale bread crumbs on his plate.

"Maybe we should order a pizza," he said.

"Pizza?" Annie's mood instantly lightened. Then she frowned. "With no olives?"

"No olives."

"Or mushrooms!"

"Okay. No mushrooms. What do you want on your pizza?"

"No onions."

"Hmm. How do you feel about pepperoni?"

"I like pepperoni."

"Good. I'll order pepperoni and olives."

"*No olives!*"

Papa laughed. "Okay, you win, princess."

That night before bed, Annie again measured herself against the doorjamb. Why had she gotten taller while she was in the hospital? Was it the medicine they gave her? Was it all the ice cream? Was it because she hadn't done anything bad for five whole days?

She looked into Miss Mekas's room. The bed was neatly made. All her things were gone. Annie looked through the closet and dresser to see if she'd forgotten anything. She wondered if Mekas had missed her Saint Christopher's medal. She didn't feel bad about stealing it, but she hoped Mekas had traveled safely.

As she turned to leave, she saw the thing behind the door. Annie jumped back—for a second she thought it was an animal. But it didn't move. It was about six inches tall, made of some fuzzy-looking material. She bent over it for a closer look and poked it with the toe of her shoe. The clump fell apart, leaving nothing but a pile of dusty fragments. Annie blew on it. The dust bunnies scattered.

She laughed at herself. Dust bunnies! Miss Mekas had probably swept them up before she left but forgot to put them in the trash. Annie went to her room and took out her tablet.

I got sick and made Miss Mekas go away.

PART THREE

OZOLS

25

RAT-BITE GIRL

Annie woke to the smell of bacon. Still in her pajamas, she went downstairs. A woman with white hair was standing at the stove.

"Hello?" Annie said.

The woman turned around. It was Mr. O'Connor's mother.

"Mama Dara?"

"Good morning, sunshine!" Mama Dara said. "Are you hungry?"

Annie nodded.

"I'll make you a nice bacon sandwich, just like my Irish mother used to make for breakfast."

Annie had never heard of a bacon sandwich. She sat down at the table.

"Are you my new *aukle*?" she asked.

"I don't know what that is," Mama Dara said. "Your father had to go to work early. He asked me to keep an eye on you."

"All day?"

"If it's all right with you."

"I guess so," Annie said. "But who will take care of Mr. O'Connor?"

Mama Dara smiled. "I imagine he'll muddle by." She put the sandwich in front of Annie: two slices of buttered white bread with some strips of bacon in the middle.

"I like pancakes for breakfast," Annie said.

"I'll make you pancakes tomorrow."

Annie regarded the sandwich suspiciously.

"Can I have some ketchup?" she asked. She was pretty sure she could eat it if it had ketchup on it.

"Where do you keep the ketchup?" Mama Dara asked.

"In the refrigerator."

Mama Dara opened the refrigerator. It took her a long time to find the ketchup. While she was waiting, Annie took an experimental bite of the sandwich. It tasted like bread and bacon, two things she liked. Mama Dara returned with the ketchup. Annie opened the sandwich and squirted a generous blob onto the bacon.

Much better. Bread, bacon, and ketchup. Three things she liked.

"What do you think?" Mama Dara asked.

"I like it."

Annie hadn't seen Fiona for more than a week, so she was excited to catch up and tell her all about the hospital and how she'd had a growth spurt. She was still kind of mad at Fiona for being so mean at her birthday party, but she remembered something Arthur had said: *"Everybody's mean sometimes."* Maybe Fiona was just mean when she was with Rachel.

At three o'clock Annie heard the school bus. She put on her old jeans and a T-shirt. The jeans were shorter than she remembered, and her shoes were a little tight, but not too bad. She ran down the street and rang the doorbell. Fiona's teenage sister, Ginny, opened the door.

"Oh, hi, Annie," she said. She looked past her, smiled, and waved as a car full of teenagers pulled up at the curb.

"Is Fiona home?" Annie asked.

"She's in her room," Ginny said. She ran across the yard to the car. Annie watched them drive off, then went upstairs to Fiona's room.

Fiona was not alone. Rachel was sitting on the bed with her. They both looked up when Annie came in.

"Oh, it's the rat-bite girl," Rachel said.

Annie's body reacted almost before Rachel's words

reached her brain. She launched herself at Rachel and grabbed her hair and yanked her off the bed. Rachel screamed and clawed at Annie's face. Annie knocked her hand away and clawed back. Fiona was screaming, and so was Rachel, and maybe Annie was screaming, too. It was all a blur until Mrs. Bray rushed in and pulled Annie off.

Rachel's face was bleeding from four long scratches on her cheek, and she was crying. Mrs. Bray was holding Annie by the shoulders and shouting at her. Her words seemed to be coming from far away, and made no sense. Annie twisted out of her grip and ran out of the house and down the street.

Mama Dara was sitting on the porch in Papa's rocking chair. She peered at Annie through her thick glasses. "You have something on your face, dear."

Annie touched her cheek and looked at her hand. Blood. She ran upstairs and looked in the bathroom mirror. A small scratch—not nearly as bad as the scratches on Rachel's face. She wiped the blood away with a moist tissue. Would Papa notice? Maybe not.

She went to her room and wrote down what had happened. After feeding the paper to the *burna*, she felt much better.

26

THE LASS
AND THE
THREE

Mama Dara was still sitting in the rocking chair on the porch. Annie sat in the other chair.

"Will you tell me a story?" she asked.

Mama Dara twitched, as if she had been sleeping. Maybe she *had* been sleeping—with those thick glasses it was hard to tell.

"What sort of story?"

"A fairy tale. I'll show you." Annie ran into the house and came back with the book of Litvanian fairy tales. "One of these."

Mama Dara took the book in her ancient hands, peered at it through her chunky glasses, and smiled. "Dear, I'm afraid this is quite beyond me. My eyes, you see, are not so keen as they once were."

"Oh," said Annie, disappointed but not surprised. "You probably couldn't read it anyway because it's Litvanian."

"That is true!" Mama Dara laughed. Her laugh was like that of a little girl, and for a moment Annie caught a glimpse of what the old woman had looked like when she was a child. "Would you like to hear a story from Ireland?"

"Does it have dragons?"

"I could put a dragon in if you like."

"That's okay. You don't have to."

"This is a story my grandmother told me when I was about your age. It is called 'The Lass and the Three.'"

"The three what?" Annie asked.

"That is the question! The lass, whose name was Anne of the Fields, lived in a stone cottage far from the nearest village."

"In Ireland?"

"Yes, but it was not named Ireland back then. It was called Éire, after the goddess Ériu."

"Was Ériu real?"

"We shall see. Now, Anne of the Fields woke up every morning and made a pot of porridge for her da. They would have porridge with honey and fresh butter while her father told her stories about her ma, who had gone to heaven when Anne was a wee one."

"I wish Papa would tell me stories about my mama,"

Annie said. "But he says thinking about her makes him sad."

"If you wish, I will tell you a story about your mama. But first, let me finish telling you about Anne of the Fields.

"After breakfast, Anne's da would go off to work in the fields while Anne milked the cow, fed the chickens, and weeded the garden. After, she would make a lunch of boiled eggs, garden greens, and rashers of bacon fried up crisp in an iron pan.

"At noon, Anne's da's da—her granddad, that is—would come from his home deep in the woods. He and Anne would eat, and then he would braid her hair and tell her the secrets of the forest. Afterward, he would go off to the fields to help Anne's da. Anne would stay behind and clean the cottage, mend clothes, and bake bread. While the bread was baking, she would hang a pot of soup over the fire for supper.

"At sunset, Anne's *great*-granddad—her da's father's father—would arrive with a jug of cider and a sack of red apples. Anne and he would make a meal of soup and fresh bread, with cider to drink.

"Over a dessert of baked apples sweetened with honey, he would tell her tales of the old days when the land was ruled by three goddesses: Ériu, Banba, and Fódla. The goddesses, he told her, had granted him a life three times longer than that of most men. 'But,' he said, 'she told me I would live only a third of it. I am older than the eldest man in Éire, though I have lived no more of life than he.'"

"What about Anne's father and grandfather?" Annie asked. "Were they still out in the fields?"

"That is a very good question!" said Mama Dara.

"Didn't Anne of the Fields wonder where they were?"

"No, because it had been that way ever since she could remember. She knew no other life. Anne would wash up after supper, and she and her great-granddad would retire to their straw pallets and sleep soundly through the night. And in the morning, Anne's great-grandfather would be gone, and she would make porridge again, and her da would be there to eat it."

Annie thought for a moment, then asked, "Didn't they ever all eat at the same time?"

"No."

Annie thought some more. "They were all the same person, weren't they?"

"The same, but different. My grandmother called it goddess magic."

"Ireland is where leprechauns are from, isn't it?"

Mama Dara laughed, and again, for a moment, she

seemed to become younger. "Leprechauns and goddesses both. Your mother was a goddess, for a goddess is a strong woman who matters, and that is all there is to it."

"My mama mattered?"

"Indeed she did! Your mama loved you, and she was *fierce.*"

"Fierce?"

"Like a mama tiger, she was. She would have fought off an army to protect you. Why, I remember one day—you were probably two years old—she came to buy some eggs from us, and she brought you with her. We were in the henhouse. Kundze would buy only our freshest eggs. You wandered outside, and a moment later we heard you scream. Kundze dropped the eggs and flew out of the henhouse.

"Back then we had this bull. A huge, bad-tempered fellow named Brutus. We kept him fenced off from the other animals because he was so mean and nasty. Well, on that day he had managed to break down the fence and escape. You were standing in the barnyard face-to-face with him.

"Kundze didn't hesitate for an instant. She scooped you up in one arm and punched that bull right in the snout.

"I'd never seen anything like it. I was afraid Brutus would kill the both of you, but that bull just shook his head, took one good look at your mama, and ran off."

"How big was Brutus?"

"More than two thousand pounds."

"That's really big."

"Your mama didn't care. As I said, she was *fierce*. That bull knew he was not her equal."

That evening, Papa and Annie drove Mama Dara back to her farm. On the way home, he looked over at Annie. She could tell he was looking at the scratch on her cheek.

"Mrs. Bray phoned me at my office," he said.

Annie nodded.

"Did you write down what you did?" he asked.

She nodded again.

"Good girl." He smiled a tired smile. "When we get home, we will order a pizza."

"No olives!"

"Of course."

27

THE CROW LADY

Mama Dara came again the next day. She made breakfast, and lunch, and then she fell asleep on the porch. Annie sat with her and read a book until she heard the distinctive screech of the school bus braking. She ran down the street to the bus stop and intercepted Fiona as she was walking home.

"Hi!" Annie said.

Fiona stopped, hugging her book bag to her chest. She had a swollen-eyed look, as if she was about to cry or lose her temper.

"Hi," she said, looking down at Annie's feet.

"How was school?" Annie asked.

Fiona looked up and her eyes hardened. "You mean how is *Rachel*?"

Annie shrugged. She hadn't been thinking about Rachel

at all. Their fight felt far away, like something that had happened in another lifetime. Annie knew it was just yesterday, and she remembered what had happened, but since she had confessed to the *burna*, it no longer seemed very important.

"She's got *scratches* all over her *face*," Fiona said.

"I have a scratch, too!"

"My mom says you can't come over anymore."

"Oh!" Annie was startled, but she knew she shouldn't be.

Fiona hugged her book bag harder and looked away. "And she says I can't be your friend anymore."

Annie felt as if she'd been punched. "But . . . don't you want to be?"

"You can't just hit people. It's *immature*." Fiona pushed past her. "I'm going home."

As Annie watched Fiona walking away from her, a sickening, painful lump formed in her throat. Hot tears welled up.

"I don't want to be your friend, either," Annie called after her.

Fiona quickened her pace without looking back.

"I hate you!" Annie shouted as tears of anger and pain flowed down her cheeks. "You and Rachel both!"

Fiona broke into a run. A few seconds later she was at her house. Even from a hundred yards away, Annie could hear the door slam.

As she walked home, Annie imagined that Fiona was watching her from a window. She tried to make her walk look nonchalant, even skipping for a few yards because she didn't want Fiona to know how hurt she was. As she got closer to home, a black, boxy-looking Jeep drove past her and pulled into the driveway where Papa usually parked.

A young woman stepped out of the Jeep. Her features were sharp and crisp, her hair was black and shiny, and she was tall—almost as tall as Papa. She was wearing a long black coat, even though the weather was mild. A big leather purse hung from one shoulder. She looked up at the tower, her wide mouth set in a frown. Annie was sure she had seen that frown before, as if from a half-remembered dream. After a few seconds the woman lowered her gaze and zeroed in on Annie.

"Annike Klimas," she said. Her voice was as sharp and crisp as her features. Again, it had a familiarity to it—maybe it was the slight accent. "Why are you crying?"

"I'm not crying." Annie dragged her sleeve across her eyes.

"I see. Is your father at home?"

"He's at work."

The woman nodded and sniffed the air. "What is that smell?"

Annie was a bit offended. The dead rat smell wasn't *that* bad.

"I don't smell anything," she said.

"Smells like something died." She stepped up onto the porch. Annie did not think she liked this woman.

"How old are you?" the woman asked.

"Eleven," Annie said.

"You are rather small."

"Well, *you* look like a crow," Annie said. It just popped out of her mouth.

The woman did not seem to be offended. She tipped her head in a crowlike manner and said, "It is interesting that you should say that. My given name is very close to *vairia*, the Litvanian word for crow. I am Vaira Ozols. You may call me Ozols."

Annie did not want to call her anything at all.

"Who is looking after you?" Ozols asked.

"Mama Dara."

"Take me to her."

After introducing the crow lady to Mama Dara, Annie went upstairs and wrote down what had happened with Fiona. *I told Fiona I hated her,* she wrote. The fresh memory brought a new flood of tears. She clamped her jaw tight and willed herself not to cry, and after another minute the tears stopped. She rolled up the yellow paper and carried it downstairs.

Mama Dara and the crow lady were in the kitchen, talking. Annie took the paper into Papa's study and fed it to the *burna*, then sat in one of the big chairs. *"I hate you!"* she had shouted at Fiona. That didn't seem so bad anymore, but losing Fiona as her friend still felt awful. She hugged her legs to her chest. It was so unfair! She hadn't done anything to Fiona, and Rachel was a mean, hateful, horrible person.

Maybe it was just temporary. She imagined Fiona knocking on the door and saying she was sorry, and that they could still be friends after all. Mrs. Bray would say it was okay for her to come over, and Fiona would realize that Rachel was a bad person who deserved to have her face scratched.

Everything would go back to normal.

Annie was enjoying that fantasy when she heard Papa's car. She hopped off the chair and ran outside. Papa had to park in the street because Ozols had stolen his parking space. He got out of his car looking puzzled and irritated.

"Annike, whose car is this?" he asked.

Annie pointed into the house. "The crow lady."

She followed him inside.

Ozols was still in the kitchen talking with Mama Dara. Papa stopped at the kitchen door so suddenly it was as if he had hit an invisible wall. His mouth opened, but he didn't say anything. Annie had never seen him look so surprised.

Ozols looked up and said, "Hello, Lukas."

It took Papa a moment to reply.

"Vaira?" he said. His voice sounded funny.

"You look as handsome as ever, and younger than I would have expected." Ozols made it sound like a bad thing.

"What are you . . . what are you doing here?"

"The question is, what are *you* doing here, Lukas? Mekas has fled back home for fear of the *zelty maras*, and your daughter is without an *aukle*."

"Annike is fine," Papa said. "I have arranged for a new *aukle*, and a *mokytojas*. They will be flying in from Litvania this week."

"I have canceled their flights. I will be Annike's new *aukle*. And her *mokytojas* as well."

"That is hardly necessary," Papa said.

"It is entirely necessary. I made a promise to Kundze."

Annie's heart thumped at the mention of her mother.

Ozols continued. "Annike will become a young woman soon. Mekas is back in Litvania, and Mama Dara here must attend to her own home."

Mama Dara, who was standing back by the pantry smiling uncomfortably, nodded. "It is true," she said. "I should be getting back to the farm."

"Therefore," Ozols said, "I will undertake Annike's care and education, as the girl has no other family."

Papa said nothing, so Annie spoke up. "You're not my family!"

Ozols gave her a look. "Of course I am, Annike. I am your *tanta*. Your aunt. I am your mother's sister."

28

INCORRIGIBLE

Ozols wasted no time in taking charge. As soon as Papa left to drive Mama Dara home, Ozols undertook a complete reorganization of the kitchen. She sorted through the cupboards and pantry, threw out half the contents of the refrigerator, and scrubbed the counters and the floor, which she described as "worse than a barn."

It was fascinating to watch the crow woman work. Ozols was all elbows and hands, and very fast—at times it seemed like there were two of her.

At one point she stopped suddenly and shot a look at Annie, who was watching from the doorway.

"You could help, rather than stand there gaping like a beached carp!"

"Miss Mekas always said I would just be in the way," Annie said.

"You need training," Ozols said. She launched into a fury of sink scrubbing.

"Are you from Litvania?"

"Yes. But now, for the time being, I live here."

Annie went upstairs to her room. She opened her tablet and wrote,

I told Ozols she looked like a crow.

She thought for a moment, then added,

Because she does.

That night Papa carried Ozols's two enormous suitcases up to Miss Mekas's old room. Annie watched from the doorway as she opened them. The first one was all clothes, mostly black, and shoes, all black. Ozols folded, hung, and arranged her wardrobe with great vigor, ignoring Annie.

The second suitcase was filled with books. Ozols selected several of them and quickly filled the small bookcase next to her bed. The remaining books, about two dozen of them, she placed in a cardboard box.

"These are for you," she said.

"What are they?"

"Obviously, they are books."

The blue book on top of the stack was called *Basic Algebra*.

"I don't even know what that is," Annie said.

"One day you will. Take them down to the library. We begin your education tomorrow."

To her relief, Annie's first lesson was not from *Basic Algebra*. It was from a history book about Litvania. She couldn't read it herself because it was written in Litvanian, so Ozols sat next to her on the sofa and read it out loud in English.

"The Queendom of Litvania is a beautiful country located between Latvia and Lithuania, along the Nemunélis River. With a landmass of two hundred forty square kilometers and a population of eighty-two thousand, it is one of the smallest and most mysterious countries in the world."

"What's mysterious about it?" Annie asked.

"For one thing, many people don't even know it exists."

"My teacher at school told me there was no such place."

"Perhaps that is why your father wishes you to be homeschooled. Now listen. Litvania is a monarchy ruled by Queen Zurka, who lives in the capital city of Zük, which is also the name of its primary currency. It is the only Baltic nation to retain its independence while its neighbors succumbed, variously, to Mongol, Swedish, German, and Russian rule. The main agricultural products are . . ."

Annie drifted off. She would much rather hear about dragons and changelings than agricultural products or currencies. Ozols droned on for some time before she noticed the glazed look in Annie's eyes.

"Annike!" she snapped. "What did I just read?"

Annie had no idea. "Something about Litvania?"

Ozols slapped the book shut. "You are incorrigible!"

"I don't know what that means," Annie said.

"Come to think of it, neither do I! But it is not good." She narrowed her eyes and glared at Annie.

Annie glared back at her. They sat like that for several heartbeats. Suddenly, to Annie's astonishment, Ozols's frown turned into a smile and she began to laugh. It was not the witchlike cackle that Annie had expected, but a full belly laugh. For the first time, Annie noticed the resemblance between Ozols and the photo of her mother. In an instant, Annie was laughing, too, even though she didn't know what was so funny.

Ozols stopped laughing first. She sank back into the sofa cushions and wiped her eyes with the backs of her hands.

"You are so like your mother," she said.

"She was incorrigible, too?"

"Kundze was many things. Tell me, how did . . . what was your former *mokytojas*'s name again?"

"Ona Smetona," Annie said.

"Yes. Did this Ona Smetona succeed in teaching you anything at all?"

"She taught me fractions, and all about the planets and moons and stars, and she told me everybody in Litvania is related to Queen Zurka."

Ozols nodded. "That is almost true."

"And she read me stories sometimes."

"What sort of stories?"

Annie jumped up and ran to the bookshelves. She came back with the fairy-tale book and thrust it at Ozols.

"She read you fairy tales?" Ozols asked as she flipped through the book.

"She read me the story about the dragon and the twins."

"I see. And what did you learn from that?"

"That girls are smarter than dragons."

"That is quite true." She continued paging through the book, then paused at a story halfway through. "But some girls can be rather foolish."

Annie looked to see which story she was looking at. It had a picture of a girl looking into a mirror.

"I will read you one story," said Ozols.

29

THE PRINCESS
AND THE MIRROR

✦Once upon a time, a princess was born into the world with a full head of bouncing golden curls, rosy pink lips, and bright blue sparkling eyes. Her name was Princess Raisa. Her father, the king, proclaimed her to be the most beautiful child in all the land, and no one dared to disagree.

Remarkably, the princess became even more beautiful as she grew into a young woman. Princes and princelings came from far and wide in hopes of gaining her favor. The princess knew how beautiful she was, and she used her beauty to charm and befuddle her suitors. Many young men came and went, but not one of them did she deem worthy.

Alas, she was a rather foolish girl. Because her beauty was so great, she had no need for her wits, and therefore had little practice at using them. This is true of many beautiful people.

Time passed, and the queen, who was wise with years, saw changes in her daughter that others overlooked: a slight crease at the left corner of her lips, a hint of dryness at the tips of her golden tresses, a tiny mole just above her collarbone.

"Soon, you must choose amongst your many suitors," she advised the princess. "The day will come when your beauty fades. You will want the love of a man who remembers you as you are at this moment."

The princess shook her golden curls and laughed.

"I need no man," she proclaimed. "As for growing old, I refuse to do so."

The queen sighed. "Would that it were so simple."

That night, when the princess retired to her rooms, her maidservant brought her a silver tray with two slices of toasted bread, a small ramekin of juneberry jam, and a flask of sweet rosewater, as was her custom. The princess ate the toast and jam, leaving the crusts on the tray, as always. In the morning they would be gone; she had never thought to wonder why.

She drank the rosewater, then examined herself in the full-length mirror. She was as perfect as ever. She picked up her hand mirror, which was bordered with gold filigree and had once belonged to her great-great-great-great-grandmother, and smiled at her reflection. Her teeth were white and even, her lips were plump, her skin was flawless . . . except . . . was that a tiny wrinkle at the corner of her eye? And where had that mole on her collarbone come from?

The princess threw the hand mirror across the room, crying out, "I refuse!" The mirror shattered against the stone wall. "I will not grow old!"

With that, she threw herself onto her feather bed, pulled the covers up over her head, and after many long minutes of tossing and turning, she slept.

Sometime later, the princess was awakened by the sound of gnawing. The princess was not afraid, as nothing bad had ever happened to her. She sat up. At the foot of her bed, illuminated by moonlight, sat a creature larger than a rabbit but smaller than a goose. It had shiny black eyes, long white whiskers, and a glossy sable pelt. It was eating the crust of toast the princess had left.

"It is true, as they say, you are quite lovely," said the creature in a voice that sounded like paper tearing. "Despite your lack of a tail." It twitched the tip of its long pink naked tail. "Would you like a tail?"

"No, thank you, Your Majesty," the princess said politely. She did not know what sort of creature this was, but she recognized royalty when she saw it, a useful talent shared by all of royal blood.

"Are you sure? I can give you a tail. You should consider it."

The princess considered it for only the briefest of moments, then said, "I fear my dresses would not accommodate such an appurtenance."

The creature shrugged. "As you wish. Is there anything else I can do for you?"

"Er . . . what are you?" the princess asked.

"I am the Queen of the Rats," said the Rat Queen.

The princess accepted this immediately, although she had never seen a rat, and had always assumed they were somewhat smaller.

"I'm pleased to meet you, Your Majesty."

"As you should be. I come to offer you a boon." The Rat Queen smiled. Now, a smile on a rat looks nothing like the smile on a person. It is more of a wrinkling of the nose and a flash of pink tongue, but the princess grasped the queen's intent, and smiled back at her.

The Rat Queen frowned. In rats, frowning is a rapid blinking of the eyes. She said, "When you contort your face in that manner, you cause your skin to stretch and wrinkle."

"I do not wrinkle," said the princess.

"Ah, but you will! You will grow old and lined and your lips will narrow and your golden curls will grow thin and limp and gray. Your belly will sag, your ankles will thicken, and your back will curve. Brown age spots will speckle the backs of your hands."

The princess stared at the Rat Queen in shock. Even her mother, the queen, had never spoken to her so harshly.

"Why are you saying these horrible things to me?" she asked.

"Because they are true . . . but perhaps not unavoidable! Would you like to remain as you are—young and beautiful?"

"I would like that," said the princess.

"I can help," said the Rat Queen. "As I said, I come to offer you a boon."

"Why?" asked the princess.

The Rat Queen shrugged. "I could say it is because you are the firstborn daughter of a first-born daughter of a firstborn daughter, but that is not an uncommon thing amongst royalty. Or I could tell you it is because our families have shared these walls and crevices for a hundred generations—"

"Is that true?"

"A hundred *rat* generations. It would be seven generations for you."

"Oh, I see."

"The truth is, you made a wish as you broke the mirror that belonged to your great-great-great-great-grandmother, who made a pact with my great-great-great . . . I will not bore you with all the greats. Your family and mine have lived in harmony ever since. For our part, we eat only such scraps of food as will not be missed—such as this delicious crust. For your part, you permit us to live in your walls and secret spaces, so long as we remain out of sight. Every night while you sleep, my subjects emerge silently from their cracks and holes and devour every last crumb of food or splash of grease left on the floor, on the counters, on the dining tables, in the garbage bins, and on your nightstand." The Rat Queen ate the last bit of crust, as if to demonstrate. "This is why every morning your silver tray is empty, and your cooks wake up to a perfectly clean kitchen."

"That sounds like an excellent arrangement! But what does it have to do with mirrors and wishes?"

"I don't know," said the Rat Queen. "There is probably more to it. For example, every month at the full moon, we rats all leave the castle and gather around the moat holding paws, and the queen—your mother—stands upon the draw-bridge and hurls handfuls of buckwheat into the water. A waste of buckwheat, in my opinion, but it is what we do, and no one knows why. Not even the queen.

"In any case, because of the mirror, I am compelled to grant your wish. Henceforth, you will not age, and your beauty will remain intact."

"Thank you!" said the princess.

"There is a price, however. There is always a price."

"I have gold," said the princess.

The Rat Queen shook her head. "Gold is of no use to me. It must be a part of you. A finger, a toe, an ear . . ."

"But then I would not be beautiful!"

"Yes, that is a conundrum. But you have things to offer that will not make you less beautiful. A bit of your intelligence, perhaps?"

The princess was not terribly smart, as has been mentioned, but she was smart enough to know that intelligence was not a thing she possessed in excess.

"I am afraid I need what wits I have," she said.

"How about joy? I would not need it all at once—say, a tenth of a tenth for each year that passes."

The princess considered. The mathematics were beyond her, but a tenth of a tenth did not sound like a lot. Still, she was not overflowing with joy.

"No?" said the Rat Queen. "Is there nothing you have in excess?"

"My mother says I am too foolish."

"I have no use for foolishness."

"She also says I am too stubborn, too vain, and too proud."

"I do not want your stubbornness, and vanity is something you will need if you wish to remain beautiful, for if you are not vain you will let yourself go. But pride? That I can accept."

"A tenth of a tenth of my pride?"

"That should be sufficient."

And so the princess remained young and beautiful to the end of her days. ✦

Ozols stopped speaking, but continued to read for a few seconds, then lowered the book to her lap.

"That's it?" Annie said.

Ozols roused herself. "Is that not enough?"

"How long did she live?"

"A long time."

"But what about her *pride*?" Annie asked.

"I imagine she became less and less proud as the years passed."

"A tenth of a tenth. That's not so much."

"At first, but with each passing year she grew less and less proud, and after a hundred and seventeen years her pride was mostly gone."

"Then what?"

"I will read you the end, but first you must tell me about the crying."

"I'm not crying."

"When I first arrived yesterday you were crying. Why?"

Annie was too startled to say anything but the truth. "My best friend in the whole world doesn't want to be my friend anymore."

Ozols nodded. "That is deserving of your tears. But you are both young, and things change." She lifted the book and continued to read.

"On the last day of her one hundred seventeenth year, the princess Raisa was as beautiful as ever, but when she beheld herself in her full-length mirror, she took no pleasure in it. Her pride had deserted her. She thought herself as plain as any peasant woman.

"She took up the silver tray by her bed and hurled it at her reflection. The mirror broke into a thousand shards, and as the glass shattered, so did the princess. The next morning, when her handmaid brought the princess her morning tea, she found nothing but a sea of broken glass and an empty nightgown."

Annie thought for a moment.

"You are right," she said. "I do not like it."

Ozols shrugged. "One ought not expect a Litvanian tale to end happily, but there is always a lesson."

"What's the lesson?"

Ozols pursed her thin lips and gave her head a little shake. "It is different for every reader. It may be that pride is an essential part of us all, but pride in excess is unseemly. When I first read that story, I was no older than you, and I thought the lesson was to never give away one's pride. Reading it now, I learned that everything has a price. What did you learn?"

"To never trust a talking rat?"

Ozols laughed. "You are indeed incorrigible!"

"I still don't know what that means!"

"Do you know how to look things up in a dictionary?"

"Usually, I just ask."

Ozols *tsked* and stood up. She went to the bookshelf, lifted the heavy dictionary, and set it on Annie's lap.

"Look up *incorrigible*," she said.

. . . . .

That night before bed, Annie made herself a piece of toast and spread it with strawberry jam. She put it on a plate and carried it up to her room and placed it on her bedside table.

In the morning, the toast was still there. Annie laughed at herself.

"Fairy tales," she said.

30

MOON BITES

Mr. Wendell came home the next day. Annie ran across the street.

"Welcome home, Mr. Wendell!" she said.

"Thank you, Miss Klimas," he said as he unlocked his front door.

"You were in the hospital a long time!"

"At my age, it takes a bit longer to recover."

"How are you feeling now?"

"Quite well, thank you! In fact, I feel better than I did before I got sick. Why, I feel like a young man of seventy!"

"That's not very young," Annie said.

"It is younger than eighty, which is what I am."

"Oh." Annie didn't think there was much difference between seventy and eighty. "Will TomTom be coming home soon?"

"He'll be in quarantine for another week, just to make sure he doesn't make anyone else sick. I'm sorry you caught that bug from him."

"That's okay. I'm cured. What is quarantine?"

"They keep him in his own room and test him to make sure he isn't still contagious."

"Oh. Guess what? I have a new *aukle*!"

"Miss Mekas is gone?"

"She went back to Litvania. Papa said she was scared of the rats, but the exterminators think all the rats in the neighborhood are dead now."

"Let's hope so. I would not wish that disease on anyone. Truth is, for a while there I thought I was a goner."

"But you're okay now."

"One hundred percent! And I have a souvenir." He stuck out his wrist. Where he had been bitten were two small pink scars, like two new moons pointing at each other.

At dinner that night, Papa noticed Annie examining her wrist.

"What are you looking at?" he asked.

"My moon bites. Mr. Wendell has moon bites now, too. From when the rat bit him."

"I see." Papa nodded and went back to eating his salad as if there was no more to be said.

"Did I get bit by a rat?" Annie asked.

Ozols had stopped eating and was listening intently.

"You fell down the stairs," Papa said. "I told you."

"But why do my moon bites look exactly like Mr. Wendell's?"

"There are many things that could leave similar scars. The head of a nail sticking out from a step, a piece of broken glass . . . all sorts of things can leave a mark. You mustn't let your imagination carry you away."

Ozols picked up her plate—even though she had not finished her dinner—and took it into the kitchen.

"Maybe I fell down the steps because a rat bit me."

"Or maybe the moon really did come down from the sky to nibble on you." Papa winked and grinned. Annie didn't smile back. He shrugged and became serious. "Are you finished eating?"

Annie nodded. Her appetite had gone away.

"All right, then, let's go to my study. I have something to tell you."

"Do I have to write things down for the *burna*?" she asked.

"Did you do anything regrettable today?"

"I don't think so."

"Then just bring your lovely self."

. . . . .

They sat in the big chairs in front of the fireplace. Papa asked her how she was feeling.

"I'm not sick," Annie said.

"How are you feeling about Ozols?"

Annie hesitated. She wasn't sure, because her feelings about Ozols had gone through several changes. At first, she hadn't liked her at all. Especially at breakfast, when Ozols had served her a bowl of plain oatmeal. But then she had put out a bowl of whipped cream, and another bowl of fresh strawberries, and a bowl of sugar. "Oatmeal needs lots of toppings," Ozols had said. After that Annie liked her better. But then there was the boring history book, and Annie hadn't liked that at all. But then Ozols had read Annie the story about the princess . . .

"I like her sometimes," Annie said.

Papa nodded slowly. "She can be difficult," he said. "But Vaira is family. She will be staying with us for a while. Tomorrow I will be flying back to Litvania to take care of some business. Ozols will be in charge while I am gone."

"Isn't she sort of in charge already?"

Papa laughed. "She can be a bit bossy!"

"How long will you be gone?"

"A week. Perhaps longer. And while I am gone, you must continue to feed the *nuodeema burna*. Remember, it is only for you and me. Do not mention it to Ozols."

"Okay."

"Vaira may tell you stories. You should take them all with a grain of salt."

"Salt?"

"That means you should not believe everything she tells you."

"She told me a story today."

"What story?"

"The one about the princess and the mirror."

"Ah, a fairy tale."

"And she helped me look up *incorrigible*. It means I don't like to be corrected."

31.
FUDGE

Seven days after Papa left for Litvania, the telephone rang in the middle of the night. Annie sat up in bed and rubbed her eyes. Faintly, she could hear Ozols talking. She opened her door. Ozols was at the other end of the hall, holding the phone to her ear.

"I see, are you sure? I don't . . . all right. All right. Yes, yes, we'll be fine. Don't worry about a thing . . . okay . . . Goodbye." She hung up.

"Who was that?" Annie asked.

"That was your father, calling from Litvania. He's going to be a bit longer than he thought."

"Why?"

"He has been detained. Now go back to bed. We can talk more in the morning."

. . . . .

First thing every morning, Annie measured herself against the doorjamb. It was always the same. She hadn't grown at all since her stay in the hospital. She was sure that Fiona and all her friends were getting bigger. And the last time she saw Arthur, he came all the way up to her nose. She was stuck at four feet, four and a half inches. It wasn't fair.

Ozols asked her why she was measuring herself.

"To see if I grew," Annie said.

"Yes, but every day? You would hardly see the difference!"

"When I was in the hospital, I grew a whole inch in just a few days."

"That's very impressive! But usually children grow more slowly. I bet you're taller now than you were when you got home from the hospital."

Annie shook her head. "I haven't grown even a squidgen."

"Not even a squidgen?" Ozols laughed. "Try not measuring yourself for a month. I bet you'll gain a squidgen or two."

"I wish Papa would come home."

"He will, when he can."

"Why can't he? Is he in a dungeon?"

"What? Certainly not! He has been detained at the

border—apparently, his visa has been revoked. He can't enter or leave the country until Queen Zurka gives her consent, and she keeps putting him off."

"But that's not fair!"

"Litvania is many things. *Fair* is not one of them."

"Does she know that Papa is related to her?"

"Related? Your father is not related to Queen Zurka."

"But he told me I was related!"

"Yes. Through your mother."

While Papa was gone, Ozols and Annie fell into a routine. Mornings were for schooling. Annie had to read, or do the vocabulary worksheets Ozols made up, or do some activity like writing or drawing, or listen to Ozols tell her about the history of Litvania. If Annie did her work and wasn't too *incorrigible*, Ozols would take her on a field trip. They visited a science museum, an art museum, and best of all, the zoo.

Afternoons were free, except for some housework that Ozols insisted upon. Annie was in charge of dusting, putting away the dishes, making her bed, sweeping the mudroom, and anything else Ozols thought up. Annie didn't particularly like doing chores, so she usually went outside where Ozols wouldn't assign her some new job.

The neighborhood didn't smell like dead rats anymore.

The exterminators had packed up all their bait boxes and gone away. Sometimes Annie would just walk around, pretending she was an orphan. She felt like one, since Fiona didn't want to be her friend anymore, and Arthur was in school all day so there was nobody else around.

Mr. Wendell recovered completely from his illness and was working hard to catch up on his yard work. He spent hours cutting tiny branches from his bushes and cleaning up the edges of his lawn. TomTom was back at home, but Mr. Wendell never let him out of the house anymore.

September came and went, and Papa was still gone. He called once a week or so and reassured Annie that he would be home soon, but his voice sounded weak and he had been gone for more than a month, and Annie was afraid she'd never see him again. Ozols was worried, too—Annie could tell.

The days were getting shorter and colder. The turtles hardly ever ventured up onto their log anymore. The leaves had turned yellow and orange and red. Mr. O'Connor had harvested his corn, leaving only a fringe of tall stalks between the house and his field. Annie thought about walking across the field to visit Mama Dara, but she was afraid she'd run into Matilda and her brood.

"I'm bored all the boring time!" she announced.

Ozols looked up from the book she was reading.

"Read a book," she said.

"I'm sick of books, and there's nothing to do."

Ozols tried to remain stern, but her face softened, and she said, "I understand. Your friends are all in school." She thought for a moment, then said, "Have you ever made fudge?"

"Is fudge Litvanian?" Annie asked as she watched Ozols pour the warm, chocolaty goop into a cake pan.

"No. Litvanian candy is hard and sour."

"Then how come you know how to make it?"

Ozols wiggled the cake pan to level out the fudge, then evened it out with a rubber spatula. "When I was your age and Kundze was sixteen, we were sent to a boarding school in New England. That is where I learned to make fudge."

"Why did they send you away?"

"Litvania is a beautiful, magical, and mysterious country, but the schools are not so good."

"Were there really dragons there?"

"Who told you that?"

"Ona Smetona."

"That silly girl. No, of course there are no dragons."

"But *were* there?"

"In stories, yes. But only in stories."

"Was my mother like you?"

Ozols snorted. "You could not imagine two sisters more different than Kundze and I. As a child, Kundze was a ray of sunshine. I was dour and sad. Kundze laughed more than anyone I have ever known. Open the refrigerator, please."

Annie opened the refrigerator. Ozols slid the fudge onto a shelf.

"We must wait for it to cool now. Waiting is the hardest part." Ozols closed the refrigerator. "Do you remember your mother?"

Annie shook her head. "I was only three."

"Do you have any pictures?"

"Just one. I'll show you." Annie ran up to her room and got the framed photo from her dresser. She brought it downstairs.

"I took this picture!" Ozols said. "We were on the coast. She was laughing because a seagull was dive-bombing us as I was trying to take the picture. The seagull terrified me, but Kundze was afraid of nothing. It was the year before she married your father. Is this the only photo you have?"

"Papa doesn't like to remember her. It makes him sad."

"I imagine it does." She stared at the photo for a few seconds, then looked at Annie. "You look a lot like her, when she was your age."

"Did she have moon bites, too?" She held out her wrist.

Ozols peered at Annie's scars. Her frown deepened.

"You really don't remember." She made it a statement, not a question.

"I was little."

"Yes, you were." Ozols had a curious expression on her face, as if she had something to say but was holding it back. It lasted only a second. "Would you like to hear a story about the moon?"

"From the book?"

"No. This is a story our mother told us when we were little girls. Come. It is a nice day. We can sit on the porch."

32

THE *ZILZEM*

"Once upon a time in the middle of a forest in the middle of Litvania, an old woman lived inside a tree," Ozols began.

"How could she live inside a tree?" Annie asked.

"It was a big tree, and it was hollow."

"How big?"

"Big enough that the woman had three rooms, one on top of another. The bottom room was her sitting room, where she would entertain guests. The middle room was her bedroom. The top room, high up in the tree, was her *laboratorium*, where she performed her experiments. You see, the woman was a witch and a healer. People came from far and wide for her elixirs."

"What's an *elixir*?"

"A magical potion. The woman had a way with plants.

She knew every plant in the forest, and by mixing their saps and seeds and leaves and flowers and spores, she created marvelous substances for curing gout, dropsy, pox, and many other maladies. And she had learned over the years that her potions were enhanced by exposing them to the light of the full moon. Back then, the moon was very bright, and when it was full you could not look at it directly lest you burn your eyes.

"But the full moon came only once a month, and many of the woman's potions were effective for only a short time. For example, her poultice for treating pleurisy required seven warts of the fly agaric mushroom bathed in the light of the full moon for no less than three hours. The poultice had to be applied to the chest that same night, and left in place for a full day. Unless a patient was lucky enough to become ill when the moon was full, the woman could not help them.

"So she spoke to the tree, and commanded it to use its millions of leaves to gather the light of the full moon and let it drip down into her *laboratorium*. She bottled the moonlight in a special jar made of pure moonstone. And do you know what? It worked. With the help of the tree, the woman was able to capture enough moonlight to treat all her patients. For a time, all was well, but as her reputation grew, so did the number of people who came asking for her help. The tree could not gather enough moonlight to help them all, so the woman asked the other trees to help. Soon, the entire forest was storing moonlight for her, and again, for a time, all was well. Can you guess what happened next?"

"No," Annie said, because she just wanted Ozols to get on with the story.

"The moon lost its brilliance. You see, the moon gets much of its power from the earth. When moonlight strikes the leaves of a forest, that light is imbued with life energy and reflected back to the moon. So when all the trees in the forest captured that moonlight and didn't reflect it back, the moon became weaker and weaker, and soon there was not enough moonlight for the woman's potions.

"And that is why today, you can look at the full moon without being blinded. It is also the reason we no longer have magical potions."

"That's *it*?" Annie said after a moment.

Ozols shrugged. "It is a Litvanian story."

"Tell me another."

Ozols smiled. "You will have stories coming out of your ears!" She looked out at the street, where the first fallen leaves of autumn were gathering in the gutters. "Have you ever heard of the eater of sins?"

Annie's mouth fell open and her heart went *ka-thump*.

"Eater of sins" was what Papa said *nuodeema burna* meant. Fortunately, Ozols was not looking at her and didn't notice her reaction.

"What's that?" Annie asked.

"Long ago, when the moon was bright and magicians were common, the Queen-Whose-Name-Is-Forgotten ordered her court magician to create a vessel into which she could dispose of her regrets.

"The magician fabricated an urn. He called it the eater of sins. The queen ordered it placed in a secret room deep below the castle dungeons where only she could go.

"You see, a queen must make difficult judgments almost every day. How to punish a thief who has seven children to feed. How to tax a farmer whose wheat has been blighted by fungus. How to distribute food when not everyone can be fed, or what to do with a condemned prisoner who might possibly be innocent.

"Often there is no simple or fair solution. A queen— even a very good queen—is tormented by her conscience because every decision she makes causes pain to someone.

"Every night before retiring, the queen would go down the stairs to the dungeon and walk past all the poor wretches imprisoned there. She would enter a winding staircase and descend to the *zilzem*, a circular room where the bronze sarcophagi of Litvania's most ancient rulers stood along the walls. In the center of the room stood the eater of sins, a midnight-black urn with a bulging body and a gaping mouth. The queen would face the urn and speak her regrets. It is said that as the words left her lips, she could see the urn come alive and suck her confessions into its hungry mouth.

"Afterward, the Queen-Whose-Name-Is-Forgotten would climb the steps to the dungeon and walk past the wretches, and it would not bother her that they were filthy and miserable. She would climb the next staircase to her chambers and she would sleep the sleep of innocence, and all would be well.

"The queen's decisions became increasingly cruel. For example, when two barons came to her with a dispute about the ownership of a fine stallion, the queen had the poor horse cut in two. In another case, when the baker could not deliver the castle's daily bread allotment because his flour had been infested by weevils, she imprisoned the baker in her dungeon and fed him nothing but weevil pie until he devoured every last weevil in the land.

"The Queen-Whose-Name-Is-Forgotten lived two hundred and fifty years. When she finally died, her bones were placed in a bronze sarcophagus, and the sarcophagus joined the sarcophagi of her forebears against the walls of the *zilzem*. The new queen, whose name was Kintija, had the staircase leading down to the *zilzem* filled with rubble. So far as anyone knows, the eater of sins remains there to this day."

Ozols looked at Annie and raised her eyebrows. "What do you think?"

"Is that a true story?" Annie asked.

"Probably not," Ozols said with a shrug.

"Is the fudge ready?"

"Let's find out."

Ozols was not as good a cook as Miss Mekas. For breakfast it was usually oatmeal or cold cereal. Lunch was sandwiches. And for dinner, Ozols usually made soup, or a stew of some sort.

But the fudge was heavenly—sweet and smooth and possibly the very best thing she had ever put in her mouth.

"It's perfect!" she declared.

Ozols smiled, and Annie could almost remember her mother's face.

33

THiN ICE

The cold snap came hard and fast, as if the entire region had been hit with a freeze ray overnight. There was no snow, just a steady, frigid wind from the north. The walls of the house were popping and creaking from the sudden cooling. Chilly gusts stripped the last of the leaves from the trees. The thermometer outside the kitchen window read one degree below zero.

"Is it winter already?" Annie asked.

"It's still October," Ozols said, looking out the window. "This weather is freakish. It is going to be hard on the trees. Hard on the birds, too. The geese and ducks haven't even migrated yet."

"Will they die?"

"I hope not."

Annie got out her winter coat, her mittens, her favorite

stocking cap, and the suede boots she had copied from Fiona.

"Where are you going?" Ozols asked.

"I'm going to see if the ducks are frozen on the pond."

Outside, the wind tried to suck the air out of her lungs. Annie pulled her cap low over her forehead and breathed through her nose. Frozen leaves were blowing around her, making *tick-tick-tick* sounds. The pond was only a five-minute walk, but it felt longer. When she got there, she found a lacy fringe of ice around the shore and four ducks paddling around on the far side. The turtles were not on their log.

"Hey, ducks!" Annie yelled. "Time to fly south!"

The ducks ignored her. She went home and reported her findings to Ozols.

"They say it will be cold again tonight and tomorrow," Ozols said.

The next day was even colder. That afternoon, Annie went back to the pond. It was frozen over, a perfectly smooth, crystalline sheet of ice. The ducks had flown. She walked up to the edge. The ice was like glass—she could see the bottom. She tested it with her toe. It felt solid, but she could tell it wasn't very thick, so she backed away and bumped into something soft.

Annie let out a yelp and spun around. A ball of puffy,

down-stuffed nylon parka tumbled to the ground.

"Arthur! I told you not to sneak up on me!"

Arthur rolled onto his mittened hands and climbed to his feet.

"Not sneaking," he said.

"You came up right behind me!"

"I want to see the turtles."

"They're down in the muck with the frogs and the other slimy creatures."

"I'm going to look." He walked to the edge of the pond and stepped out onto the ice.

"I can see the bottom!" he said, sliding his feet around. "It's slippery."

"Come back here!" Annie said.

"No!"

"Arthur, it's not safe!"

He took two sliding steps toward the log in the middle of the pond. "Look, I'm skating!"

"Arthur, you stupid boy, you come back here right now!"

"You're not my mom," Arthur said. "I don't have to do what you say. And you can't come and get me 'cause you're scared!"

"Fine!" Annie shouted. "I hope you fall through and

drown!" She turned her back to him and started to walk off, but got only a few steps away before she looked back.

Arthur was slide-stepping toward the log. He was almost there when one of his feet went through the ice. He yelled something, and in an instant his entire body disappeared into the pond.

Annie stared at the hole in the ice.

Arthur did not reappear. Annie screamed his name and ran toward the pond. She hit the ice at a run. Her feet flew out from under her and she slid on her butt toward the hole. It felt like slow motion. The ice broke as she reached the edge of the hole and she went under.

The water was shockingly cold. She flailed and kicked and got her head above the water for long enough to take a breath. The log was almost in reach. She clawed at it but missed, and sank again, pulled down by her sodden coat and heavy boots. Her feet hit the soft muddy bottom and she pushed herself back up. This time she was able to fling off one of her mittens and grab on to the log—but where was Arthur?

She gulped air and went back under, trying to see through the murky water. Her hand hit something. Arthur's parka! She held on and thrashed her way back to the log and got her arm over it and tried to pull Arthur to the surface.

He was too heavy. She broke through the ice and dragged him to the submerged end of the log. She threw one leg over the top of it and got both hands under Arthur's arms and dragged him up until his head was above water.

Arthur was unconscious. Or dead. Annie wrapped her arms around him and pulled him all the way up onto the log. She knew there was something you were supposed to do to save someone from drowning, but she didn't know how to do it. Scared, cold, and angry, she pounded Arthur on the chest, yelling, "Arthur, you stupid boy!" She hit him again.

Arthur coughed, then vomited pond water all over her.

"Hang on, I'm coming!" someone shouted.

Annie looked toward the shore. Mr. Dennison was wading toward them, crashing through the thin ice and carrying a long board on his shoulder. He was up to his knees, then waist deep.

He pushed the board across the ice between them. Arthur was gasping and coughing and looking around wildly, as if he had no idea where he was.

"Can you reach it?" Mr. Dennison asked. The water was up to his chest.

"I think so," Annie said.

"One at a time," Mr. Dennison said.

"Can you grab the board?" Annie asked Arthur.

Arthur nodded. Annie lowered him into the water and

held on to one hand as his other reached for the end of the board.

"I got it," he said.

She let go. Arthur pulled himself along the board until Mr. Dennison was able to grab him and drag him back to shore, where Mrs. Dennison and their dachshund were waiting.

Annie hadn't been thinking about the cold, but now it hit her hard. She could hardly bend her fingers and was shivering violently. It could not have been more than a minute, but it felt like hours before Mr. Dennison waded back into the pond and pushed the board to where she could reach it. Annie's fingers were too frozen to grab anything, so she threw herself onto the board and wrapped her arms around it and let Mr. Dennison pull her out of the pond. He lifted her and carried her across Circle Lane to their house. Mrs. Dennison and Arthur were right ahead of them.

Once they were inside, Mrs. Dennison stripped off their wet coats and boots and wrapped them both in warm, dry blankets. Annie was shivering so hard she could hear her teeth chatter. Arthur's lips were blue, and he was shaking, too.

Mr. Dennison, still dripping wet from his shoulders down, brought out two mugs of hot cocoa. Mrs. Dennison had to hold the mug steady so Arthur could sip it.

"That was very courageous what you did, Annie,"
Mr. Dennison said. "You are a very brave young woman.
You're a hero!"

His words warmed her even more than the hot cocoa.
Nobody had ever called her *brave* before. Or a hero. Mr.
Dennison was looking at her in a way that made her feel
strong and important.

"You were brave, too," Annie said. "You saved us both."

"You were all quite brave," Mrs. Dennison said with a
smile.

Mr. Dennison shook his head and said, "If I hadn't seen
you through the window, I don't know what might have
happened."

"Now, Harry, let's not be morbid," said Mrs. Dennison.
"You go get out of those wet clothes and pour some cocoa
for yourself. I'll call the children's parents and have them
bring over some dry clothing."

"Papa is in Litvania," Annie said.

"I will call your caretaker. What is her name again?"

"Ozols."

Annie was shivering less now. Arthur was looking at
her with an odd expression—almost as if he was grateful
but mad at her at the same time.

"I *told* you to come back," she said.

34.
APOLOGIES

The first thing Ozols did when they got home was to run a hot bath.

"Let's get that pond scum out of your hair and get you warmed up."

Annie wasn't shaking anymore. Her face felt prickly and hot, but she was still cold inside.

"What would your father say if he came home and I told him you had drowned?" Ozols asked.

"I didn't drown," Annie said. "Arthur almost drowned. I almost froze to death. And it was his fault."

"You should never have let him go out onto the ice."

"I told him not to."

"You could have stopped him."

That was true. She could have grabbed him. But then

Arthur had made her mad. She'd told him she hoped he would fall through and drown.

"He was being a brat," she said.

"I suppose you're never a brat? Ha! Now get in the tub."

The bath felt wonderful—she sank in all the way to her chin and stayed there until her fingertips were wrinkly. She kept thinking about what had happened. Ozols was right. She could have stopped Arthur. She should have. But she had *saved* him! Mr. Dennison told her she was brave. He said she was a *hero*.

Still, she felt bad. *"I hope you fall through and drown,"* she had shouted at him. She had called him *stupid*. But he'd said mean things to her, too.

But Arthur was just a little kid.

But she was a kid, too. She shouldn't have to be responsible.

Annie took a breath and slid down until her whole head was underwater. She held her breath and counted all the way to thirty before she had to sit up. How long had she been underwater at the pond? Not that long. How long had Arthur been under? Longer.

She had *saved* him. She was *brave*. She was a *hero*.

After her bath and a big bowl of hot chicken noodle soup, Annie was ready to go to bed, even though it was hours before her usual bedtime. Her brain was still buzzing, replaying the events at the pond over and over. *I could have stopped him. But I saved him. But I let him go out there. But I saved him. It was my fault. But I saved him!*

She took out her tablet and chose a pencil. Brown, the color of pond muck. She wrote down what had happened. She filled two whole pages and had to sharpen the pencil three times. She read what she had written. She tore out the pages and rolled them tightly. All she had to do was put them in the *burna* and everything would be okay. She wouldn't feel bad about letting Arthur go out on the ice. She wouldn't feel bad about saying those mean things to him.

Ozols was in the library reading a book. Annie tiptoed past the doorway and quietly opened the door to Papa's study. She stepped inside and closed it after her. The sun had just set, but there was still enough light coming in through the windows for her to see. She peeled back the corner of the rug. The *burna* stared back at her, a single black eye.

For the hundredth time, Annie wondered what was down there. A magical urn, like the one in the Queen-Whose-Name-Is-Forgotten's castle? Or just a big dark room full of rotting paper?

Annie knelt down. She pressed her ear to the hole and listened, as she had done many times before. A faint hiss, like the sound she heard listening to the big seashell in her bedroom.

She sat up and regarded the tube of paper in her hand. She looked at the hole. All she had to do was put the paper in the hole. It would disappear, and drag the guilt and shame and bad feelings down into the dark. She had done it . . . how many times before? Fifty? A hundred? Her tablet was more than half gone.

She thought again about what had happened with Arthur. Her bad feelings about letting him go on the ice and saying those mean things to him were all mixed up with how she felt about being a courageous, brave hero. What if the *burna* took away the good feelings, too? She never felt *wonderful* after feeding the *burna*. She just felt numb. Like the way her face felt after coming inside from the cold. The way her fingers had felt while she was in the pond waiting for Mr. Dennison to save her.

Annie stood up and stuffed the tube of paper into her pocket. She did not want to forget how it felt to be a hero.

That night, Annie woke up with a terrible leg ache—first in her left leg, and then in both legs. She hadn't had a leg ache since she was sick in the hospital.

She sat up and rubbed her shins the way the nurse in the hospital had done. It helped only a little. She thought about waking up Ozols, but her legs hurt so bad she didn't think she could walk.

The leg ache went on and on, and when finally it faded to a dull throb, Annie heard a sound, a bare whisper: *scrish-scrash, scrish-scrash, scrish-scrash*. She had to concentrate to hear it. It reminded her of the scratching sound she had heard in the cellar, but much fainter, as if it was coming from far, far away. There was a soothing rhythm to it, but at the same time an eeriness that prickled the back of her neck. Annie wrapped her pillow around her head and squeezed it against her ears. *Scrish-scrash, scrish-scrash*. The sound continued, now seeming to come from deep inside her. *Maybe my heart is talking to me,* she thought. She listened, trying to understand what it was saying. After a time, she let the rhythm carry her away, and she slept.

In the morning she felt fine. She woke to the sound of crows cawing outside, and for a few seconds she didn't even remember that she'd had a leg ache. She put on her jeans and a T-shirt, grabbed a red pencil from her box, and went downstairs. Ozols was in the kitchen stirring a pot of oatmeal. Annie went to the library doorway and measured herself. She wasn't expecting her height to be any different, but she had grown a quarter of an inch overnight!

Annie stared at the red pencil mark. The last time she had grown taller was while she was in the hospital, and she'd had leg aches there, too. Dr. Bray had called them "growing pains."

Maybe it was the *burna*, she thought. In the hospital she had not been feeding the *burna*, and she had grown. And yesterday she had written down what had happened with Arthur but hadn't put the paper in the *burna*. Did feeding the *burna* keep her from growing?

She measured herself again, just to make sure. Definitely one-fourth of an inch, maybe even a little more. She put the pencil in her pocket and felt the crumpled paper tube there. She unrolled the tube and read what she had written, remembering everything that had happened with crystal clarity. It was her fault that Arthur had almost died. But she had saved him. If you do a bad thing, and then later do something that undoes the bad thing, was the first thing still bad?

Annie didn't know, but the two things were connected. Saving Arthur had definitely made the bad thing *less* bad. She stuffed the two pages back in her pocket, not bothering to roll them up. She wasn't ready to forget her feelings about it, even if they were confusing.

All day long she felt alternately guilty and proud of herself. When Ozols asked her to sweep the stairs, she didn't do a very good job. She kept thinking about what it would be like if Arthur had drowned. Would she have just written "I let Arthur drown" on her tablet and fed her guilt to the *burna*?

But I saved him, she said to herself. *I saved him.*

So why did she feel so awful?

"You seem preoccupied," Ozols said. Annie had only swept half the stairs, and she had started it several minutes ago. "Or are you making the task last because you are enjoying it so much?"

"I was just thinking about Arthur," Annie said. "I feel bad that I let him go out on the ice. What if he'd drowned?"

"You are feeling remorseful. It is perfectly natural that you should feel bad."

"But I don't *want* to feel bad!"

"Perhaps you should apologize to Arthur and his mother. Tell them you're sorry."

"But I'm not sorry I saved him!"

"No, but the two things—saving him, and putting him in danger in the first place—are not the same. You can have different feelings about each of them."

Annie felt the crumpled paper in her pocket, and again considered feeding it to the *burna*. If Ozols was right about the two things being different, she could keep the good feelings about saving Arthur.

The problem was that in her head, the two things were all one thing.

"Annie? Are you all right?"

Annie ran down the stairs.

"Annie!" Ozols shouted.

Annie ignored her and ran out the front door.

Emily Golden answered the door. Annie was panting from running all the way over there. Her breath was making clouds in the cold air.

"Annie? Why aren't you wearing a coat?"

"I just came over for a minute. I came to apologize."

"For what, Annie?"

"For letting Arthur go out on the ice. Is he okay?"

"He's fine. He's watching TV." She looked over her shoulder. Annie could hear the television in the other room.

"Annie, what you did yesterday was very brave. But why didn't you stop Arthur in the first place?"

"He made me mad. Then I called him names and said I hoped he fell through the ice. I didn't mean it. I'm sorry."

"But what if you hadn't been able to save him?"

"I don't know. I think about it all the time now. I am really, really, *really* sorry."

Emily Golden put her hands on Annie's shoulders. "I accept your apology. I am so grateful that you were there to save Arthur. Would you like to come in and warm up?"

"That's okay. I should get back." With that, she turned and ran back home.

"And where have you been?" Ozols asked when Annie charged in through the front door.

"Over at Arthur's house."

"Dressed like that? In this weather?"

"I had to apologize."

Ozols pressed her lips tight together and gave a sharp nod. "That's good. But next time wear a jacket. You don't have to be cold to apologize. Now finish sweeping those stairs and I'll read you a story from your book."

"The one about the rat with the raspberry?"

Ozols pursed her lips, gave her head a little shake, then said, "If you wish."

35.
MATAS AND THE
RAT QUEEN

◆A boy named Matas was sent into the woods by his mother to gather thimbleberries. As he was filling his basket, he put his hand on a bee and was stung on his finger. Matas cursed the bee and struck out at it.

The bee, who had stung the boy only because he had grabbed it, buzzed around the boy's head and spoke. "Young sir, you have laid your hand on me, and flailed at me, and befouled me with your language. Apologize, or honey shall forever be bitter on your tongue!"

The boy cursed the bee again, using language so wicked it refuses to be written upon a page.

The bee said, "Twice now you have cursed

me, and so I double my curse on you—you shall carry true remorse in your heart of hearts until the end of days."

"I am not afraid of you," Matas said. "Bees sting only once, and then they die!"

"That is true, but curses live forever. Good day, sir. I go now to die with my hive mates." And with that the bee flew off.

Matas returned to picking berries with a throbbing finger and a heart full of remorse. He regretted striking out at the bee, and the foul language he had used, and his future filled with bitter honey. He filled his basket and headed home to show his mother. On the way, he encountered a wood rat.

This was no ordinary wood rat. This was a rat the size of a cat, and she was wearing a golden crown. Instead of front paws, she had clever little hands, and her front teeth were as sparkly and golden as her crown. The boy knew immediately that he was face-to-face with the Queen of the Rats.

"Your Majesty!" The boy knelt.

The Rat Queen sniffed and twitched her naked tail. "Rise, young man," she said in a voice that sounded like a shovelful of dry pebbles.

Matas stood and set the basket of fruit in front of the queen. "Would you care for a thimbleberry?"

The Rat Queen peered into the basket, inspected the berries, and with her tiny pink hands, selected the largest and reddest one and set it on her head so that it was encircled by the crown.

"That is quite handsome," said Matas, who secretly thought it looked ridiculous.

"I thank you for your insincerity." The Rat Queen tilted her head and clacked her teeth. "You carry a hex, I see."

"It is nothing," said Matas. "Only a bee's curse."

"I cannot help you with the bitter honey, as honey is the domain of the Bee Queen. I fear you must henceforth sweeten your gruel with molasses. But I can help with the remorse, if you wish."

"That would be splendid!" Matas exclaimed.

"It is a simple matter. I need only take your conscience, and the remorse will go away as well."

Matas thought for a moment. Did he really

need a conscience? It was, after all, an inconvenience. Only last night it had kept him up for hours as he fretted about a lie he had told his mother.

"Your Majesty, I accept your kind offer."

The Rat Queen laughed, a sound like boulders tumbling down a distant mountain. "I will need the rest of your berries as well."

"It would be my honor," said Matas.

The Rat Queen waved her tiny hands, and the deed was done.

Sometime later, Matas returned empty-handed to the small stone house where he lived with his mother.

"I thought you went to pick berries, Matas!" she said.

"I could find none," he said, and his lie caused him no discomfort whatsoever.

"Your fingers are stained red," said his mother.

"I found a few. Only a few." Another lie, and it felt exactly the same as telling the truth.

"Where is the basket?"

"Lost."

She shook her gray head and said, "Yanna needs milking."

Matas went to the small lean-to shed where their aging nanny goat lived. Yanna was well past her prime years; her milk was scant and thin. He managed to coax only a few paltry gills from her shriveled udder.

"So little!" his mother said when he returned. She always said the same. That night, for supper, they ate a stew of cabbage, burdock root, and goat milk thickened with dried pigweed.

The next day, Matas's mother harvested six cabbages and fifteen parsnips from their garden.

"Take them to Hamm the butcher and trade them for a knob of salt and a royal pound of fatty pork belly," she said to Matas. "Do not let him cheat you. The knob of salt must be as big as a baby's fist, and if you are not watchful, he will give you the lean end of the belly."

As Matas filled a sack with the vegetables, he noticed that several of the cabbages were a bit moldy. He arranged them so the mold was hidden on the bottom, slung the sack over his shoulder, and trudged off toward town. He arrived at the abattoir shortly and displayed his wares to Hamm the butcher.

Hamm glanced into the sack.

"How many cabbages?" he asked.

"Eight," said Matas, increasing their number by two. *It is only fair,* he thought, *as the butcher will try to give me the dry end of the pork belly.*

"And how many parsnips?"

"Nineteen," said Matas, increasing their number by four. *It is only fair,* he thought, *as Hamm will try to cheat me on the salt.*

Hamm nodded, accepting Matas's count. He eyeballed a slab of pork belly and cut off a large chunk. Matas saw that it was nicely marbled with fat, and somewhat larger than a royal pound. The butcher reached into a barrel and came up with a lump of rock salt much larger than a baby's fist. He placed both items in a muslin sack and gave them over.

Matas was delighted to find that he felt no remorse about lying to the butcher. He congratulated himself on the bargain he had struck with the Rat Queen, and made his way home with a light heart. When he arrived, his mother was pleased with the pork belly and salt. "Such a clever boy!" she said proudly. "Tonight we will have pork and nettle soup, with molasses pie for dessert!"

Matas took himself out to the edge of the field to pick nettles for the soup. As he was working, he heard a horse-drawn cart approaching along the lane. It was Hamm the butcher, and he did not look happy.

Matas backed into the nettles to conceal himself, but Hamm saw him and came to a halt.

"Matas!" he said. "I have a grievance! Your parsnips were too few, as were your cabbages! And moldy as well!"

"A bargain is a bargain," Matas retorted.

"I will not be gulled by such as you!" Hamm took up a cudgel and sprang from his cart. Matas fled, but the butcher was faster. He caught up with him and struck him down with the cudgel.

"Stop! I will give you back your salt, and such pork as remains!" Matas cried.

"I do not want your pork and salt," said the butcher. "I want only to beat you bloody for your deceit!"

With that, the butcher struck the boy again and again until he lay senseless and bleeding on the ground. Sometime later, Matas woke in a haze of pain, and found himself looking up at the Rat Queen.

"Young Matas, you are looking poorly," she said. "But at least you have no regrets."

"I regret my aches and pains," Matas muttered through broken teeth. "And it is all your fault!"

"My fault!" exclaimed the Rat Queen. "Ungrateful child, since that is how you feel, I will undo what I have done!" She waved her tiny pink hands, turned her back, and scampered off. In an instant, Matas's conscience returned, and he saw he had only himself to blame for the miseries that had befallen him.

His mother found him in the field. She carried him home, made a poultice of jewelweed and wood ash, and applied it to his wounds. Several days later, when he was able to stand and walk, Matas returned to the butcher's shop.

"I am sorry," he said to the butcher.

Hamm, who was a good man at heart, nodded. "I am sorry as well," he said. "For a few paltry coppers' worth of pig meat and salt, I beat you senseless. I have felt remorse every day since."

And so the butcher returned to his trade, and the Rat Queen to her underground throne. Matas went back to his life of farming oats and cabbage and parsnips, and all was well, except that he spent the rest of his days without once tasting the sweetness of honey on his tongue.✦

"He couldn't eat honey?" Annie asked.

"The bee's curse never left him. For Matas, all honey became unbearably bitter."

"I asked Papa to read me that story, but he wouldn't."

"Perhaps because it was too sad?"

"He said it was not *nice*. He read me the story about the changeling instead."

"I know that story!" Ozols said. "The one where the changeling becomes a wolf and eats the princess for stealing his berries."

"That is not the way Papa told it! He said it was a girl named Annike, and she made the changeling turn into a beetle and then stomped on it."

Ozols laughed. "I guess everybody reads it differently."

"But it's written down, so shouldn't it always be the same?"

"Stories change every time they are told."

"Does that mean if you read the Rat Queen story again, Matas might live *happily* ever after?"

"Possibly. But we would have to read through the whole story again to find out."

36

FOOL'S SUMMER

The weather grew warm over the next few days. The temperature reached seventy degrees, and Ozols opened all the windows.

"It is Fool's Summer," Ozols said. "This may be our last chance to air out the house before true winter arrives."

"Why is it called Fool's Summer?" Annie asked.

"That is what we called it in Litvania. Because only a fool thinks the warm spell will last."

Annie had not been writing anything in her yellow tablet. She had not fed the *burna*, even though she did several regrettable things, including lying to Ozols about how much she had read. Every night she had leg aches. She still heard the whispering, but it was fainter. Every morning when she measured herself, she was a little bit taller. In one week she grew almost an inch.

It's the burna, she thought.

When Papa called to say he'd be home in a week, he asked her if she was writing things down and putting them in the *burna.*

"Yes, Papa," she said.

"Good girl!"

Annie felt so bad, she wrote down that she had lied to Papa. She took the rolled-up page to his study, folded back the corner of the rug, and stared at the little hole. If she put the paper in there, would she feel better about lying to Papa? Would she stop growing?

She heard Ozols's footsteps approaching. She covered the hole and stood up.

"Hello!" Ozols said from the doorway. "What mischief are you up to?"

"Nothing." Annie looked at the paper in her hand. "I wrote a note for Papa to welcome him home." Another lie.

"Well, he won't be back for another week." Ozols looked Annie up and down. "You're shooting up like a bean sprout!"

"I think I'm having a growth spurt. I grew almost an inch this week."

"That is quite a spurt! Look at you—your arms are sticking out of your sleeves."

"I know. And my new shoes are kind of tight."

Ozols shook her head, smiling. "I suppose you're catching up. You *were* rather on the small side."

Annie kept growing, but much more slowly. She gained only about a quarter of an inch over the next week, and her legs hardly hurt at all during the night. Ozols took her shopping for new shoes, a pair of winter boots, and a sweater. Annie made sure to pick out clothes that were nothing like Fiona's. She didn't want to look like Fiona anymore.

On Saturday morning, Papa finally came home. Ozols and Annie drove to the airport in Papa's car because Ozols's Jeep wasn't big enough for the three of them. He had called and said he would be waiting for them on the sidewalk outside the baggage claim area. When they arrived, the only person there was an old man in a wheelchair flanked by two large suitcases. He saw them coming and stood up shakily.

It was Papa.

Ozols stopped the car. Both she and Annie jumped out and ran to him.

"Papa!" Annie wrapped her arms around his hunched shoulders. "Welcome home! Why do you have a wheelchair? Are you hurt? Are you sick?"

"No, and no," he said with a dry chuckle. "Just tired from my journey. The airport let me borrow this excellent chair. I'm fine."

He did not look fine. The skin around his eyes was gray and pouchy, and he was bent over as if his back hurt. He appeared to have aged years in the weeks he had been gone.

On the drive home, Papa had little to say. He sat slumped in the passenger seat while Ozols drove and Annie chattered from the back seat, telling him about making fudge, and how Arthur had fallen through the ice, and how she had saved him. She hardly knew what she was saying. She was talking out of nervousness. Papa always looked tired after his trips to Litvania, but she had never seen him like this. He didn't even seem to be listening to her. Ozols was worried, too. She kept glancing at him as she drove.

"I had another growth spurt," Annie said.

That got his attention. He looked back at her.

"What's that you say?" he asked.

"I grew more than an inch," Annie said.

Ozols said, "It's true, Lukas. She sprouted like a mushroom."

"Is that a fact?" he said with a frown.

"Ozols says I'm catching up."

Papa shook his head and stared out the windshield and didn't say another word. When they got home, he walked unsteadily from the car to the porch and gripped the railing as he climbed the steps. Moments later he was in his study with the door closed.

Ozols and Annie carried his suitcases up to his bedroom.

"I'm worried," Annie said.

"He does not look well. But I'm sure he'll get better."

"He always looks bad when he comes back from his travels. But not this bad."

"I will make lamb stew," Ozols said. "He needs food and rest."

"He needs to *cicenja*," Annie said.

"*Cicenja*? Do you know what that means?"

"It makes him not so tired."

"In Litvanian it means to cleanse."

"But he doesn't wash. He just writes on his tablet."

Ozols frowned. "Some things cannot be cleansed with soap and water."

37

COINCIDENCE

Papa stayed in his study all day. When it came time for dinner, Ozols knocked on his door.

"Lukas? Are you all right in there?"

"I'm fine."

"Are you hungry?"

"I'll eat later."

Ozols shook her head and frowned. "That man is stubborn as a cat," she muttered, and walked stiffly back to the kitchen. Annie knelt down and peeked through the keyhole. She could see Papa's hand, writing furiously. A moment later he stopped writing and said, "Annike, I know you are there."

Annie's heart went *thump*.

"Come in here, if you would."

Annie opened the door and stepped into the study.

"Close the door, please."

Annie closed the door. Papa stood and walked around his desk. He looked much better—still tired, but he was no longer hunched over, and the skin under his eyes was no longer so dark and pouchy.

"You *cicenjaed*," she said.

"I have a ways to go, but yes, I'm feeling much better."

"Ozols made lamb stew."

"Good. I'll be done here soon, but you two should not wait for me." He looked Annie up and down. "You have grown."

"An inch and a quarter."

"Have you been writing in your tablet?"

"Yes, Papa." She had already lied about it once. It was easy to keep on lying.

"Have you been feeding the *burna*?"

"Yes, Papa."

"Hmm." He walked over to the fireplace and looked at the framed photo of his granduncle Valdemaras. Annie could tell he didn't believe her, but she didn't know how to undo her lies.

"Is it true what you said in the car?" he asked. "You saved that boy when he fell through the ice?"

He *had* been listening! "Yes! Mr. Dennison said I was a

hero. He's a hero, too. He jumped in the pond and saved us both."

"I will have to thank him for that." He fixed Annie with an intent gaze. "I would not want to lose you to some reckless impulse."

"I won't go on the ice," Annie said. "Anyway, it melted. It's Fool's Summer."

Papa smiled. "I have not heard that expression in many years."

"Ozols told it to me."

"Have you told Ozols about our *burna*?"

"No! You said not to!"

"Why have you not been feeding the *burna*, Annike?"

Thunk. His question felt like a punch to the gut. He *knew*.

"I'm sorry." Her words came out like a squeak.

Papa pressed his lips tight together. Annie braced herself for a scolding, but he only sighed. His shoulders sagged and suddenly he appeared old again. He lowered himself into his big leather chair and closed his eyes.

"Why?" he asked again, in a voice so quiet she almost couldn't hear it.

"Because I think it keeps me from growing up," she said.

Papa did not reply immediately.

Annie waited. After a few more seconds she asked, "What is down there?"

Still with his eyes closed, Papa gave his head a little shake. "It is nothing."

"You said it was magic."

"*Magic* is a word we use for things we do not understand." He opened his eyes and looked at her. "Annike, the *burna* is nothing but a family ritual and a hole in the floor. The important thing is that we confess the things we have done—things we ought not have done—and make them go away. You *will* grow up—eventually."

"But all my friends are growing up faster!"

"Annike . . . I want you to be happy, and at peace. Would you rather grow up bearing the burden of your regrets?"

Annie did not know how to answer that, so she asked, "Why doesn't Ozols do it? Isn't she family?"

"Yes, but she is Ozols. We are Klimas."

"Did my mother?"

He shook his head. "Your mother was an angel. She performed no regrettable acts."

"So why is it only for us?"

"Because that is the way of it."

Which was no answer at all. "Why do I get taller when I don't feed the *burna*?"

Papa looked away. "That is coincidence," he said.

Annie didn't believe him, and that made her feel sick inside.

"You must continue to write things down," he said. "You must feed the *burna*."

Did he want her to stay a little girl forever? *Never grow up.* He was always saying that.

"Are you listening to me?" He was looking at her again, his eyes dark and tight.

Annie looked down. "Yes, Papa."

"Look at me. Promise me."

Annie looked at his face. She had never seen him so serious.

"I promise," she said.

"Good. Now go eat your supper. After dinner, you will write down all the things you have done—including disobeying me—and feed them to the *burna*."

Annie picked at her dinner. The lamb stew was good, but she wasn't hungry. She told Ozol that she wasn't feeling well and went to her room. She wrote down everything she had done wrong while Papa was in Litvania. She filled six whole pages. Some of it made her feel bad, but at the same time she remembered the sweet taste of stolen fudge, and the feeling she'd had when she saved Arthur's life, and the fact that she disobeyed Papa and grew more than an inch.

She would feel better about the things she had done when she put the pages in the *burna*, but what about the things she didn't feel bad about? Would she forget how good the fudge had tasted? She read what she had written, then tore up all the pages. She didn't want to forget about saving Arthur. She didn't want to stop growing. She rolled a blank piece of paper into a tight tube, took it downstairs, and put it in the *burna*. Papa, sitting at his desk, nodded approvingly. He looked tired, but much better than before. He was almost completely *cicenjaed*.

Annie had another leg ache that night, but it did not last long. She heard only the faintest whisper of the whispery sound. The next morning when she measured herself, she had grown another eighth of an inch.

Papa didn't notice.

38.
AUKLES

Every night, Papa would ask her, "Did you feed the *burna* today?"

"Yes, Papa," she would lie. And then she would feel bad. She started writing down other things—nonsense like,

I'm a winky dinky wuzzle puzzle

or

Once upon a time there was a girl so big she could touch the moon.

She would roll up the paper and put it in the hole so that when Papa asked her if she'd fed the *burna*, she could say yes and not be lying.

She measured herself every day. Some days she couldn't tell any difference, but some days she could. She was growing, but it was so gradual that Papa didn't notice—or he pretended not to notice. Every week her shoes got a little tighter and her pants got a tiny bit shorter. When she sat on the swing set in the side yard, she had to tuck her feet up high or they would drag on the ground.

Fool's Summer lasted only three days. For the next two weeks, the days stayed in the forties. Annie was on the swing set wearing a sweater and a hoodie. She was thinking about going back inside to get a pair of gloves because the chains holding up the swing were cold on her hands, but if Ozols spotted her, she'd assign her some chore to do.

Wondering whether she could sneak in through the back door, she looked up and saw Arthur's mother standing on the porch talking with Ozols. Arthur, wearing a brand-new puffy parka with the hood up, was coming toward her.

"Hey, Arthur," Annie said.

He sat on the other swing.

"How come your mom's here?" she asked.

"She has to go to work," Arthur said.

"Where does she work?"

"She got a job, so you have to take care of me."

"I do?" Annie was confused.

"Push me," Arthur said.

"Okay, but just for a minute," Annie said. She got behind him and pushed him up as high as she could, then backed away quickly. When he reached the end of his backswing, she ran forward and pushed again.

"I bet if I pushed even harder you could go all the way around in a circle."

"Don't!" Arthur yelled.

"I won't. I'm just saying."

Arthur dragged his feet to stop. He got off and looked up at Annie. "You're bigger than you used to be," he said.

"I know. I was under a magic spell that kept me from growing. But I defeated the spell, so now I'm getting bigger."

"You're lying. There's no such thing as magic," Arthur said confidently.

Annie did not like to be told she was lying, even if she *was* lying.

"You are very irritating," she said.

"My mom says that, too."

The two women had gone into the house.

"Come on, let's find out what they're talking about," Annie said.

When they got inside, Arthur's mother put her hands on his shoulders.

"You be good," she said. "Do what Ozols and Annie

say. No running off, and no mischief. I'll be back in a few hours."

"Okay," Arthur said.

Emily Golden stood up and looked at Annie. "Thank you, Annie."

"For what?" Annie asked.

"For looking after Arthur."

Annie looked at Ozols, trying to make sense of things.

"Arthur will stay with us three afternoons a week while his mother works at the bookstore," Ozols said. "You can be his babysitter!"

"Do I get paid?" Annie asked.

Ozols said, "Dear, we are neighbors! Neighbors help neighbors."

"I'm sure I can bring you something, Annie," Emily Golden said.

After Arthur's mother left, Ozols told Annie that she had been rude.

"I wasn't trying to be," Annie said. "But Fiona's sister gets paid for babysitting, so I thought I would, too."

"That is understandable, but your timing was not nice."

Annie didn't understand that, but she said, "I'll apologize when she comes to get Arthur."

"Good. Now, I trust you'll keep Arthur amused while I hang out the sheets."

After Ozols left, Annie asked Arthur what he wanted to do.

Arthur shrugged.

"How about if I read you a story?" Annie said.

"What story?"

"A Litvanian story."

39.
THERE IS
MAGIC
HERE

Annie couldn't read any of the stories in the Litvanian fairy-tale book, but she remembered them. She sat Arthur down on the sofa in the library, opened the book, and pretended to read.

"Once upon a time a little boy named Arthur was picking berries, and he ran into a changeling." She knew that wasn't exactly right.

"What's a changeling?" Arthur asked.

"A funny-looking little creature who can turn into a bear. And the bear chased the little boy away and ate his goat."

"What goat?"

"The little boy had a goat."

Arthur leaned across her arm and looked at the picture. "That's a little girl and a big dog," he pointed out.

"Actually, it's a wolf. And it's not really a wolf, it's the changeling."

"But you said it was a bear."

"It was, but changelings can change. The changeling turned into a wolf to scare away a dragon and then a girl named Annie came along."

"Did the wolf eat her?"

"No. Annie made the wolf turn into a bug, and she stomped it to death." She was pretty sure she had that part right.

"Then what happened?"

"That's the whole story."

"That's not a very good story," Arthur said.

"It's Litvanian," said Annie, closing the book. "Litvanian stories are always like that. But they have magic in Litvania."

"Where is that?"

"I'll show you." She led him over to the big globe and pointed out Litvania.

Arthur put his nose to the globe so his eyes were only an inch from Litvania. "I don't see any magic."

"It's not the kind of magic you can see."

"Then how do you know it's real?"

"I have a magic amulet." She pulled up the chain around

her neck and showed him the Saint Christopher medallion she had stolen from Miss Mekas. She had been wearing it ever since Mekas left. "And we have a magic room."

"Where?"

"In the cellar." Annie pointed at the floor.

Arthur thought for a moment. "Show me."

"I can't. It's locked."

"You're just saying that!"

Annie rolled her eyes and dragged him out of the library and into the kitchen. She grabbed the knob on the cellar door and shook it. "See? Locked. And I don't have a key."

"Did you ever go down there?"

"Yes, but I couldn't open the door to the magic room because it has a padlock."

Arthur looked closely at the old-fashioned doorknob and the keyhole-shaped keyhole. "How did you get in this door?"

"With a screwdriver."

"Let's do it again."

"I'm not supposed to." Annie wished she hadn't said anything. The thought of going back into that cellar made her neck all prickly.

"Hello! What's this mischief?"

Annie spun around. Ozols was standing in the doorway looking at them with her arms crossed.

"Nothing," Annie said. "Arthur was just asking about the cellar. I told him we couldn't go down there."

"Hmm," Ozols said with narrowed eyes. "See that you don't."

Annie said, mostly to escape her *tanta*'s distrustful gaze, "Let's go outside, Arthur."

Still with her arms crossed, Ozols watched them leave through the back door.

"She's kind of scary," Arthur said once they reached the street.

"She's okay," Annie said. "Only she's kind of weird about some things."

"Like your basement?"

"It's a cellar."

"What's the difference?"

"I don't know."

When they reached the sewer grate, Arthur stopped. He didn't get on his hands and knees and press his face to the grate like he used to; he just looked down.

"You know what?" he said.

"No, what?"

"We should go down there sometime."

"In the sewer? No, thank you!"

"I mean your basement." He started walking again. "If they keep it locked, there must be something interesting down there."

When Arthur's mother came to get him, she handed Annie a big fat book with a shiny red cover: *The Complete Grimm's Fairy Tales*.

"Ozols said you like fairy tales," she said.

"She certainly does," said Ozols.

Annie paged through the book. The print was small, and there were very few pictures. But at least it was in English.

"Thank you," Annie said. "I'm sorry if I was rude earlier."

"Oh, you weren't rude, Annie. Thank *you* for looking after Arthur," she said. "I'm scheduled to work again tomorrow afternoon. Will you be able to watch him then?"

"I guess so," Annie said.

"Of course we will," said Ozols.

40

THE ARGUMENT

Every time Annie walked past the cellar door, she thought about what Arthur had said: *"If they keep it locked, there must be something interesting down there."* According to Papa, there was nothing under the tower, just a dark space filled with scraps of pink and yellow paper. But Arthur had a point—why did Papa keep it locked? There had to be something there, something magical—like the magic urn that ate the sins of the Queen-Whose-Name-Is-Forgotten. Something that kept her from growing. It wasn't just writing down what she had done, and it wasn't just putting tubes of paper in the *burna*. It was only when she did *both* things that she stopped growing.

She asked Ozols why Papa kept the cellar door locked.

Ozols stopped wiping the stove top and just stood there for a few seconds before saying, without looking at Annie, "I'm sure he has his reasons." Which was the same as saying nothing at all.

"Like what?" Annie said.

Ozols turned to Annie and said, "Annie . . . your father wants you to be safe. You know you got hurt when you were a little girl—"

"I'm not a little girl now! I don't fall down stairs anymore."

"Yes, but your father, he worries. That cellar holds unhappy memories for him. It was just after you fell that Kundze—your mother—became ill."

This was new information. Annie held her breath, waiting for more, but Ozols went back to cleaning the stove top. Annie let her breath out and asked, "Was it the *zelty maras*?"

Ozols pressed her lips together and gave her head a little shake, then a nod. "I believe so. She never got better. I should not be telling you this."

Annie stared at her. "You mean my mom died because of me?"

"No! No, you must never think that! She did not respond well to treatment here, so your father flew with her back to Litvania, where the *zelty maras* is better known, but the Litvanian doctors could not cure her. You don't remember, but I came here to take care of you while your father was gone. Annie, you must understand that your father has strong feelings about you never going in that cellar again. You should respect his wishes."

"He goes down there sometimes," Annie said.

Ozols frowned.

"At night," Annie added.

"Probably he is just checking on the furnace," Ozols said.

Annie didn't argue anymore. In truth, she did not want to go back into the cellar. Her curiosity was not great enough to overcome her fear of what she might find if she were to open the door to the room under the tower. It wasn't just the whispery scratching she had heard. It was more than that. She was afraid to find out what happened to all the papers swallowed by the *nuodeema burna*. Papa did not want her to know. Ozols did not want her to know. And without Papa—without Ozols—she had nobody.

That night, Annie was awakened by the dull drone of Papa and Ozols talking downstairs. She listened sleepily, not able to make out the words. She was drifting back to sleep when the tone of the voices changed. Papa's voice became deeper; Ozols's voice rose in pitch. Annie sat up. It sounded as if they were arguing.

She slid off her bed, moved quietly to the door, and pushed it open a few inches.

"—don't care, Lukas! If you must have this life of yours, fine! Leave Annike out of it!"

Annie crept to the top of the stairs.

"Annike is my daughter." Papa lowered his voice and added, "I will do as I think best."

"As you did for Kundze?"

"Annike is strong. She is a Klimas."

"Only half!"

"Lower your voice," Papa said. "You'll wake her."

"I'll do more than that! She is old enough to know the truth."

What truth? Annie wondered.

"This is not your concern, Vaira. If you cannot do as I wish, then leave."

"I will not! I promised my sister I would care for Annike if anything happened to her, and now it has. *You* happened to her. What if she hadn't recovered from the *maras*? What if she gets sick again? She could have died!"

"She won't get sick. I have the situation under control. And you will say nothing to her."

"Am I to lie, then, Lukas?"

"Simply say nothing."

Ozols muttered something Annie could not make out.

She heard her father's footsteps coming toward the stairs and quickly returned to her room and slid beneath the covers. A few seconds later, Papa looked in on her. She lay perfectly still with her eyes closed. He backed out and closed the door.

The next morning, Annie woke up to the sound of Papa's car driving off. She went downstairs and measured herself against the doorjamb. She hadn't had a leg ache in three days, but she had gotten a bit taller—maybe another tenth of an inch? It was hard to tell. She went to the kitchen. Ozols was sitting at the table nibbling on dry toast and sipping tea.

"Good morning!" Ozols said with a bright, fake-looking smile.

Annie put two slices of bread in the toaster.

"How did you sleep?" Ozols asked.

Annie shrugged, waiting for Ozols to start lying to her, but Ozols just gave her that fake smile again. Annie looked away and watched the toaster until her toast popped up. When she turned back to the table, Ozols wasn't smiling anymore.

"What?" Annie said.

Ozols said nothing.

Annie sat down across from her and buttered her toast.

She spread it with a layer of strawberry preserves almost as thick as the toast itself, and waited for Ozols to tell her it was too much. Ozols remained silent. Annie looked at the cellar door and ate her toast and jam.

Ozols stirred her tea, sipped from her spoon, and said, "Did you hear us talking last night?"

"Papa wants you to lie to me," Annie said.

"I *thought* I heard you stirring around up there."

"You said I was old enough to hear the truth."

"I may have been wrong. Your father is your father."

"You said I almost died."

"Yes, you were very sick. But you are fine now."

"So, what aren't you supposed to tell me?"

Ozols frowned. "It is nothing." She stood up and took her plate and cup to the sink. "The weather has turned. Fool's Summer is long gone. It's going to snow. Arthur will be here soon. You can read him a story from your new fairy-tale book."

"Okay."

"They say the snow will be heavy."

41.

THE GOLDEN KEY

Arthur and his mother arrived just as the first flakes came drifting down.

"I may be back early today," Emily Golden said. "Depending on the weather."

"They say we might get a foot of snow," Ozols said.

"I hope to be back before *that* happens!"

After his mother left, Arthur pointed at Annie's chest. "What's that?"

She looked down. "It's a brooch," she said.

"Is it a rat?"

"No, it's Litvania."

"It looks like a rat."

Annie rolled her eyes. Arthur could be so *irritating*. "Do you want to hear a story?"

"I guess."

They sat at either end of the library sofa. Annie didn't feel like reading Arthur a long story, so she flipped through the book until she found one that was only half a page long. She read through it quickly to make sure it wasn't too weird or scary for a little kid.

Arthur was being very squirmy.

"What's wrong?" Annie asked.

"My feet are hot."

"Take off your boots."

"No."

"Okay, then, don't. This story is called 'The Golden Key.'"

"My name is Golden!"

"Yes, that's why I'm telling it to you." Annie cleared her throat and began. "One winter when the snow was very deep, a boy had to go outside to gather wood on his sled."

"Why on a sled?" Arthur asked.

"It doesn't say."

"Why?"

"Because it's a fairy tale. So, the boy had to gather wood, and when he had piled up all the wood on his sled, he was freezing cold."

"Was he wearing boots?"

"Yes. But he was still cold, so he decided to build a fire."

Annie told the story in her own words, hardly looking at the book. "The boy scraped away the snow to make a place for the fire, and he found a little golden key. He kept on digging and soon came to an iron casket."

"What's that?"

"Like a metal box, I think. The boy thought the casket might hold a treasure, so he looked and looked and at first he couldn't find a keyhole, but finally he did, and the key fit perfectly! He twisted the key, and the box opened."

Annie closed the book.

"What was in the box?" Arthur asked.

"It doesn't say. That's the end of the story."

"That's not a good story!"

"I'm just telling you what it says."

"I don't want to hear any more stories." Arthur slid off the sofa and stomped out of the room. A moment later, Annie heard him talking to Ozols in the kitchen.

Annie looked out the window. The wind had picked up and the snow was coming down harder. She would be stuck in the house with Arthur all afternoon. She took the book up to her room and paged through it until she came to a story called "The Ratcatcher."

The title alone sent a prickle up her spine. She had just started reading—*A very long time ago the town of Hamel in Germany was invaded by bands of rats, the like of which had never been seen before*—when Ozols called her from downstairs.

Arthur was sitting at the kitchen table eating a cookie. Ozols was putting on her winter coat. "Annie, I have to run out. Will you and Arthur be okay on your own for a while?"

"How long is a while?"

"Not long. Your father called, and his car won't start. He asked me to come and pick him up at his office."

"We can come with you," Annie said.

"There's not enough room in my little Jeep, and I need you to stay here and look after Arthur. Can you do that?"

"I guess so."

"If you need help with something, Mr. Wendell is right across the street." Ozols clapped her wide-brimmed hat on her head and rushed outside. Annie watched through the front window as the Jeep disappeared into the snowstorm. She turned back to Arthur.

"I guess I'm in charge now."

"No, you're not. I'm in charge of you!"

"Oh. Okay. So, what do you want to do?"

Arthur put the last piece of cookie in his mouth and chewed thoughtfully.

"Let's go in the basement," he said.

"No!"

"Can I have another cookie?" Arthur asked.

Annie ignored him and went to look out the kitchen window. Usually, she could see across the backyard to Mr. O'Connor's cornfield, but the snow was coming down so hard that all she saw were white slashes against gray shadows.

"Why is it so dark out?" Arthur asked.

"Because of the clouds," Annie said. She climbed onto the step stool and got the package of vanilla wafers from the cupboard. Arthur took two. She watched him eat them. Outside, the snow continued to fall.

"Can we play a game?" Arthur asked.

"What game?" Annie did not really want to play a game. She wanted to go back to her room and read about the ratcatcher.

"We could go outside and run in the snow!"

Annie looked out the window. "I think we should stay inside," she said.

"I know, let's play hide-and-seek! I get to hide."

"No! It's my house. I'll hide and you look for me. Cover your eyes and count to a hundred."

"A hundred? That's too many."

"Then count to fifty, only count really slow."

"Okay." Arthur put his hands over his eyes and started counting out loud.

"Slower," Annie said. She ran out of the kitchen and clomped noisily up to her room so he would think that she was upstairs. She grabbed the red fairy-tale book and tiptoed back down. She heard Arthur counting faster and faster: ". . . forty-two, forty-three, forty-four . . ." Annie ran back to the library and ducked behind the sofa. When she heard Arthur pounding up the stairs, she crept silently to the skinny closet next to the staircase and opened the door. It creaked, but Arthur was making so much noise running from room to room upstairs that he didn't hear. She closed the door, felt around for the light cord, and pulled it. The closet was even dirtier than she remembered. She brushed the dust off the wooden chair and sat down and opened her book.

"The Ratcatcher" turned out to be a super-creepy story, especially when read in an old closet surrounded by a lot of dirty old junk. This town called Hamel was overrun with big rats, and they hired this weird rat guy to get rid of them. That sounded way too familiar! Annie had to stop several times and look around to make sure there weren't any rats in the closet with her.

The ratcatcher played strange music on a magic pipe and lured all the rats to the river, where they were trapped in a whirlpool and drowned. When the townspeople refused to pay the ratcatcher for getting rid of the rats, he took all their kids to a hole in a mountain and they disappeared forever, and that was the end.

Annie closed the book and imagined West Exterminating coming back to Pond Tree Acres and taking her and Arthur away in their white vans. She would refuse to go! Anyway, it was just a fairy tale.

She sat quietly and listened for Arthur, but she didn't hear him. What was he doing? She was surprised he hadn't found her yet. Surely he would open every door in the house looking for her. She waited for another minute, then opened the closet door.

"Arthur?" she said.

She heard only the howl of the wind. It was blowing so hard the snow was going sideways, and it had gotten even darker out. She turned on the lights.

"Arthur!" she yelled.

Nothing. She wandered through the house, turning on the lights in every room and calling his name. She hoped he hadn't gone outside, or tried to go home. She hadn't been hiding that long—maybe ten minutes. She checked the kitchen, expecting him to be sitting at the counter eating vanilla wafers.

Arthur wasn't in the kitchen, but the cellar door was

standing open. The cellar light was on, dim and yellow. She heard something. A faint scuffling, scraping sound, and a grunt of effort.

"Arthur?" Her voice sounded hollow.

"I'm down here."

"What are you *doing*?"

Arthur appeared at the bottom of the steps. His face was filthy. He was holding a screwdriver.

"I thought maybe you were hiding in the magic room," he said.

"Well, I'm not. I'm up here. You're not supposed to be down there!"

"I got it open," he said.

"Got what open?"

"The door."

"I can see that—I'm standing in it."

"Not that door. The other door."

42

THE PINK MAN

"You should come down and see," Arthur said.

"Why?" Annie felt her heart pounding. Half of her wanted to see what was in the room under the *burna*, and the other half wanted to run away.

"It's kind of dark," Arthur said. He ducked out of sight.

"Arthur! Get back up here!"

No reply.

"Arthur!"

At that moment there came a loud cracking sound from outside, then a splintering crash that shook the whole house.

The lights went out.

For a second, Annie stood without moving. She knew

right away what had happened. The old cottonwood had fallen on the back of the house and taken the power line with it, just like Mr. O'Connor had warned Papa it would.

Arthur shouted, "I can't see!"

"I'm coming!" Annie ran to the drawer where Papa kept the flashlight.

She turned it on, but nothing happened. The batteries were dead. Annie ran to Papa's study. On the way there, she looked in the library and saw that the windows had shattered. Part of a tree branch was jutting through and snow was swirling into the room. She ran to the study and grabbed the candelabra from the mantel. Where were the matches? There, in the box next to the fireplace. She lit one of the long wooden matches and set fire to the candles.

"Annieeee!" Arthur yelled. "Where are you?"

"Just a minute!" she yelled back. She carried the candelabra to the cellar door.

"Arthur! Can you see the light? Come up here!"

"What happened?" he asked.

"The electricity went out. Come up here!"

"No! You come here. I want you to see."

"See what?"

"The pink man."

Pink man? Annie's curiosity overcame her fear. She

descended the steep wooden steps. Her hand holding the candelabra was shaking. When she reached the bottom, she saw Arthur standing in front of the small door. Several empty NutriRodent Rat & Mouse Food bags were piled next to it.

The hasp that held the padlock hung loose—Arthur had removed the screws that held it in place. The door was open.

"Look." He pointed.

Annie approached, holding the candelabra out in front of her. She peered through the open doorway and gasped. Inside was a tall pink man. For a moment she froze, too frightened to move.

The pink man did not move, either. He wasn't real. It was a life-size statue. She held the candles as far out in front of her as she could and poked her head into the room.

The statue stood atop a solid-looking mound of compacted paper scraps and corn husks. The rest of the floor was covered with an ankle-deep layer of leaves and twigs.

The room itself was round, and smelled like rotting leaves and wet fur. The walls were brick. Annie stepped inside and looked up at the heavy rafters holding up the ceiling. Somewhere up there was the *nuodeema burna*.

The statue was finely sculpted out of what looked

like papier-mâché. She could see the individual sheets of paper, torn into strips and pasted over one another. Bits of scribbles and fragments of words were visible in places. The figure stood with its arms crossed, feet spread apart, hair swept back, and a strong chin jutting forward defiantly. Even the facial features were lifelike.

Arthur stepped in through the doorway. "It looks like your dad," he said.

It *did* look like Papa—a statue made from all the pink pages he had stuffed through the hole in his study over the years. Annie imagined all those tubes of pink paper dropping into this space, year after year, thousands and thousands of them. But what about the yellow pages she had put in the *burna*?

She looked back at the statue of her father, then stepped to the side and saw behind it a second, smaller, yellow statue. It was less finished, the arms only half-formed, the head a rough, egg-shaped blob. Annie had no doubt who it was meant to be.

It was her.

"Papa must have made these," she said, thinking about how she had heard him going into the basement in the middle of the night.

"Uh-uh," Arthur said. "Look." He pointed up at where the brick walls met the rafters. "I think it was them."

Annie looked where he was pointing. Along the top of the wall, between the rafters, was a ledge. Six pairs of eyes glittered red in the candlelight.

"Are those . . . *rats?*"

"There's more," Arthur said.

Annie swung the candelabra around. More rats were perched on the cross braces between the rafters, clinging to the brick walls, and sitting in a ragged circle along the base of the wall. Dozens of them, all looking at her, none of them moving. Annie was screaming inside, but all that came out of her mouth was a squeak. She grabbed Arthur's hand and turned. A big black rat was sitting on the doorsill. It chittered, showing its yellow teeth. Annie froze.

"I give them cookies and sticks," Arthur said in a quavery voice. "They won't hurt us."

Annie heard a scrabbling sound behind her. She turned and saw a rat climbing up the statue of her father. It had a curl of pink paper in its mouth. The rat perched on the statue's shoulder, grasped the slip of paper in its paws, licked it, then stuck it on Papa's cheek. It licked its paws and smoothed the paper, over and over again, until the paper became part of the face.

They watched, fascinated.

The rat's tiny paws looked like hands, but with four fingers instead of five. When the rat had completed its work, it looked at Annie and Arthur and chirped—a chirp so high-pitched that Annie wasn't sure if she had heard or imagined it.

"It's showing us," Arthur said.

The rat made a *churr* sound, like a file on toenails.

Annie took a step toward it, holding the candelabra as far in front of her as she could. The rat squealed, jumped off the statue's shoulder, and disappeared into the leaves.

Annie turned and pushed the candelabra toward the rat guarding the doorway. It squeaked and ran up the wall to the rafters. There were at least two dozen rats up there, plus the ones clinging to the back wall. The floor was moving, trembling and shifting from more rats tunneling through the leaves.

"They don't like the candles," Arthur said. "We should go."

All the rats were chirping. Annie backed toward the door, waving the candelabra wildly, shouting, "Go away!"

As she swung the candelabra back and forth, one of the candles fell into the dry leaves. There was a curl of smoke, then a small flame. Annie tried to stomp it out, but the flame spread too quickly.

"Annie!" Arthur called from the doorway.

The tentacles of fire writhed out in every direction.

Rats erupted from the leaves and ran up the walls, their high-pitched squeals stabbing into Annie's ears like needles. She backed out of the room just as the flames licked at the legs of her father's statue.

"Annie!" Arthur was tugging at her arm. "Annie! Come on!"

She watched through the doorway as the flames snaked up the statue's legs and torso. Acrid smoke billowed from the doorway and hit her lungs. She coughed.

"Annie!" Arthur yanked hard at her arm.

Annie dropped the candelabra and let Arthur lead her up the steps. They were both coughing and hacking. The smoke followed them into the kitchen. Annie looked down the stairs. Dozens of rats were fleeing the round room and scrabbling up the steps toward them. Annie slammed the door.

"Grab your jacket," she said to Arthur. "We have to get out of here." She had her coat half on when she remembered the picture of her mother.

"Go outside." She pushed him out the front door. "I'll be right out."

Annie knew it was a bad idea—the whole house could go up in flames any second now—but she couldn't leave the picture behind. She ran up the stairs to her room and grabbed the photo from her dresser. She noticed the book of Litvanian fairy tales beside her bed. She snatched it up and ran downstairs. Smoke was pouring from the kitchen. Arthur was standing in the front door, coughing.

"Let's go!" she yelled, grabbing his hand. They ran out into the snow.

43.

EVEN MAGICAL
CREATURES DIE

Annie and Arthur watched from across the street as the tower became a roaring, crackling pillar of flame. They could feel the heat on their faces. The fire was so hot it turned the falling snow to dirty gray rain. Ash flecked the snow in Mr. Wendell's front yard. Several of the neighbors came out to watch, including Mr. Wendell. Fiona ran up the street followed by her parents and her sister. She saw Annie and ran over and hugged her.

"I'm sorry," she said.

Annie wasn't sure whether Fiona was sorry about the house burning or about not wanting to be her friend. It didn't matter. Annie hugged her back.

By the time the fire trucks arrived, it was too late. The

peak on top of the tower had collapsed, sending a fountain of sparks high into the night sky, and the fire had spread to the house.

The firefighters turned their hoses on the blaze. Everybody backed away as a cloud of smoke and steam rolled out from the house.

Annie saw a pair of headlights coming up Klimas Avenue—Ozols's Jeep. Ozols pulled over in front of the vacant lot. Annie ran to meet them. Papa got out from the passenger side and stared open-mouthed at the inferno that had been his home. Even the fallen cottonwood tree was in flames. A layer of dense black fog was oozing out onto the street.

Papa took a few steps toward the burning house, staggered, and dropped to his knees. The dark fog came up to his chest.

"Papa!" Annie cried out.

Papa held out his arms, but he wasn't looking at her; he was fixated on the house. His firelit face appeared contorted and ashen.

Annie stopped in front of him. "Papa?"

His eyes glittered orange with reflected flame. He did not seem to see her at all.

Ozols appeared beside him, her scarf wrapped across her mouth and nose. She grasped his arm. "Lukas, get up.

We have to get away from this smoke." She pulled him up. His legs seemed to barely support his weight.

Annie grabbed his other arm. As they dragged him to the Jeep, his legs failed completely. The best they could do was to prop his back against the front bumper, where he sat like an abandoned puppet, legs splayed out, eyes empty. He looked dazed and deflated, as if all the life and energy had gone out of him.

"Papa?" Annie said.

He turned his head toward her and contorted his face into a twisted mockery of a smile. His hair was thick and black with silver streaks across his temples, and he had the same perfect bright white teeth as before, but his eyes were buried in a nest of wrinkles and the skin of his face sagged on his skull.

"I am sorry, Annike," he said in a barely audible rasp.

He closed his eyes and exhaled. The sour scent of rotting leaves and rancid smoke filled the air.

Annie stood with Arthur and Mr. Wendell as the paramedics loaded Papa into the ambulance. The snow had let up. The house was no longer burning, though it was still smoking. The top half of the tower was completely gone. The firefighters were moving around the wreckage, dousing the remaining hot spots.

One of the paramedics was asking Ozols questions. When he asked her how old Papa was, she said he was in his early fifties.

"Are you sure?" he said. "This man looks much older than that!"

"It's a . . . family trait," Ozols said.

Moments later the ambulance drove off, lights flashing.

"Are we going to the hospital, too?" Annie asked Ozols.

"Yes. In a bit. I called Arthur's mother and told her what happened. She's on her way home now. As soon as she gets here to take care of Arthur, we'll go."

"Is your papa going to die?" Arthur asked.

Annie blinked back tears.

Ozols put her arm around Annie's shoulders and said, "Let's hope not. I'm sure he'll be fine." She looked up at the pillar of smoke rising into the clouds. "But I cannot say the same for your home."

"It was full of rats," Arthur said.

Ozols nodded. "I suspected as much. And now they are no more."

"Even magical creatures die," Annie said. "That's what Papa told me."

They sat in the waiting room for almost an hour before Dr. Bray came to talk to them. He looked tired, and anxious.

"Annie, Vaira, I don't have much news. We're waiting for the blood-test results."

"But he's okay?" Annie said.

"He's resting comfortably, but I'm afraid this is quite serious, and unlike anything I've seen before. I spoke with him less than two weeks ago and he looked normal, but now—" He looked at Ozols. "How has Lukas been lately? I mean, he seems to have suffered severe weight loss."

"He's been fine," Ozols said.

Dr. Bray shook his head. "I don't see how he could deteriorate so quickly."

"Can we see him?" Annie asked.

"Of course. He may be sleeping, but you can sit with him for a bit."

Annie could hardly believe this was her father. He looked small, as if the bed was swallowing him. His eyes were closed and sunken deep in their sockets. His cheeks were hollow, his skin pale, and his arms looked bony and wrinkly against the white hospital sheets. A tube leading to a bag of fluid was taped to one wrist. A monitor was attached to his other hand.

"Papa?"

He opened his eyes. The whites were yellow and bloodshot.

"Annike," he whispered.

"Are you okay?" she asked, even though it was clear he was not. She forced herself to take his veiny hand. His lips twisted as if he had something in his mouth. He lifted his other hand and spat weakly; a tooth fell into his palm. He stared at it, then let his hand fall back. Annie heard the tooth hit the floor.

"I need . . . to . . . *cicenja*," he said, his voice barely audible.

Ozols said, "The house is gone, Lukas. I'm afraid that is no longer an option."

His shoulders came up off the mattress. His eyes narrowed and grew hard.

"Yes, it is," he said to her, his words strong and clear. "You must make arrangements." He slumped back. "It is time to go home," he said in a fading voice. He looked at Annie. "This time, Annike, you must come with me. To Litvania."

PART FOUR

THE
RAT
QUEEN

44.

WELCOME TO LITVANIA

Five days later the private jet touched down at Riga International Airport at four o'clock in the morning. Ozols wheeled Papa down the ramp and across the runway to a long black car. Annie followed.

The driver, a blocky man wearing a dark blue suit and a short-brimmed cap, helped Papa out of the wheelchair and into the back seat. Annie got in the other side. Ozols took the seat next to the driver and spoke to him in Litvanian. The driver put the car in gear and drove out of the airport and onto a highway.

"Are we in Litvania?" Annie asked.

"No, this is Latvia," Ozols said. "We still have a long drive ahead of us."

"How long?" Annie asked.

Ozols spoke with the driver in Litvanian.

"Guntis says it will be about six hours, depending on the roads."

Annie looked over at her father. He was slumped against the door, eyes closed, jaw slack, his mouth hanging open. He had spent most of the twelve-hour flight filling the pages of his pink tablet. Annie had peeked to see what he was writing. His usually strong, clear handwriting had become weak, shaky, and hard to read. Also, it was in Litvanian.

"And then Papa can *cicenja?*" she said.

"He must first plead his case to Queen Zurka," Ozols said.

"Why?"

"Because that is the way things are done in Litvania."

Annie was tired and cranky and confused, but mostly she felt horribly guilty. It was all her fault. Their house was gone, and Papa had turned into a sick old man she hardly recognized. Her brain hurt from bouncing back and forth from anger to hope to fear to desperate longing. For years she had dreamed of going to Litvania with Papa, of meeting Queen Zurka—but not like this. She'd hardly slept at all during the flight, and when she had managed to drift off, she dreamed of rats and fire. And now they were speeding over twisty roads in the dark, the headlights glancing off fence posts, trees, and unreadable road signs. She reached into her shirt and held the Saint Christopher medallion. With her other hand, she gripped the bag tucked in next to her and felt the squarish outlines of the fairy-tale book and the framed photo of her mother.

She looked at her father. He seemed so small now, so weak. She touched his hand. It was cold. She squeezed his fingers. He twitched. Annie let her breath out and relaxed—for a moment she'd thought he had died. She didn't want him to die. She wanted him to be young and strong and smiling again.

She looked out the window, trying to guess what the dark shapes might be. Barns and houses, she thought. The hum of the tires on the road went on and on, and finally she fell into a restless sleep.

Annie woke up with a bright light in her eyes—a flashlight shining in through the window. A man in a uniform was speaking Litvanian, harsh and insistent. Guntis spoke back to him. Ozols rolled down her window and handed a sheaf of documents to a second uniformed man. Through the windshield Annie could see a gated, wrought-iron arch blocking their way. The arch spelled out the words LAIPNI GA LITVANJA.

Next to her, Papa stirred. He sat up and rolled down his

window and said something to the man, who was sorting through the papers Ozols had given him, examining them with a flashlight. The man looked at him.

"*Kastu esa?*"

"Klimas," Papa said. "Valdemaras."

Valdemaras? That was Papa's granduncle's name!

The man looked closer and frowned. "*Tiessa?*"

"*Ta tiessa,*" Papa said.

The guards spoke to each other rapidly in Litvanian.

"What are they saying?" Annie asked Ozols.

"The border guard says that his visa has been revoked," Ozols said. She leaned out the car window and spoke sternly to the two guards. They looked startled, and again started arguing with each other. Ozols raised her voice and spoke again. One of the guards threw up his hands and walked over to the guard station beneath the arch.

"What did you say?" Annie asked.

"I told them that we have special permission to enter the country, by order of Queen Zurka. I spoke with her on the phone just two days ago. Apparently, these guards were not informed."

They could see the guard talking on the phone.

"What's he doing?"

"Getting the queen out of bed, I imagine. She will not be pleased about that."

"You really talked to the queen?"

"I certainly did. She is, after all, my *vanama*."

Annie started to ask what *vanama* meant, but before she could speak, the guard returned and shoved the papers back through the car window. He did not look happy.

"*Laipni ga Litvanja,*" he said.

"What did he say?" Annie asked.

"He said, 'Welcome to Litvania.'"

The roads in Litvania were narrower and bumpier than the Latvian highways. Ahead of them the sky brightened, and as the sun rose Annie could see the surrounding country-side. They passed through rolling golden fields dotted with rough stone walls, stone barns, and thatch-roofed stone houses. The road was mostly empty; they passed an ancient-looking truck carrying a load of hay bales, and a couple of rusty old cars that were somehow still running. Annie saw goats, a small herd of cattle, and a swayback horse.

"I was born not far from here," Papa said. "In a tiny cottage much like that one." He pointed a shaky finger at a stone hut no bigger than Annie's bedroom. He sighed and shook his head slowly. "So very long ago."

"Everything looks really old," Annie said.

"In Litvania nothing is thrown away. You see that trac-tor?" They were passing a farmer driving an odd-looking tractor across a field. Instead of rubber tires it had ridged metal wheels. "That tractor is a hundred years old. Many of the farmers here still use horse-drawn plows."

"Why?"

"Because they always have."

As they neared Zük, the capital city, the houses they passed became larger, and were made of brick rather than rough stone. The highway widened, and there was more traffic: horse-drawn carts and buggies mixed with cars and trucks that looked like they belonged in a museum or a junkyard. A few newer cars raced past the slower vehicles.

As the city came into view, Annie saw that it was built upon a towering hill. Four tall turrets were visible at the top.

"Is that Queen Zurka's castle?" Annie asked. She looked at her father, but he was sleeping again.

"It is," said Ozols.

"Is that where the Queen-Whose-Name-Is-Forgotten lived?"

Ozols smiled. "That was just a fairy tale," she said.

"It looks like a fairy-tale castle."

"I imagine it does. It is nearly a thousand years old. You'll be able to see it up close soon enough."

The highway branched into a dozen smaller roads, and soon they were making their way up a narrow cobblestone street, past open-air markets, tiny shops, and apartment buildings wedged tightly together. Most of the buildings were constructed of reddish brick, but some of the older-looking ones were stone, and still others were made of wood. The street was crowded with people, carts, cars, and wagons. They swerved around a girl pushing a wheel-barrow piled high with colorful squashes, and almost ran into a man wearing a suit and tie and talking on a cell phone. A moment later Guntis had to slam on the brakes to avoid hitting an aproned, broom-wielding man who was chasing a group of laughing boys. The street rose and con-tinued to curve slightly to the left, following the base of the hill. Every so often, between the buildings, Annie could see the castle turrets rising above them.

"This is the Great Spiral Way," Ozols explained. "The road slowly rises as it curves around the Castle Mount. We'll circle it four times before arriving at the gates."

"Why?" Annie asked.

"It was built this way so that those who wish to petition the queen have time to consider their thoughts carefully."

The driver said something in Litvanian. Ozols laughed. "Guntis says it is more likely to make them tired and cranky." They were stuck behind an old woman herding a flock of geese, using a pair of long sticks to urge them along. "I expect that when the Spiral Way was built, it was not so busy. And of course it was not designed for cars and trucks."

They continued up the narrow, slowly rising, gently curved street. Annie gawked at the strange mix of modern and old-fashioned vehicles, buildings, and clothing. As they wound their way slowly upward, the castle seemed to grow larger and taller. Each turret had several colorful pennants flying from flagpoles: red, blue, yellow, white, and purple. The road finally opened onto an elevated, circular brick causeway that formed a crown on the hill. To their left was a dry moat and, rising above it, the castle. They followed the causeway around the castle to a bridge that crossed the moat and led to a set of tall double doors. Next to the doors stood a bronze statue of a rat the size of a horse, standing on its hind legs and brandishing a sword.

Guntis parked the car at the bridge. "We're here," Ozols said. She helped Guntis get Papa out of the car and into his wheelchair. She wheeled him across the bridge as Guntis drove off.

Annie, following right behind Ozols, looked up at the rat statue. "That's a big rat," she said.

"When I was a little girl, we called him *Zurkukzen*," Ozols said.

"What does that mean?"

"Crazy Rat Boy."

Annie leaned over the balustrade and looked into the moat. There were a few puddles at the bottom, littered with leaves and plastic bags and every other sort of trash that could be blown by the wind.

"Did this used to be full of water?" she asked.

"I suppose it was, but not in my lifetime," Ozols said.

"Nor mine," Papa said in a barely audible croak.

The doors, made of heavy wooden panels held together by iron bars, were big enough to drive a truck through. Set into the right-hand door was a smaller, normal-size door.

"Go ahead and ring the bell," Ozols said. "You see that handle hanging from the chain? Next to the small door?"

Annie grabbed the worn brass handle and pulled down. It didn't budge.

"Harder," Ozols said.

Annie grasped it with both hands and yanked as hard as she could. This time she was rewarded by a metallic boom, more like a gong than a bell. "Now what?"

"Now we wait."

45.
LITTLE MOONS

The small door swung open only seconds after Annie rang the bell. She was not sure what she had expected—some sort of doorman, or a guard, or maybe even the queen herself. But the door was opened by the last person Annie expected to see.

"Miss Mekas!" Annie exclaimed, and wrapped her arms around Mekas's doughy body. Startled, Mekas patted Annie on the back, then pushed her out to arm's length to get a better look.

"You so big!" she said.

"I had a growth spurt."

Miss Mekas looked at the man in the wheelchair. Papa had fallen asleep again; his head hung off to the side, seeming to be barely attached to his body by his neck. Mekas's eyes and mouth went completely round. If she hadn't been so obviously horrified, it would have been funny.

"Mr. Lukas?" She clapped her hands to her chest.

Papa roused himself and lifted his head. "Hello, Mekas," he croaked.

Mekas was swaying as if she was about to fall over, still staring in shock at Papa. Annie grabbed her arm to steady her.

"Papa got sick when the house burned down," she said.

Mekas tore her eyes away from Papa and looked at Annie. "House is burned?"

Annie nodded. Mekas crossed herself. *"Labas Dievas!"*

"Much has happened," Ozols said. "Queen Zurka is expecting us."

Mekas nodded and stepped aside. Ozols pushed the wheelchair through the door. They entered a large, open courtyard. A carriage heavily decorated with gold leaf and silver filigree stood to their left. A long silver limousine and two smaller cars were parked against the opposite wall.

"You come with me," Mekas said. "I will bring food. She say to feed you first."

As much as she wanted to meet the queen, food sounded good to Annie. They'd had a snack on the airplane, but that was hours ago. They followed Mekas across the courtyard and entered the castle.

Once again, Annie was surprised by the odd mix of old and new. The walls of the hallway were hung with ornate tapestries, faded with age, that reminded her of the rug in Papa's study. Between the tapestries were lamps plugged into modern electrical outlets. The floor was closely fitted blocks of stone, and it was being cleaned by a man wearing jeans and a T-shirt using an electric floor-polishing machine like the one the janitor had used at her old school. Mekas led them down the hall and into a large room with six stone-arched doorways and a long wooden table.

Miss Mekas quickly filled the table with a feast: roast chicken, cabbage and pear salad, tart cherry *kolduny*, mashed potatoes with sour cream and buttered apples, and thick slices of rye bread warm from the oven.

Annie ate until she was full. She had missed Mekas's cooking. Papa managed a few spoonfuls of potato, and Ozols coaxed him to eat a single chicken wing. Mekas kept looking at him and shaking her head.

"This is all wonderful!" Ozols declared. "It tastes like my childhood."

"I cook for you then," Mekas said.

"Exactly!" Ozols helped herself to the last *kolduny*.

"You cooked for Ozols?" Annie said.

Mekas nodded. "When she and Kundze were little girls." She waited patiently until everyone had finished,

305

then stood up and began clearing the table. "You go see her now. She is at assizes."

"What is *assizes*?" Annie asked.

"A sort of court," Ozols explained. "It is where Queen Zurka hears petitions from her subjects." She looked at Mekas. "In the Low Hall?"

Mekas nodded.

Ozols pulled Papa's chair back from the table and set off through one of the arches.

Annie hung back. "Miss Mekas?"

"Yes, child?"

Annie lifted the chain with the Saint Christopher medallion over her head and pulled it out from under her shirt.

"I stole your Saint Christopher medal. I'm sorry."

Mekas smiled. "I know you took." She accepted the medallion.

"I'm sorry."

"Is no need. Svetais Kristofers deliver you safe to *Litvanja*." Mekas tucked the medallion into her apron pocket. "Now you go with your papa."

Annie ran out of the dining hall and quickly caught up with Ozols and her father. The castle was like a maze— they turned left, then right, then walked through a hallway lined with life-size portraits of regal-looking women wearing enormous dresses. The first ones they passed were of stern, older women; as they neared the end of the hall, the women became younger and happier-looking.

"Are these all queens?" Annie asked.

"Yes," Ozols said.

"They kind of look like the same person."

"Most of them are. Queen Zurka sits for a new portrait every ten years."

Annie stopped before a painting that showed a very young queen. "This one looks like that picture of my mother," she said.

"It certainly does," Ozols said.

They soon reached the Low Hall. It was laid out like a church, but with a low ceiling held up by massive wooden beams, and six rows of benches facing a dais. On the dais was a straight-backed throne with gilded legs, and on the throne sat Queen Zurka. Annie recognized her from the portraits in the hallway. But the portraits had failed to capture the aura of authority and power exuded by the woman on the throne. Her hair, whiter than white, was gathered in a tight, elaborate coiffure; her lips were scarlet and hard as rubies, and her black eyes shone like polished onyx. She was small, ancient, and unmoving, but blazing with vitality.

To the left of the throne, two girls were sitting on the dais playing with dolls. They looked to be four or five years old. A dark-haired woman, whose back was to Annie, was sitting with them. Annie thought she might be the girls' *aukle*. The three of them were giggling and paying no attention to the queen, or to the two men who were standing before the throne. The men were taking turns addressing the queen, arguing in Litvanian. The queen's bright eyes moved from one to the other as she listened, the corners of her mouth turned down in a frown. She raised one hand. The men stopped talking and stood at attention.

The queen spoke. Her voice was like a knife made of ice. The shorter man dropped his chin to his chest. The tall man smiled in triumph.

The queen spoke again. The tall man looked startled. He began to speak, but the queen cut him off with a motion of her hand. The two men filed out of the room, both looking dejected.

"Such is the essence of the assizes," Ozols whispered to Annie. "When both parties leave dissatisfied, the queen's judgment is proven to be fair and just."

The queen summoned them forward with a hand motion. Ozols rolled Papa forward to the lip of the dais. Annie went to stand beside him.

Queen Zurka's eyes fixed upon Papa. Her eyes snapped over to Ozols and finally landed on Annie. The queen's mouth tightened, her eyes darting for a split second to her left, where the girls and their *aukle*, oblivious to the queen, were chattering and playing with their dolls.

Papa cleared his throat—a disturbing rattle.

The queen spoke. "You dare to petition me, Valdo?"

Papa replied in Litvanian.

The queen held up her hand. "You will speak English, Valdo. Your daughter deserves to witness your folly."

Papa cleared his throat again and nodded. "Yes, Your Majesty."

"I agreed to see you only because my youngest *mazbe*"— she glanced at Ozols, who nodded—"has asked this of me. Not because you deserve to be heard.

"We are an insular people," the queen continued. "There is much of this world we do not know, but word of your recklessness has reached even my aging ears. And now I see that your body is paying the price for your deception and thievery, beginning with your theft of our royal *zurkas*."

"Only two," Papa said.

"*Silence!*" The queen slashed the air with her hand.

Papa bowed his head.

"Now, what is it you wish?"

Papa cleared his throat and spoke. "Your Majesty, you see that I suffer for my years. I ask only that you permit me to make my confessions to your *zurkas*, that I may live out my remaining days as a whole man. It will cost you nothing, and I will be gone tomorrow, never to return."

"That is all?" the queen said.

"Yes, Your Majesty."

"Your theft of the *zurkas* alone would be sufficient cause for denial, but your transgressions go far beyond that. You beguiled my eldest granddaughter to leave Litvania and marry you. And when she attempted to shield her own child from your *zurkas*, they attacked her." She looked over at the woman with the two girls. *"Mazbe!"*

The woman turned to the queen. *"Yah, Vanama?"*

"Speak English. Do you know this man?"

The woman turned to face them. Her face bore several small white scars shaped like new moons.

"No, Grandmother," she said.

"And the girl standing beside him?"

The woman looked at Annie with a puzzled expression. "No, Grandmother."

Annie stared in utter shock.

"You see?" the queen said to Papa. "You have stolen her life from her. Kundze doesn't even remember her own daughter."

46

VATRUKA
AND TEA

Annie stood with her mouth open, unable to speak. Kundze looked at her with her head tilted, smiling uncertainly.

"Our physicians were able to save Kundze when you brought her to us, Valdo," the queen said to Papa. "The bites left by your *zurkas* healed, but the *zelty maras* left deeper scars. Your actions have damaged your daughter as well."

Annie heard her words but barely absorbed them. She couldn't stop staring at her mother.

"*Annike!*" The queen's voice was the crack of a whip. Annie snapped to attention. "Did you know your mother was alive?"

Annie looked at her father. "You said she was dead."

"I . . ." Papa's mouth opened and closed as he searched for words. "I . . . never said she was dead, Annike. I told you she was *gone*."

"You lied to your daughter, Valdo. Yet another unforgivable sin."

Papa let out a wheezy breath, then nodded weakly. "I am sorry," he said, looking at Annie.

Kundze had returned to playing with the two girls. Queen Zurka smiled a bitter smile and shook her head.

"Your pathetic apology to your daughter changes nothing. Still, you are her father. I will consider your request."

Papa raised his head, and Annie thought she saw a gleam of hope in his rheumy eyes.

The queen made a slight motion with her right hand. From the side of the hall, two uniformed men stepped forward. They had been standing so still that Annie hadn't noticed them before. The queen spoke to them in Litvanian, then said to Annie, "Our *sargas* will escort your father to a bedchamber. He will be treated as a guest until such time as we render our final judgment. As for you, child, you know nothing. This we will change."

The queen stood up. She was even shorter than Annie had thought. "Kundze!"

"*Yah*, Vanama?"

"English, child. English. Come with Grandmama." She turned to Ozols. "Vaira, your room is as you left it. Beata and Aleska, you will go with your *aukle*." A woman whom Annie hadn't noticed stepped forth from the side of the dais and led the two young girls away.

"What about me?" Annie asked.

"You will come with us."

Queen Zurka led Annie and Kundze through a door to the side of the dais. They followed an arched hallway lit by electric wall lamps designed to resemble torches. Queen Zurka moved briskly for such an elderly woman. They soon reached a tall, ornately carved set of wooden doors attended by a guard. The guard opened the doors. They stepped into a room that reminded Annie of Papa's study, only larger. The walls were stone and the windows were tall and narrow. One wall held a fireplace as tall as Annie and wider than she could stretch her arms. A small fire was burning. Several chairs were arranged in a half circle around a low table in front of the fire.

Queen Zurka sat down in one of the chairs and indicated to Annie and Kundze to do the same. A moment later, a man entered the room carrying a silver tray on his shoulder. He set out three cups and a platter of assorted pastries, then filled the cups from a teapot with a long, curved spout.

"Thank you, Stefan," said the queen. The man left. The queen picked up the cup nearest her and took a sip. Kundze grabbed a pastry that looked like a filled donut and took a big bite. Annie wasn't sure what to do. She was still full from the meal Mekas had fed them, and she didn't really like tea.

"Er . . . Your Majesty?"

The queen smiled. The wrinkles in her face rearranged themselves and became new wrinkles.

"*Majesty?*" she said. "Do you see a throne? No? Here in this room I am no more majestic than you. You may call me *Vanamama*, or Great-grandmother, since that is what I am. You should try the tea. You will like it."

Annie took one of the cups, sniffed, and sipped. It did not taste like tea. It tasted like sweet flowers.

"It is very good," she said.

"It was once your mother's favorite, although now she prefers to stuff her face with *vatruka*. Isn't that right, child?"

Kundze, her mouth full of *vatruka*, nodded.

"When you have finished with your biting and gulping, I will tell you a story." The queen sat back and sipped her tea and waited. Annie stared at Kundze, looking at the tiny scars on her face, at her childlike expression, at the flecks of pastry on her chin. How could this be her mother? She felt as if she were dreaming, as if the universe had been turned inside out and upside down.

When Kundze had finished with the *vatruka*, the queen took a napkin and wiped the crumbs from her face. "There, now," she said. "Much better."

Kundze smiled.

"And now the story." The queen took another sip of tea and set down her cup. "Many long years ago, a country girl named Melanja petitioned the queen to become a lady-in-waiting."

"What is that, Vanama?" Kundze asked.

"A lady-in-waiting is a servant who attends the queen."

"Is this a fairy tale?" Annie asked.

"Some may regard it as such, but it is true. Back then, the queen had ruled over Litvania for one hundred and seven years. All the surrounding countries were ruled by the czar of Russia, but Litvania remained independent. Some say that it was protected by magic, but more likely the czar simply did not think it worth his while to conquer our tiny country."

This sounded a lot like a fairy tale combined with one of Ozols's history lessons. Annie's thoughts must have shown on her face, because the queen stopped speaking and gave her an intent look.

"Are you bored so soon?" she asked.

"No," Annie said. "But I don't see how the queen could be so old."

"This is Litvania. Now listen. Melanja was allowed to bring her young son to live in the castle with her. For a time, all was well. The boy was liked by all who lived in the castle. As he grew older, he explored every nook and crevice and cranny, and came to know the castle better even than the captain of the guard.

"Although the child had the run of the castle, he was still a commoner, and when he reached the age of ten, he was put to work in the kitchen. At night he pursued his explorations of the castle.

"One night the boy dared to follow the queen through a secret doorway behind her throne. The door led to a staircase that descended deep into the bowels of the castle. There he hid behind a curtain and watched as she performed the magic ritual that kept her young. He saw her communing with her familiars, the *zurkas*, who lived deep beneath the castle. As she completed her ritual, the queen heard the boy moving about. She threw aside the curtain and caught him by the ear.

"Now, in those days, to trespass in the queen's private chambers was punishable by death. But the queen could not bring herself to condemn the young man, of whom she had grown fond. Instead, she swore him to silence on pain of death. The boy was terrified, and quickly agreed to tell no one what he had seen.

"As the boy grew older, he became unhappy with his station in life. At sixteen, he ran away to join the Lithuanian revolutionary army and fight for their independence from czarist Russia. For five long years he was gone. Melanja, his mother, became ill with grief and died. No one knows what happened to him during those years, but it is likely he was captured by the Russians. When he returned to Litvania he had become a different person—bitter and resentful. The queen took pity on him and let him stay in the castle, in the room that had once been his mother's.

"Alas, the young man was not appreciative of the queen's generosity. In the darkest hour of the night, he entered the secret door behind the queen's throne.

"He descended to a room deep below the old dungeons, where he found the queen's *zurkas* gathered around an *avatus*, a statue of the queen made from paper and vellum. He snatched two of the *zurkas*, a male and a female, threw them in a heavy canvas bag, and fled the castle."

The queen paused, looked at Annie, and raised one eyebrow.

"Are *zurkas* rats?" Annie asked.

"That is the physical form they take, yes."

"So your name is Queen *Rat*?"

"In English, yes. When I ascended to the throne, I took the name Queen Zurka, to honor my familiars."

"Was the young man Papa?"

The queen nodded. "Valdemaras, yes. We called him Valdo."

47

DRESSING FOR DINNER

"Your father fled to America, where he became a wealthy farmer, and built a tower to house his stolen *zurkas*. The *zurkas* bred and made many baby *zurkas*. He used those *zurkas* to keep himself from growing old. After a time, to prevent his neighbors from wondering at his long life, he feigned his own death and returned, claiming to be his nephew Petras. Years later, Petras began to dye his hair gray, then white, so that his neighbors would not grow suspicious. But eventually he had to pretend to die again, only to return as Petras's youthful nephew Lukas.

"As Lukas, Valdemaras returned to Litvania in secret. Here he met your mother and caused her to fall in love with him. He took her to America, where they were married.

He stole away my heir, the one who should have sat on my throne after me." She looked at Kundze. "My *mazbe*. My granddaughter."

Kundze grinned and said, "Vanama!"

The queen smiled and shook her head in mock frustration. "Kundze, you are so much like your childhood self it hurts my heart."

"Can I go play now?" Kundze asked.

"Go." The queen made a shooing motion with her hands. "Play with your friends."

Kundze jumped up and left Annie alone with the queen. They sat in silence for a few seconds. The queen poured herself more tea.

"She has made a good deal of progress over the past eight years."

"She's really my mother?"

"Yes. Do you remember her at all?"

"Not really. I remember a necklace she had."

"Ah, the green and the gold? I gave that to her when she was about your age." The queen sighed. "I suppose it is for the best that you do not remember her. When Kundze came to us, she could not speak or care for herself in any way," the queen said. "She was an infant in the body of a young woman. And now, eight years later, she is still mentally a child. The *zelty maras* slowed her development. It may be decades before she is able to think and act as an adult, whereas you, Annike, are on the verge of becoming a young woman."

"I'm only eleven," Annie said.

"And growing quickly." She sipped her tea and regarded Annie with her sharp-edged gaze. "In five years you will come of age."

"I'll be sixteen."

"We of Litvanian royal blood mature quickly and live long. At sixteen you will be a young woman with all the rights and obligations of your station."

"My station? What's that?"

The queen pressed her lips together and gave her head a tiny shake. "We will discuss that later, after I deal with your father."

"Can I talk to him?"

The queen picked up a small bell from the table and rang it. The door opened and the man who had brought the tea entered. "Stefan will take you to him."

The way was long. Queen Zurka had assigned Papa to a room at the far end of the north wing. When Annie entered she found her father hunched over a small desk, a pen clutched in gnarled fingers, writing on his pad of pink paper.

He didn't notice her. Annie stood behind him and looked over his shoulder, at the same weak, spidery Litvanian script she had seen him scrawling on the airplane.

"Papa?" she said quietly.

He jerked as if he'd been stabbed, and turned to look at her.

"Annike," he said. His voice was stronger, and there was hope in his eyes.

"I came to say good night."

"Ah. Yes. Good night."

"Are you feeling better?"

He smiled, and she saw that he had lost another tooth. "I am hopeful," he said. "Zurka is stern, and she pretends to be unforgiving, but I believe she will grant me my request. After all, you are her great-granddaughter. She would not want you to be an orphan."

Annie thought for a moment, then said, "Is that why you brought me here?"

"You did not wish to come? You asked me many times to take you to Litvania."

Annie had nothing to say to that, though she could feel anger boiling up inside her.

Papa said, "Once I deliver these pages to the queen's *zurkas*, we will be able to go home."

"But our house is gone!"

"We will build a new house. All will be as before."

"Before, you made me stop growing!"

He shrugged. "The *burna* is no more. My *zurkas* are gone. But when the queen allows me to *cicenja* this one last time, I will have many more years of life. We will build a beautiful house. You can go back to school! See all your friends."

"Queen Zurka told me your real name is Valdo, and you're really old."

He chuckled, and for a moment sounded almost like his old self. "I certainly feel old! But tomorrow I will be young again."

"How old are you really?"

He didn't say anything for several long seconds. "I was born in the year 1844."

Annie worked out the numbers in her head. The answer shocked her. "Nobody is that old," she said.

"Queen Zurka is older. What else did she tell you?"

"She said you stole her *zurkas*."

"That was long ago. I hardly remember."

"She said it was your fault that Mama got sick and lost her memory."

"You mustn't believe everything you hear, Annike. It

was an accident. A terrible accident." He turned back to his pad of paper. "Now, if you will excuse me, I must finish my work."

"Are you writing down all the bad things you've done?"

He didn't answer. Annie stood there for several seconds. She had more questions, but they could wait until tomorrow. She left the room.

Ozols was waiting for her outside. "How is he doing?" she asked.

"He's writing in his tablet."

Ozols nodded slowly, then shook her head.

Annie said, "Is it true that he made my mama sick?"

"That depends on your point of view," Ozols said. "Come." She set off at a brisk pace.

"What about *your* point of view?" Annie asked.

"You might say it was my fault, as I failed to convince your mother not to marry him. Or you might say it was Kundze's fault for not listening to me."

"You might say it was my fault," Annie said.

"You were three years old," Ozols said over her shoulder. "None of this is your fault."

"The fire was my fault."

"I'd have lit it myself if I'd had the courage." Ozol's strides lengthened.

Annie had to half run to keep up with her. "Where are we going?"

"To your room."

Ozols stopped abruptly before a door and pushed it open. Inside was a small bed with tall posts and surrounding lace curtains, and two ceiling-high windows looking over a courtyard.

Ozols gave Annie's jeans and T-shirt a critical look.

"You will be having dinner with the queen in an hour," Ozols said. "You will have to dress appropriately."

"But we just ate!"

"The queen is old. She likes to eat early."

"But I don't have anything to wear!" It was true. All her other clothes had burned in the fire.

Ozols rolled back a door leading to a walk-in closet. "You should be able to find something suitable in here."

Annie stepped into the closet and stared in wonder at the hundreds of garments hung neatly in two long rows—dresses, jackets, pants, shirts, vests, and coats. A rack at the back of the closet was filled with shoes and boots.

"These were your mother's when she was a girl. Most of them should fit you."

Annie sorted through the clothes, marveling at the beautiful fabrics and peculiar styles.

"My mama lived here?" she asked.

"Both Kundze and I lived here in the castle until we were sent to boarding school in America. This was her room."

"Where does she sleep now?"

"She has a larger room just down the hall."

Annie paused at a heavy linen vest, intricately embroidered with glittering metallic threads. She lifted it off the hanger. On the back was a coiled golden dragon with twelve wings. "It's just like the fairy-tale dragon!"

"That is a traditional Litvanian *slibininka*, or dragon vest," Ozols said.

"Can I wear it to dinner?"

Ozols laughed and shook her head. "That is worn only in October, to celebrate Saint George's battle with the dragon." She pulled out a pale yellow dress with hundreds of tiny pearls sewn across the chest and shoulders. "Perhaps something like this would be more appropriate?"

"I don't know . . ." Annie put the dragon vest back and continued paging through the wardrobe. Some garments were ordinary and familiar. There were blue jeans and T-shirts much like what she was wearing, some plain skirts, and even a cotton hoodie with a New York Yankees logo. Annie kept looking, ignoring Ozols's suggestions, until she came upon a dark green matching jacket and skirt made of the thinnest, softest fabric she had ever touched. When she held it up to the light, the cloth shimmered with gold highlights.

"That is vicuña wool from Peru," Ozols said. "Interwoven with twenty-four-karat-gold threads. It was Kundze's favorite. She cried when she outgrew it."

"Can I wear it?" Annie asked.

"Only if you promise not to dribble on it. Now, if you'll excuse me, I must go. Be ready in half an hour."

48.

A ROYAL
DINNER

Annie wasn't sure what "dinner with the queen" involved.
She half expected a gala affair attended by royalty and
nobles. Maybe a roast pig in the center of a long banquet
table, a minstrel singing songs, and candles everywhere.

She changed into her mother's favorite outfit, and
brushed her hair with a jeweled hairbrush that might also
have been her mother's. She looked at herself in the mirror.
Something was missing. Sorting through the small bag she
had brought from America, she found the brooch Papa had
given her—the green-eyed rat pin in the shape of Litvania.
She pinned it up by her shoulder.

A few minutes later there came a knock at the door.
Annie was expecting Ozols, but it was Stefan. He led her
down the stone-walled passage to a set of double doors.

The hinges and handles were gold plated, as was the rat-shaped door knocker. Stefan lifted the knocker by its tail and let it fall against the metal plate. A moment later there came a voice from within.

"Enter!"

Stefan opened the doors. Annie stepped inside.

It was a bedroom, similar to the one she had just left but considerably larger and more opulent, with larger windows and a majestic curtained bed.

Queen Zurka was sitting at a small table in front of the window, sipping something purple from a wineglass.

"Welcome," said the queen. "My apologies for starting without you. Please sit." She gestured at the other place at the table.

The queen did not look like herself—not at all. Her white hair hung free over her shoulders, her lips were pale, and her eyes looked . . . softer. She was wearing a loose garment with a faint pastel pattern that suggested flowers. It looked like a housedress, like something Mama Dara would wear.

"Would you care for a cordial?" The queen lifted her glass.

Annie didn't know what a cordial was, but she nodded. "Do you always eat dinner in your bedroom?"

"When possible, yes. Sometimes Mekas joins me, but

she has little to say. I am hoping to find you more entertaining." The queen smiled and poured purple cordial into a wineglass. "Frankly, I just couldn't be bothered to get all gussied up twice in one day. My court outfits are uncomfortable, and they take forever to get into. I hope you don't mind."

Annie tasted the cordial. It was astonishingly sweet and fragrant.

"It's very good," she said.

"It is made with plums from our Royal Orchard." The queen leaned toward Annie and peered at the rat pin. "Tell me, how did you come by that lovely brooch?"

"Papa gave it to me."

"So that is what happened to it. It was once mine, you know. I haven't seen it since Valdo absconded with my *zurkas*."

"Oh!" Annie moved to take it off, but the queen stopped her.

"You may keep it, my dear. You may keep the outfit as well. It looks lovely on you."

"Thank you."

"In fact, all of Kundze's old clothes are yours now, as they no longer fit her."

Annie thought about that enormous closet full of

clothing and said, "Thank you, but I would have no place to keep them."

"Then leave them where they are, and stay."

"Stay?"

"Here. In Litvania." She lifted the domed top off a steaming platter of *kolduny*.

Annie tried to sort out what Queen Zurka had just said. Stay here? In Litvania? The idea was almost impossible to imagine. She lived in America, on the other side of the world.

The queen peered at her closely, waiting for an answer.

Annie said, "What about Papa?"

"Your father is not well."

"You can help him. You can help him *cicenja*."

"*Cicenja*? Is that what he calls it?" She shook her head. "Your father is not welcome here. In any case, he has had all the life he deserves, and more."

"What about you?" Annie asked.

The queen's eyes narrowed.

Annie said, "How old are *you*?"

The queen held her metallic gaze on Annie and did not answer for a very long time. Annie refused to look away.

"Older than your father," she said at last.

"Because of the rats?"

"*Zurkas*," said the queen. "Now eat."

"I'm not hungry. Why won't you help him?"

"Have some *kolduny*."

Annie crossed her arms and sat back in her chair.

"Ach!" Queen Zurka put the dome back over the *kolduny*. "You are incorrigible!"

"That's what Ozols says."

"She is correct. And I will not permit your father to *cicenja*, as he calls it. Tomorrow he will be sent back to America to live out his final days. For, you see, I am incorrigible as well."

Annie stood up, turned her back on the queen, and ran out the door.

49

REMEMBERING

Annie ran through the castle. Her face was hot, as if she was about to start crying, but she refused to cry. She turned left, and right, and left, until she was completely lost. She slowed down and tried to orient herself. The hallway looked familiar—had she been going in circles? No, this hallway led to a stairway that she hadn't seen before.

All she wanted at the moment was to find a quiet place to be alone. She approached the stairway. The steps were stone, and the staircase was curved. This must be one of the corner towers, she thought.

Annie started to climb. The stairs spiraled around the inside wall of the tower. She climbed until her legs hurt, then climbed some more. After what felt like a thousand steps, the stairs ended, and she found herself in a circular room, about forty feet across, illuminated by several tall, narrow windows.

The room was full of junk. Dusty old boxes, lamps, broken chairs, old rugs, and a haphazard pile of what looked like church pews. It was like an attic—a graveyard for things that would never be used again but were too nice to throw away.

Annie found a chair that looked like it wouldn't collapse. She dragged it over to one of the windows, brushed off the dust, and sat down. The window faced the central courtyard. She could see the other three towers, and the sun setting behind the rolling hills surrounding the city of Zük. Litvania! She had always wanted to visit, but not like this. Not with no home to return to, with Papa maybe dying, and with a queen who refused to save him. She squeezed her eyes shut and felt tears dribbling down. She heard herself sob—then her mother's voice.

"*Sveikia!*"

Annie shrieked and jumped up, knocking the chair over.

Kundze shrieked, too. She was peeking out from underneath a table next to the pile of church pews. They stared at each other. Annie's heart slowed as she recognized her.

"What is *sveikia*?" Annie asked.

"It means 'hello,'" Kundze said. "Why are you crying?"

Annie wiped her eyes with the back of her hand. "I'm not crying. What are you doing under there?"

"It is secret." Kundze grinned. "But I will show you." She backed under the table. Annie hesitated for a moment, then followed. There was a row of tables that made a sort of tunnel. At the back of the tunnel was a light, and an open space with church pews on one side and stacks of cardboard boxes on the other. A small rug covered the floor, and there were big pillowy cushions around the edges.

"You've made yourself a fort!" Annie said.

Kundze plopped down on one of the cushions. Annie noticed what was hanging around Kundze's neck and felt her heart speed up. She reached out to touch it. Kundze drew back and put her hand over the necklace.

"It's mine!" she said.

"I know," Annie said. The green and yellow glass beads were smaller than she remembered—only about the size of grapes. She sat down beside Kundze and asked, "Can I touch it?"

Kundze hesitated, then leaned forward and let Annie run her hands over the beads. They were as smooth and warm as she remembered.

"It's very pretty," she said. "Do you keep it here in your fort?"

Kundze nodded. "Sometimes when I hold it, I remember things."

"Like what?"

"The ocean. Seagulls."

"Do you come here a lot?" Annie asked.

"I like to hide."

"Why do you want to hide?"

"My cousins are mean sometimes."

"Who are your cousins?"

"Aleska and Beata. Miss Mekas's brother's grandchildren."

"So . . . wait, I'm related to Miss Mekas?"

"Everybody is related." Kundze pushed out her lower lip. "But they won't play with me. They say I'm too big."

"You're not too big!"

"I'm bigger than you. Aleska and Beata make fun of me because I'm big and *stoobi*."

"What is *stoobi*?"

"Stupid."

"Oh! Well, don't say *stoobi*. Or *stupid*. Not about yourself or anybody else. It's not nice."

"But I *am* stupid."

"No, you're not. You just have trouble remembering."

"I want to be smart like you."

"You're very smart. You know all the Litvanian words. I hardly know any."

"I want to be small like you."

"And I want to be big like you!" Annie said. "I once had a whole year when I did not grow at all."

"Really?"

"I thought I was never going to grow up. But then, later, I grew faster. Would you like to hear a story?"

Kundze brightened. "Yes, please!"

"Once upon a time in a faraway land, a little girl lived with her mama and papa in a house with a tower."

"I live in a castle with *four* towers," Kundze said.

"Well, this little girl had only one tower. But it was a very special tower, because underneath the tower was a cellar full of *zurkas*."

Kundze shivered. "I do not like *zurkas*. Sometimes I have bad dreams where the *zurkas* are coming to get me."

"I've had those dreams, too," Annie said.

"Why did the little girl have *zurkas* in her cellar?"

"The girl's papa put them there to capture their magic. He fed them and kept them safe. But the girl's mama did not like them because she was afraid they would make her little girl sick. One day, when the girl was only three years old, she was playing, and she went down into the cellar . . ."

As Annie spoke, long, dark memories swam into her consciousness. She remembered going down the steps backward on her hands and knees, because she was little and the stairs were steep. She remembered the hard, gritty floor on her bare feet and the rich, overpowering smell of dead leaves and wet stone.

"... where she was never, ever supposed to go. And she saw a little *zurka*, and it looked soft and furry like one of her stuffed animals. She picked it up ..."

Annie remembered the way the rat had felt at first— warm and squirmy.

"Eww! I would never do that!"

"The *zurka* did not like to be picked up. It bit her on the wrist. The little girl screamed and the *zurka* ran up her arm and bit her on the face. The girl's mama, who was very brave, heard her screams and ran down into the cellar to save her ..."

Annie remembered the sound of her mother's feet clomping down the wooden steps.

"She grabbed the *zurka* by the tail and *threw* it against the wall!" Annie could see her mother's face: strong and determined and angry and scared.

"She saved the girl!" Kundze said.

"Yes, but there were many more *zurkas*. Hundreds and hundreds of them!" Annie could see the rats as if it were happening all over again. "They dropped from the rafters onto the girl's mama and bit her and bit her and bit her. The mama fought back, kicking and stomping and hitting them." She could hear her mother screaming. "But they kept coming."

Kundze's eyes were huge. "Did the *zurkas* eat the girl and her mama?"

"Almost! But the girl's mama scooped her up and ran back up the stairs and slammed the cellar door shut and locked it."

"Were they okay?"

"Except for the bites, yes, but then the mama got sick from the *zelty maras*."

"The golden plague," Kundze said.

"She went to the hospital, but she just got sicker and sicker."

"Did she die?"

"Almost." Annie looked at the adult child who was her mother, and she remembered her as she had been before. She blinked, and tears trickled down her cheeks.

"Why are you crying?" Kundze asked.

"Because it is a sad story. The girl's mama slowly got better, but she no longer remembered her own daughter."

"But she *did* get better?"

"She is getting better every day." Annie wiped her cheeks.

"Is that the end?"

"No. When the little girl got older, she set fire to the tower and all the *zurkas* died, and she went to a faraway land to care for her mother."

"What about her papa?"

"That's another story," Annie said.

Kundze thought for a moment, then said, "I'm glad the *zurkas* got killed. Did I live in a house by a farm?"

"Yes!"

"I remember an old lady who lived on the other side of the corn."

"Mama Dara!"

Kundze's eyes widened, and she nodded. "Yes."

"Do you remember me?" Annie asked.

Kundze looked at her closely. "I remember there was a little girl."

50

THE LOW HALL

Annie's father was slumped over a pile of pink papers filled with his handwriting.

"Papa?" Annie said.

He didn't move. Annie put a hand on his shoulder—so thin, so bony! She shook him gently. "Papa?"

He stirred, blinked, and raised his head. "Kundze?"

"No. It's me. Annie."

"Annike. Of course. I must have been dreaming." He pushed himself upright in his wheelchair and dragged a withered hand across his eyes. "Is it morning?"

"It's night, Papa. Time to go to bed."

He squinted at the sheaf of pages and shook his head. "I have work."

"I talked to Mama."

He looked at her through clouded eyes.

"I remember her now," Annie said.

Papa stared down at his lap, saying nothing.

"I talked to Queen Zurka, too."

"What did she say?"

Annie almost said, *She said you don't deserve to live and she's sending you back to America.* But she couldn't do it. "She said we will talk tomorrow."

"Good." He tried to pick up his pen, but his fingers were too stiff and gnarled. "I have to finish." He clawed at the pen and knocked it off the table.

"You should rest. Lie down for just a bit." Annie pulled his chair back from the table. Papa didn't argue. She wheeled him over to the bed. "Can you stand?"

"I think so." He leaned forward, put his feet on the floor, and slowly stood. Annie held his elbow to steady him. He shifted his feet and lowered himself to the mattress. Annie lifted his legs and swung them onto the bed.

"Just for a few minutes," he mumbled. "I have work to do." He sighed and his body seemed to sink into the mattress. Moments later, he was asleep.

Annie watched his chest rise and fall. She listened to the sound of air rattling in and out of his open mouth. He had lost two more teeth and much of his hair. Tears ran down her cheeks. She didn't bother to wipe them away. She didn't want Papa to be old. She didn't want him to die. Even if what Queen Zurka said was true—that he had lived far longer than he deserved. That he was responsible for what had happened to her mother. That he had used the *zurkas* to keep her from growing up. But he was her papa—how could she leave him like this? She thought about his strong arms and his beautiful smile and his thick hair and his eyes filled with life. As angry as she was, she wanted that version of Papa to come back.

She wiped her eyes with her sleeve and flipped through the many pages covered with his spidery scrawl. What sins and secrets had he confessed? She wished she could read Litvanian, but at the same time, she was glad she could not. She gathered up the filled pages, rolled them up, tucked them in her sleeve, and went back to her room.

Annie did not sleep. She tossed and turned on the softest and most comfortable bed she had ever experienced and struggled to rein in the whirlwind of thoughts and feelings. She could not imagine what her life would be like with no home, without Papa, without anybody. Her mother was a child, her great-grandmother was hundreds of years old, and Ozols . . . did Ozols think Papa should be left to die? Just because more than a hundred years ago he had stolen two rats?

There was no clock in her room, but there was a window. The moon was full and rising, its light beaming into the room. She watched the light move slowly down the wall, watched it until it was a patch on the floor. She waited until the moon was above the castle, out of sight, then went to the door and looked out. The hallway was empty, dimly lit by wall sconces. She stepped out of her room and listened to the echoey silence. The castle was asleep.

A secret doorway behind her throne, the queen had said. Annie didn't remember seeing a door behind the throne, but maybe she just hadn't noticed.

After a few wrong turns, she found the Low Hall. The only light came from the moon shining through some slit windows high on the walls. A tapestry hung behind the throne. The space behind the tapestry was only a few inches deep. Annie felt her way along the back wall; the tapestry dragged against her back. She couldn't see at all. She came out of the far end of the tapestry without finding anything but cobwebs. No door.

Maybe there was another throne room—a *high* hall. She was about to leave when she heard footsteps. She slipped back behind the tapestry. Someone entered the hall. Peeking around the edge of the tapestry, she saw a guard coming straight toward her, carrying a lantern. She ducked back and held her breath. She heard the guard step up onto the dais, then pause. More sounds—he was very close.

A faint spot of light revealed a small tear in the tapestry. Annie put her eye to the hole. The guard was sitting on the throne. She hoped he couldn't hear the beating of her heart.

The guard said something in Litvanian, then replied to himself in a stern voice and laughed. Annie was confused for a moment, then realized that the guard had been imitating Queen Zurka.

The guard got off the throne and left the room through the doorway to the right. Annie waited half a minute to get her breathing under control. The guard probably had a nightly routine, moving from room to room, making sure everything was secure. It would be better to follow him than to go another way and risk running into him head-on, so she took the right-hand passageway. That took her through a large, formal dining hall. She heard a metallic scraping sound coming from a room off to the side. The guard was in the kitchen making himself a midnight snack. She backed into an alcove and waited. The guard was humming. She smelled bacon frying and heard the clanking of utensils.

Finally, after about twenty minutes, the guard finished eating and moved on. Annie followed. She was approaching an intersection, trying to figure out which way the guard had gone, when a shadow detached itself from the wall and a hand fell on her shoulder.

Annie let out a squeak.

"*Vaika!*" said the guard, his hand clamped firmly on her shoulder. He took a close look at her and raised his eyebrows. "You are American girl," he said, switching to English. "Why you sneak like noisy mouse?"

"I'm not a mouse. I couldn't sleep. I was just taking a walk."

"In middle of night? I think you snoop."

"I wasn't snooping."

"You snoop. I report you."

"You sat on Queen Zurka's throne!"

The guard released her and drew back, startled.

"I heard you pretending you were her."

The guard scowled. "You hear nothing."

"Maybe *I* will report *you*! Are you supposed to make food in the kitchen?"

"Just a little *uzkod*," the guard said sheepishly. "A snack. I get hungry some time."

"I bet you sat on her *other* throne, too."

The guard glanced down the hallway to the left. "No. I would not ever. Not in the High Hall."

So there *was* another throne, and the High Hall was probably in the direction the guard had looked.

"I not report you," the guard said. "But you go back to your room."

"Okay," Annie said. "Then I won't report you, either."

Annie headed back in the direction of her bedroom. She could feel the guard watching her. As soon as she turned the first corner, she stopped and waited, then peeked back around the corner. The guard was gone. She headed back past the kitchen and took the other passageway.

51

THE AVATUS

If the Low Hall resembled a small country church, the High Hall was like a cathedral. Moonlight flooded in through a domed, leaded-glass skylight. There was room for hundreds of people. The dais at the head of the room was as tall as Annie, and the gold filigree and gem-encrusted throne was as big as a car. Annie walked straight up the center aisle, feeling very small in the enormous space. She climbed the nine shallow steps and paused before the throne. The seat itself was cushioned velvet. It looked black in the reflected moonlight, but she suspected it would be purple or maroon in daylight. The piping around the edges was frayed.

Unable to resist, Annie stepped up onto the footrest and lowered herself onto the throne. For such a big, gaudy piece of furniture, it was quite comfortable. She looked out over the room and imagined it full of people. She took a deep breath and let it out slowly, feeling powerful and special. Was this how Queen Zurka felt when she sat here?

The velvet armrests were a little too high for her, and their shape was odd. She noticed a shiny gold button on each of the armrests. She touched the left one and a drawer slid out over her lap. In the drawer was a stack of deckle-edged ivory-colored stationery. She pressed the button on the right. A tray swung out. In the tray were a set of quill pens, an inkwell, and assorted other items. Annie pushed shut the tray and the drawer and climbed down off the throne.

Ten feet behind the throne was a heavy curtain. Annie went to the side and stepped behind it. An arched opening led to a short hallway with two doors on each side and one at the end. None of them looked like "secret" doors. Annie returned to the throne room and noticed a wooden rectangle set into the floor directly behind the throne. She stepped on it and felt it give slightly. A trapdoor? She tried to fit her fingers in the space between the wood and the solid stone floor around it. It was too tight. She thought about the buttons on the armrests, and searched the back of the throne for something similar.

There, at one side of the throne's back. A gold button. She pressed it. The wooden section of the floor slowly rose with a faint grinding sound, revealing a steep staircase illuminated by yellow wall sconces. Annie waited to see if the guard or anyone else had detected the noise. She heard only her own breathing.

With a pounding heart, Annie descended the iron steps, holding tightly to the cold metal handrail. The stairs went down for about twenty steps, then began to curve in a spiral. The air grew damper, and a familiar smell filled her nostrils. Like the storm sewers of Pond Tree Acres, it smelled of decaying leaves, old socks, and wet dog.

The spiral ended at a stone passageway dimly lit by wall sconces every few yards. There were rooms off to the sides of the passage—small, bare, unoccupied rooms closed off with barred doors. The dungeon! Annie shuddered, imagining how awful it would be to spend days or years in one of these dank, dark cells. She continued on, peering into each cell. They were all the same except for variations in the ancient stains on their stone walls.

At the end of the passageway was another staircase leading down, again lit by the dim yellow sconces. The wet-animal smell was stronger. Annie forced herself to go on. She counted the steps to calm herself. At step number thirty-two she reached the bottom—a short passage that led to an arched, open doorway.

Even before she entered the chamber, Annie knew what she would find.

Queen Zurka's *avatus* was stunning. It was the queen in her prime, wearing a simple robe that revealed the youthful curves of her body. She looked alive, except for the fact that she was the color of ivory, like a marble statue from ancient Greece. But Annie knew that this was not a figure carved from stone—it was made of the ivory-colored pages from the hidden drawer in Queen Zurka's throne. Thousands of pages. Centuries of pages. Every regrettable act, every slight, every sin the queen had committed.

The chamber was illuminated by electric candles set into shallow wall niches. Two marble benches faced the *avatus*. The floor was spotless, not covered in leaves and sticks and scraps of paper like there had been around Papa's *avatus*.

"Hello?" she said.

The stone absorbed her words. She heard a faint squeak, and the scrabble of claws. Rats emerged from cracks and crevices she hadn't even noticed. The *zurkas* were black, with bright pink tails and noses and glittering yellow teeth. Rats flowed from the walls like syrup, dozens of them. Annie's heart thumped—she could feel it in her throat. They kept coming. Hundreds of them, chirring and squeaking, surrounding the base of the statue as if to protect it. The *zurkas* seemed almost to be one creature with a multitude of shiny black eyes, every one of them fixed on her.

"My father needs your help," Annie said, her voice shaking. She pulled the roll of pink pages from her sleeve and held them out. "These are his words, his regrets. I can't read them, but I'm sure he is sorry for taking two of you to a land far away across the ocean, many years ago. Maybe you don't even remember, but he does, and he is sorry."

Annie set the papers on the stone floor. The rats moved toward her, a living carpet of black fur, shiny eyes, and pink tails.

"She is very pretty," Annie said. "Your queen. It is a beautiful statue."

The rats came closer, swarming over the papers, chittering angrily. Annie took several steps back. The rats kept coming.

"I just want my papa back," Annie said. Her voice cracked as her back hit the wall. The stairs were only a few feet to her right, but the rats had her blocked off. Annie jumped onto the stone bench to her left. The rats surrounded the bench, clawing at the legs, climbing over one another. She could see and hear their teeth gnashing.

"*Vaika!*" The word split the air like the crack of a whip. Queen Zurka stepped from the stairwell. She wore a long robe covered with a complex design—a chain of golden, embroidered rats holding on to one another's tails. The carpet of rats flowed away from Annie and gathered around the queen's feet like a black, pink-tailed fringe to her robe.

The queen frowned at Annie. "They sense that you are responsible for the deaths of their distant relatives, even though it happened half a world away."

"It was an accident." Annie's voice quavered, and her legs were shaking. The *zurkas'* tails were lashing back and forth. It was all she could do to remain standing.

"You may get down. Benches are for sitting, not standing. My *zurkas* will not harm you so long as I am present."

Annie climbed down slowly off the bench. She couldn't tear her eyes away from the mass of rodents.

"Azit!" the queen commanded. The *zurkas* moved away from her feet and melted silently back into their cracks and crevices, leaving Annie and the queen alone with the *avatus*.

After a long pause, the queen said, in a softer voice, "You thought to do a good thing for your father. You are young and foolish."

Both those things were true, but that didn't make what she had done *wrong*. Annie was able to nod.

"You did not think my *sarga* would report to me?" the queen asked.

Annie looked up at the queen's face and felt a flash of anger. The guard had promised not to tell on her.

"He . . . he made a snack for himself in the kitchen," she managed to get out. Her voice sounded thin and desperate to her own ears. "He sat on your throne."

"*Sargas* get hungry. That is not a serious offense. As for sitting upon my throne, who would not want to know what it feels like to be queen? I'm sure you did the same."

Annie had no reply to that.

"Do you like my *avatus*?" the queen asked.

"It's very beautiful," Annie said.

"It is my ideal self—Queen Zurka as I would wish her to be. It is perfect. My *zurkas* have little to do now. These years have taught me that perfection is an illusion. I have learned to face my sins, and to live with them. I sense that you have learned this as well."

Annie nodded.

"You are wiser than I was at your age. Tell me, child, what do you imagine for your future?"

"I imagine you will let your *zurkas* fix Papa, and then we will go home."

"You have no home."

"Papa will build a new house."

"You exhaust me, child. Even if I were to allow your father to . . . *cicenja* . . . he would not be as you remember. The *zurkas* do not confer immortality. They only slow time. We all grow old eventually. We all die."

"But couldn't it make him better?"

"Somewhat, perhaps. Would you like to hear a story?"

Annie thought for a moment, then said, "No, thank you. I've had enough Litvanian stories. They always end badly."

The queen laughed. "You are more grown-up than you know. But this story is very short, and it is no fairy tale." She sat on one of the benches and gestured for Annie to sit beside her.

"As you know, Litvania is a queendom. In all of our recorded history, we have never had a king. Our rules of succession state that the throne passes from the queen to the queen's eldest daughter. Alas, my firstborn daughter, Alyssa, died giving birth to Vaira, her second child. And so it was that Alyssa's elder daughter, Kundze, was to be elevated upon my death. Unfortunately, your father beguiled her. Kundze defied me and went with him to America, where she was . . . well, you know what happened.

"Over the years I have learned patience. I would happily wait for Kundze to grow into the woman she may one day become, but I fear my time is coming sooner rather than later. Do you understand what I am telling you?"

"No," Annie said.

"You are Kundze's firstborn child. When I die, it is you who must take the throne."

52

THE CHOICE

Annie said, "What?"

She thought she must have heard wrong. Either that, or the queen was teasing her.

"Are your ears not working?"

"You want *me* to be queen?"

"When I pass, yes."

"But isn't Ozols your granddaughter?"

"Vaira was not firstborn."

"I'm only eleven!"

"I am not leaving this life quite yet." The queen smiled, and for just a moment she looked younger. "We will have a few years to get to know each other."

"No, we won't!" Annie felt herself getting mad, but she didn't care—it was better than being scared. "I'm going home with Papa, and you can't make me stay."

The queen rose to her feet and glared down at her. "You forget to whom you are speaking."

Annie stood and faced the queen, anger blotting out her fear. "I don't care who you are. You can't make me do anything."

"Bah!" The queen threw up her hands. "You are as stubborn and foolish as your mother. I can see I will be forced to negotiate. What do you want?"

"I told you! I want to go home. And I want to make Papa better."

"Which do you want more?" asked the queen.

"Both!"

"You must choose. One or the other. Choose, and I will grant your wish."

"I can't," Annie said.

"You can. I make difficult decisions every day. You must learn to do the same."

Annie thought furiously. It sounded like the queen would let her and Papa go home, but without letting Papa *cicenja*. He was so sick and frail! Annie knew she couldn't take care of him alone.

"If we go home, will Ozols come, too?"

"No," said the queen. "Vaira has decided to remain in Litvania."

"If you let Papa *cicenja*, then what?"

"He will go back to America and you will remain here. With me. With Ozols. With your mother."

"For how long?" she asked. "How long would I have to stay?"

"For as long as I wish it. Or until I die. Once you become queen, you can do as you wish."

"But you might live another hundred years!"

"That is unlikely. Now you must choose."

Annie drew a shaky breath and looked at the pile of pink pages on the floor: all of the bad things her father had done, from stealing the *zurkas* to letting them destroy her mother's mind to trying to stop her from growing up. Without the *zurkas'* magic, he would die soon. Queen Zurka said he had already lived more life than he deserved, but who was she to say? If Papa didn't have his *zurkas* anymore, would he still do bad things? And what about her mother?

"We all deserve another chance," Annie said under her breath.

"What was that?" said the queen, leaning forward.

Annie cleared her throat. "I said, *I choose.*"

The sun was rising when Papa finally stirred.

Annie had been sitting beside his bed for hours, dozing

in her chair, waking frequently to check on him. Below, in the deepest chamber of the castle, the *zurkas* were hard at work, chewing sheets of pink paper and forming them into an *avatus*. Papa's *avatus* would not be as tall as Queen Zurka's. Hers was built on centuries of regrets. But maybe even a small *avatus* would be enough to bring back the Papa she knew.

He still looked frighteningly old. The queen had warned her—the *zurkas* could do only so much. But his wrinkles were fewer, his skin looked less ashen, and when he opened his eyes, they were clear and bright.

"Papa?" Annie said.

He cleared his throat. "Annike."

"How do you feel?"

He sat up and swung his legs over the edge of the bed.

"Do you want your chair?"

"No." He stood up and walked over to the table where his papers had been spread out. He turned to Annie. "What have you done?"

"I *cicenjaed* you."

"I wasn't finished!"

Annie said, "Last night you couldn't even pick up your pen."

He clenched and unclenched his wrinkled and age-spotted hands. They were the hands of an old man, but far better than the crabbed and twisted claws they had been last night. He moved to the window and gazed out at the sun rising over the city of Zük.

"Queen Zurka says you have to leave today," Annie said.

Papa nodded. "We will start over. We will rebuild our house."

"I can't come with you," Annie said.

"Of course you can!"

"No, Papa. I'm staying here. With Mama."

Papa stared at her, his gap-toothed mouth hanging open.

"She remembers me," Annie said.

"Does she remember *me*?" he asked.

"I don't know. I don't think so."

Papa's shoulders sagged. He shuffled back to the bed and sat down. "I'd like to see her."

"The queen has forbidden it," said Ozols, who had appeared in the doorway. She entered the room, followed by two guards. "She does not want to upset Kundze."

"I demand an audience with the queen!"

"She will not see you, Lukas," said Ozols. "What is done is done. Annie will be safe here with me and her mother."

"She is my daughter!"

"I am sorry, Lukas." The two guards stepped forward. "There is a car waiting to take you to the airport."

53.
THE WAY OF THINGS

Happy Birthday, Annike!

I am well. Our new home is almost finished.
You will hardly notice a difference! Except,
of course, the new house will have no tower.
Still, it is enough house for me, and for
you, when you return home.

I have sold all of my rental properties. I
am staying with Mr. Wendell during the
construction. He and I have become good
friends.

Your friend Arthur stopped by to watch the

builders. He asked about you. I told him
you are planning to come home soon. Are
you? It has been nearly two years.

I miss you.

Papa

Annie read the letter twice. Nearly two years? Had it
really been so long? She put the letter in her desk drawer
with all of Papa's other letters, took out a sheet of ivory-
colored royal stationery, and picked up a pen.

Dear Papa,

I'm glad that you are well. I would love to
see your new house. Can you send me a
picture? Queen Zurka is keeping me very
busy here. I am learning to speak Litvanian,
and all about history and other things.

Annie set down her pen and thought. Pond Tree Acres,
the house with the tower, the fire . . . all that seemed like a
faraway dream to her now. Just as Litvania had once been
a dream. She did want to see Papa, but she had made a

bargain with Queen Zurka. And had to stay in Litvania.
She picked up her pen and added to her letter.

> One of my jobs here is to help teach English
> to the other children. Usually, I just read them
> stories.
>
> Please say hi to Mr. Wendell, and Arthur, and
> everybody else. I will come visit when I can, but
> it may be a while.
>
> Your daughter,
>
> Annie

Annie sealed the letter in an envelope and left it at the door for the Royal Post.

"Once upon a time, there was a little girl who wanted to grow up, but her father put a secret spell on her so she couldn't." Annie looked at the three girls who were sitting before her: Aleska, Beata, and Kundze.

"Why?" Beata asked.

"So that she would stay a little girl," Kundze said.

"Was her papa *noudabis*?" asked Beata.

"English, Beata," Annie said.

"Um . . . was he *bad man?*"

"No, at least he didn't think so. Even good people do bad things."

"Did the little girl ever grow up?" Beata asked.

"Yes! She found out about the spell, and undid it so she could grow up. But before she could grow up completely, she and her father were swept away to a far-off land, where the girl discovered that she was a princess, and that one day she would become queen. The girl was not happy, at least not at first, because becoming the queen of a strange new country meant she had to leave her home, her friends, and the world she knew. She had to learn a new language, and study numbers, and most of all, learn to tell people things they did not wish to hear."

"Why, Annike?" Kundze asked.

"Because it is the way of things," Annie said.

"Why couldn't her friends come with her?" Beata asked.

"I suppose they had their own lives to live."

"But that's not fair," said Aleska.

"No," Annie said, "it is not."

"What happened to her *tevis?*"

"*Father*, Aleska. We must speak English here."

"Why?"

"Because the queen has decreed that you are all to learn better English, just as I have to learn to speak *Litvanjis*. As for the father, he grew old and returned to his home to live alone with his regrets."

"Did the princess get to be queen?" Beata asked.

"Not yet, but one day she will." *I am only thirteen,* she thought. *Too young to be a queen.*

"Is this a fairy tale?" Aleska asked.

"I suppose it is. Maybe someday, when the story is told over and over, it will be in a book."

"Please do not let us interrupt," said Queen Zurka, who had appeared in the doorway with one of her *sargas*.

"I was just telling a story," Annie said.

"Have you reached the end of your tale?"

"Yes." Annie stood and helped Kundze to her feet. Her mother was still taller than her, but not by much.

"Excellent!" said the queen. "We would ask you to attend assizes. There are several petitions being brought before us. A dispute over a prize steer that broke through a neighbor's fence, a request for a marriage annulment, a widow whose late husband ran behind on his taxes without telling her, and a request to extend delivery times on the Royal Guard's new livery. It should be both fascinating and educational."

And deadly dull, Annie thought, but she said, "Of course, Your Majesty, I would be delighted." As they walked to the Low Hall, she noticed that the queen held tightly to the arm of her guard. Over the past two years, she had grown increasingly frail. Annie was worried about her.

54

THE PRINCESS
AND THE *ZURKA*

Queen Zurka grew even more unsteady as the months and years passed, but her mind remained sharp. "I will live until the day you are ready to take my place," she told Annie.

Annie grew to love Litvania. She made friends with several of the young people who lived in and around the castle, and got to know the shops and the citizens of Zük. The queen named her the Royal Tutor and assigned her to teach all the children who lived in the castle. Annie enjoyed teaching, and found that she learned as much as the children.

She thought of her father often. She tried to stay mad at him because it was easier to be mad than it was to miss him. He had stolen the rats, and the rats had stolen her mother's mind, and it was all his fault. He had tried to keep her from growing up. If he'd had his way, she would still be stuck in the body of a ten-year-old girl.

But he was still her papa. He wrote less and less often, and his handwriting grew worse with each letter. Sometimes they were hard to read, but she always wrote back.

Papa had moved into his new house. He said they had several new neighbors. Arthur and Fiona were still there, but the Dennisons had moved away. A few months earlier, Mr. Wendell suffered a heart attack while working in his yard and had to move to a nursing home. Papa said there was a FOR SALE sign on his front lawn.

On the morning of Annie's sixteenth birthday, Queen Zurka summoned her to her chambers. The queen rarely left her bed these days, so Annie was surprised to find her standing at the window looking out over the city. Annie joined her.

"It is lovely, is it not?" said the queen.

"It is," Annie said. The colorful roofs of Zük glittered with dew in the morning light. A cool mist blanketed the valleys beyond. It was truly beautiful.

"It pleases me that you like it." The queen took her arm. "I would like to visit my *avatus*," she said. "Will you walk with me?"

"Now?"

"It is as good a time as any."

Annie had not seen the queen's *avatus* since the day she brought Papa's papers to the *zurkas*.

Stefan was waiting attentively outside. The queen waved him away and clasped Annie's arm. They walked slowly through the castle, stopping frequently to rest. The queen weighed nothing, so thin and frail had she become. *It might be easier to pick her up and carry her,* Annie thought.

"You are taller already than I ever was," the queen said, as if reading Annie's thoughts.

"It is Miss Mekas's *koldunys,*" Annie said.

The queen laughed.

When they reached the High Hall, she asked Annie to help her up onto the throne. Once seated, she gazed out over the empty hall with a sad smile on her wizened features.

"So many memories." The queen settled back into the cushioned velvet. The throne was large enough for three of her, but she filled it with the force of her personality. "Would you like to hear a story, *liel mazbe?*"

"Yes, Vanamama." Annie sat at the foot of the throne. Queen Zurka's stories could be lengthy.

"Once upon a time, there was a princess who wanted to live forever . . . Have I told you this one?"

"Is it the story about the princess and the mirror? Ozols read that one to me."

"No. 'The Princess and the Mirror' is a fairy tale about the consequences of excessive vanity. This is a different story, about . . . well . . . a different sort of vanity."

"Is it a true story or a fairy tale?"

"Like all the best stories, it is both. Now listen. One day a princess sneaked into the kitchen to steal one of the blueberry tarts that the baker had left to cool on the sideboard. Alas, a *zurka* who lived behind the pantry had the same thought. It was sitting right in the middle of the tray, as big and fat as you please, with blueberry filling dribbling from its whiskers.

"'Hello,' said the princess, who loved all furry things, even those with naked tails. The creature wiped its whiskers with its paws and looked back at her without speaking, for *zurkas*, clever as they are, cannot speak the language of humans.

"Suddenly, the princess heard a scream of rage. One of the cooks had come into the kitchen and snatched up a cleaver. The cook swung the cleaver at the *zurka*. The princess threw herself between them, and instead of chopping the *zurka* in two, the blade bit deep into the princess's arm." The queen paused and rubbed her forearm with her hand.

"Was she killed?" Annie asked.

"No, but she nearly lost her arm. Later that day, of course, the cook lost her head, as it was frowned upon to attack a princess with a cleaver, even though it was an accident. The princess lost a great deal of blood, and the wound became infected. For many long days she lay in bed, delirious with fever and pain, her throbbing arm wrapped in bloodstained bandages. 'Am I going to die?' she asked the queen. The queen shook her head sadly and said, 'I do not know. It is possible.' The princess asked the Royal Physician, 'Am I going to die?' The physician said, 'Perhaps. We shall see.'

"One night the princess woke to find a *zurka* perched upon her chest. She thought she was dreaming, or hallucinating. 'Are you real?' she asked the *zurka*. The *zurka* squeaked, and to her amazement the princess understood that it was laughing.

"She asked the *zurka*, 'Am I going to die?'

"The *zurka* chirred, and the princess understood what it was saying: *Do you want to die?*

" 'No!' the princess exclaimed.

" 'Very well,' squeaked the *zurka*. 'I will show you how you might live.'

"The creature hopped off the bed and scampered to the door. It stopped and looked back at the princess and chittered insistently. The princess understood that it was waiting for her. She followed the *zurka* out of her chamber and down the hallway."

The queen gripped the arms of her throne and pulled herself forward. Annie reached out and helped her stand.

The queen continued. "The *zurka* led the young princess to the High Hall and showed her a secret door behind the throne."

They walked around the throne, the queen gripping Annie's arm tightly. She pressed the button and the trap-door lifted, revealing the illuminated staircase. As they made their way slowly down the steps, the queen continued her story.

"As the *zurka* hopped down the steps before her, the princess thought about the stories she had heard of dark magic concealed deep beneath the castle. She was afraid, but her bandaged, throbbing arm reminded her that life was short. Both her mother and the Royal Physician had said she might die of her wound. The *zurka* had promised her life, so she followed."

"Were there prisoners in these cages then?" Annie asked as they passed the row of empty cells.

"No. The dungeons had long been empty."

They descended the final staircase and soon stood before the *avatus*. The queen lowered herself to one of the marble benches. Annie noticed a misshapen lump of pink paper next to the queen's *avatus*—the unfinished *avatus* of her father. It looked like a giant, dried-up wad of bubble gum. She saw something else she had not noticed before—the left arm of the queen's *avatus* had a ragged scar just below its elbow.

"Were you the princess?"

"Of course—have you not been listening?" The queen sat on the bench and continued. "I had heard the old tales, so I was not surprised when the *zurka* who brought me here was joined by the others." She fell silent for a moment. "You know the rest. I used the *zurkas'* magic to heal my wound, to cleanse my conscience, to extend my life far beyond what nature intended."

As the queen spoke, a single rat poked its nose out from a crack in the wall. Its muzzle was gray. Its whiskers drooped. It oozed out from the crack and plopped to the floor, where it regarded Annie and the queen with clouded eyes.

"Did your mother have an *avatus*?" Annie asked.

"My mother did not like *zurkas*, and she believed the life she was given at birth was sufficient. She lived a normal life span and had no regrets. I was different. I was greedy for life. I wanted to live forever." She sighed and shook her head. "My mother was a wise woman. I have lived, perhaps, too long."

They sat without speaking. The queen's eyes were closed, her face deathly pale, her head tipped back and resting on the wall behind the stone bench. For a moment, Annie feared she had died.

"Vanamama?"

Eyes still closed, the queen spoke. "In my grand-parents' day, there was much magic in the land. Those days are long gone. Only vestiges remain with the *zurkas*, and now they, too, are leaving us." She opened her eyes. "You see this *zurka*? He is among the last of his kind." The queen smiled. "You will make a good ruler, Annike. I envy you the precious, spectacular years you have yet to live."

Her face went slack. Her eyes did not close, but they saw no more. The *zurka* turned and squeezed its body back into the crack in the wall.

"Vanamama?"

The queen was dead.

55.
POND TREE ACRES

Six weeks later, a limousine, black with tinted windows and diplomatic license plates, turned off the highway and rolled to a stop at the head of Klimas Avenue. The driver climbed out and opened the passenger door.

"Thank you, Guntis," Annie said as she stepped out of the car.

"It is my pleasure to serve, Your Majesty," Guntis said in Litvanian. Guntis could not bring himself to call her Annie, though she had asked him to do so. She still wasn't used to the way people treated her now.

Annie ducked her head back into the car. "Do you want to come?" she asked.

"You go ahead," Ozols said. "I'll wait here with Guntis."

Annie reached into the back seat and pulled out a

·shoulder bag. "I won't be long." Annie slung the bag over her shoulder and squinted in the bright autumn sun. Pond Tree Acres had changed. The street looked narrower. The trees were taller. The vacant lots had been filled with new houses. There were three little kids playing on the street. She wondered if one them was Arthur, then reminded herself that Arthur would be five years older now.

She started down the street. Fiona's house hadn't changed except for the little maple tree, twice as tall now and resplendent with bright red fall foliage.

Annie paused in front of Arthur's house, hoping he would look out the window and see her, but he didn't. The kids playing on the street noticed her and came running up—twin boys, maybe six years old, and a younger girl who looked as if she might be their sister.

"Who are *you*?" one of the identical boys asked.

Annie smiled and said, "I am the Queen of Litvania."

The boy's eyes widened, then narrowed. "No, you're not!"

"Yes, I am," Annie said.

The little girl said, "I'm a princess."

Annie laughed. "I can tell! We royalty always recognize each other!"

"I'm a prince," said the boy who had not yet spoken.

"No, you're not!" said his brother.

"Am, too!" The boy pushed his brother and took off running. His brother chased him down the street.

"What are you *wearing?*" the little girl asked.

Annie looked down at her outfit: a black silk shirt beneath her mother's embroidered *slibininka* and soft, goat-leather, knee-high boots with sterling silver toe caps. In Litvania, such garb was considered proper for royalty. She had almost forgotten how normal people dressed.

"These are my clothes," she said.

The girl was circling her, checking her out from all sides.

"Is that a flying snake?" she asked, looking at the twelve-winged dragon on the back of the vest.

"It's a dragon," Annie said.

"It's very pretty."

"Thank you." Annie pointed at the twins, who were wrestling in Mr. Wendell's front yard. "I think you should see to your brothers before they hurt each other." The house had been painted blue. The front yard was littered with bicycles and kids' toys, and the bushes were shaggy and unkempt. Annie hoped Mr. Wendell would never see what had happened to his immaculate yard.

The girl ran off to join her brothers.

Annie turned to look at the place she had once called home. No traces of the burned-down house remained. In its place was a new house that looked exactly like their old house, but without the tower. The row of pine trees was still there, as was Mr. O'Connor's cornfield and the picnic table—although one of the benches had collapsed. The lawn was neatly mown, but there were no flowers or other plantings. Papa's car was parked in the driveway, covered with leaves. One of the tires was flat.

Annie walked up onto the porch of the new house and pressed the doorbell. She waited. When no one answered, she turned the knob. The door was unlocked. She stepped inside.

The door opened directly into the living room, as before, but the room was bare of furniture.

"Papa?" she called out.

From the back of the house, she heard a croak that might have been her name. She followed the sound down the short hallway to the library. The blinds were drawn. The bookshelves were empty. The room smelled stale. There was a bed with rumpled covers, and a reclining chair with a single occupant.

"Papa?"

"Annike." His voice sounded as if he were speaking through a mask of dry corn husks. "You have grown."

"I'm sixteen now, Papa." Annie opened the window blinds; light flooded the room.

Papa winced. "Too bright," he said.

Annie closed the blinds halfway and looked at her father. He had left Litvania five years ago looking like a reasonably healthy man in his seventies. He now appeared to be much, much older. Most of his hair was gone. The whites of his eyes were yellow. A network of blue veins showed through papery skin.

"This is where you sleep now?" she asked.

"The stairs are difficult for me," he said. "My world has grown smaller."

"What do you do with yourself all day?"

"I sleep a lot. I listen to radio. I live with my regrets. I think about you." He peered at her. "You look like your mother. How is she? Does she remember me?"

"She remembers some things. She remembers the rats, but she has never mentioned you."

Papa sighed, a long, rattling exhalation, and sank deeper into his recliner. Annie sat on the edge of his bed and stared at the shell of the man who was her father. After five years, she thought that she had forgiven him. She had thought that seeing him would bring her peace. But this brought her no peace. She could feel the repressed anger gnawing at her insides.

"Papa, I have a question. Why? Why did you try to keep me from growing up?"

"I just . . . I wanted your childhood to last."

"But why?"

"I wanted your mother to see you as you were. I wanted you to stay a little girl so that when Kundze grew up . . . when she recovered . . . she could see you as a mother sees her child. I wanted you to be happy."

"I was not happy."

Papa's head dropped.

Annie looked away from him, at the empty bookshelves. "You have no books."

"They burned, as you well know. I have magazines." He gestured at the pile of old magazines next to his chair. "Reading is difficult for me. I look at the pictures."

Annie pulled back the flap on her shoulder bag and took out the book of Litvanian fairy tales. "I brought this with me to Litvania." She crossed the room and placed it on the shelf. "Now it is back again."

Neither of them spoke for many long seconds. The silence became uncomfortable. Annie didn't know what to say. Finally, she spoke.

"Would you like to hear a story?"

"A Litvanian story?" he asked.

"Yes."

Papa shifted in his chair and pulled his lap blanket up over his chest.

Annie began, telling the story from memory, in Litvanian. *"Sen zenos laitkos . . ."*

✦ . . . there was a boy who stole an egg. The farmer, alerted by the squawking of his hen, took up a pitchfork and chased after the boy, who sought refuge amongst the tall trees of the Great Forest.

No one knew where the Great Forest ended. The trees grew so close together they blocked the sun. Noon was dark as night, and night was blacker than the blackest molasses. The boy soon lost his way. Day after day, he threaded his way between the enormous tree trunks, living on nuts and seeds and berries and mushrooms.

One day the boy looked into a hole in a tree and discovered a nest containing three little brown-speckled eggs. Delighted, he ate them on the spot. As he was cracking the last egg into his mouth, a small owl landed on a low branch above him and let out a furious screech.

The boy looked up and said, "Hello."

"Hello yourself, you wicked, gluttonous beast!"

"I am no beast," the boy objected, taken

aback by the bird's fury.

"If you are not a beast, then why have you devoured my future children?"

"I was hungry," said the boy. He jumped up and grabbed the owl by her legs. The bird screeched and flapped and pecked, but the boy just laughed. "I will be hungry again soon, and you are a very tasty-looking morsel." He pushed the owl down into his jacket pocket.

"Wait!" screeched the owl. "I will make you a bargain."

"Bargain? What have you to bargain with?"

"Eggs," said the owl.

"I have already eaten all your eggs."

"I can make more. If you spare me, you will have an egg for your breakfast every morning, and I will guide you through the forest."

The boy considered the owl's offer. "How do I know you won't just fly away?"

"I give you my solemn oath, which will bind me to you until we reach the edge of the woods."

"How do I know I can trust you?"

"It is well-known that owls cannot lie."

And so the boy set off through the trees with

the owl perched on his shoulder. For days and days they wandered. Every morning the owl produced a warm, brown-speckled egg for the boy's breakfast, then soared high above the treetops to search for the edge of the forest.

Days became weeks, and still they were as lost as ever.

"If we continue, sooner or later, we will find our way," the owl said.

"I trust you," said the boy, "as owls cannot lie."

In time, the boy and the owl became friends. They wandered the Great Forest together and did not think so much about leaving the trees behind.

One day as she soared over the treetops, the owl saw in the distance fields and roads and houses and barns.

"Did you see anything?" the boy asked upon her return.

The owl opened her beak to tell him what she had seen . . . but she had come to love the boy more than she loved her freedom. She did not want their journey to end.

"Trees and more trees and nothing else," the

owl said. And that was the first and last time an
owl ever told a lie. From that moment on, all the
owls lost their ability to speak.✦

Annie paused and looked at her father, who was slumped in
his recliner with his chin resting on his chest. She was wondering at what point in the story he had fallen asleep when
he lifted his head and asked, "What happened to the boy?"

"The boy and the owl continued their journey through
the Great Forest. As far as anyone knows, they are still
there."

"Is that the end?"

"It's a Litvanian story."

Papa nodded.

"Papa, you can't live like this. I am queen now. You are
no longer banished. You can come live with me. I will see
that you are cared for."

"I doubt I could survive the journey."

"You can try." Annie stood up. "I'll be flying back
tonight. Come with me."

Papa smiled, showing several missing teeth, while shaking his head slowly. "I will think about it," he said. "But
right now I need to rest." He closed his eyes and let his head
fall back against the cushion.

Annie stood and started to leave the room.

"Annike!"

She turned back. He was looking at her.

"When my time comes, I would like to be buried in Litvania."

"Yes, Papa."

He sank back into the cushioned chair. A moment later he was snoring.

Annie heard the front door open.

"Lukas? It's me!" The voice was familiar. Annie ran out to see who it was.

"Mama Dara!"

The old woman peered at her through thick eyeglasses. "Is that Annie?" she said.

"Yes!" Annie rushed forward to help her with the bag she was carrying.

"My, but you have grown!"

"It's been five years," Annie said. "You are looking remarkably well!"

Mama Dara tittered. "Thank you, dear. I'll turn one hundred and five soon, but I don't feel a day over ninety-nine."

"That's amazing!"

"I just came by to drop off your father's supper," said Mama Dara. "He likes to eat early."

"That's very kind of you."

"I make supper for Hal and myself. It's easy enough to make a bit more."

"Do you do this every day?"

"It is no trouble. How is he today?"

Annie looked over her shoulder toward the library. "He's kind of sleepy."

Mama Dara nodded. "I am due for a little nap myself, and Hal is waiting in the car. How long will you be staying?"

"I leave tonight. I have to get back to Litvania."

"Ah yes, your father told me. You have a country to rule now."

"Ozols and Miss Mekas are helping me."

"The women will take care of things. They always do."

Annie walked Mama Dara to the front door and waved at Mr. O'Connor. She went back inside to the library. Papa looked as if he had melted into his chair, his chest slowly rising and falling. She went back to the kitchen to see what Mama Dara had brought. A bacon sandwich. A plastic container of fruit salad. A brownie. Nothing that wouldn't keep for a bit.

She went outside and took in great lungfuls of the crisp autumn air. The kids who lived in Mr. Wendell's house had gone inside. Dry leaves danced along the curb and gathered at the sewer grate. A boy, tall and gangly in yellow jeans and a green sweatshirt, came strolling down the street, his freckled face framed by a wild corona of pale, orangish hair.

"Arthur!" Annie ran to him and wrapped him in a hug. "Wow, you're as big as me!"

"I'm almost twelve. I'm in middle school now!"

"Are you still finding those little statues the rats were making?"

"Not since the fire. Are you back?"

"I just came to see my father. I'm returning to Litvania tonight."

"Oh."

"You should come and visit sometime!"

"Okay. Um . . . I'll have to ask my mom. Can TomTom come?"

"TomTom?" Annie had almost forgotten about Mr. Wendell's cat.

"He lives with me now. Mr. Wendell can't have pets where he's living." Arthur looked past her. "Look who's here."

A girl dressed all in black with long black hair was coming up the street toward them.

"Who is that?" Annie asked.

"Fiona."

"Seriously?" Annie watched as Fiona drew closer. Black

leather jacket, black jeans, black lipstick, and lots of eyeliner.

"Hey," Fiona said when she was about twenty feet away. "You're back."

"I am. Just for today. You look . . . wow."

"Yeah, thanks." Fiona flipped her hair back on one side, revealing an ear studded in six places. "So, what's up? I hear you're, like, a princess now. What's that about?"

"Actually, I'm a queen," Annie said.

"Really? Do you get to wear a crown?"

"Only on special occasions."

"Cool." Fiona looked her up and down. "Cool vest. Cool boots."

"Thanks," Annie said. "It's my new style."

Fiona looked away. "So . . . me and Kellick and Rachel are going into town to hear the Riffs tonight. Want to come?"

Annie had no idea who Kellick was, or what the Riffs might be, and she certainly had no interest in seeing Rachel.

"No, thanks," she said. "I have to get back home to, you know, do queen stuff."

"Oh, okay . . . well, I gotta go. Nice to see you." She walked off.

Annie looked around for Arthur. He was over by the picnic table on his hands and knees, looking intently at something on the ground.

Annie started toward him, then changed her mind and went back into the house to check on her father.

He was still in his chair, not moving.

"Papa?" No response. She leaned over him. He was utterly still. Annie touched his neck, searching for a pulse that wasn't there. She breathed in and out through her mouth, and sat numbly in the silence for what felt like a very long time. She felt as if her soul had separated from her body. As if her body were simply a thing that she occupied, a vessel, a living *avatus*. She stood up and backed away from the husk of the ancient, flawed man who had raised her.

"Goodbye, Papa," she whispered.

She stepped out of the house and was astonished by how beautiful everything was: the green of the grass, the flame-red leaves of the maples, the blue of the sky. She took a deep breath and let it out shakily. The children were back outside, shouting and running. That would have made Mr. Wendell happy, even if his yard was a mess. She looked over toward the picnic table.

Arthur was still there, staring at the grass. Annie walked over to him.

"What are you looking at, Arthur?"

"Beetle."

Annie dropped down on her knees for a closer look.

A beetle, green with metallic gold sparkles, was moving through the grass. They watched it struggle up onto a fallen red maple leaf. The insect paused at the center of the leaf, a brilliant, sparkly green eye on a field of red.

"Look, it's showing off," Annie said.

The beetle crawled off the leaf and continued its slow journey through the forest of grass.

"Are you really going back tonight?" Arthur asked.

"Not tonight," Annie said. She thought about her father. He had asked to be buried in Litvania. She would have to make arrangements. There would be laws to follow and papers to sign and so forth—she didn't know what all that would involve, but Ozols would help her figure it out. She opened her mouth to tell Arthur that Papa had died, but nothing came out. She could tell him later.

"I'll be here for a few more days," she said.

"Good."

The beetle reached the picnic table and began to climb.

"Do you think it knows where it's going?" Annie asked.

"I doubt it," Arthur said. "But maybe it will know once it gets there."

AUTHOR'S NOTE

The imaginary country of Litvania is a tiny, isolated Baltic
state nestled between Lithuania and Latvia. The Litvanian
language is related to Lithuanian and Latvian, with Russian
and Estonian influences. Litvanian words used in this book
are approximate translations. A glossary follows.

Rat-bite fever, also known as Haverhill fever, is a real
disease, but in our world the effects are not so dramatic.

The fairy tales in this book are original, with the excep-
tions of "The Ratcatcher" and "The Golden Key," ver-
sions of which can be found in the stories collected by the
Brothers Grimm.

GLOSSARY OF LITVANIAN TERMS

aukle: nanny or caregiver

avatus: physical avatar or representation

Azit: Leave us

brolis: brother

burna: mouth

cicenja: cleanse

Kastu esa?: Who are you? / What is your name?

kolduny: stuffed pastry

Labas Dievas: Good Lord

Laipni ga Litvanja: Welcome to Litvania

liel mazbe: great-granddaughter

Litvanjis: Litvanian

mazbe: granddaughter

mokytojas: teacher

noudabis: bad, evil, sinful

nuodeema: bad thing

nuodeema burna: eater of sins

pamises: crazy

sargas: guards

Sen zenos laitkos: Once upon a time

slibinas: dragon

slibininka: traditional Litvanian dragon vest

slibliakom: dragonstone

stoobi: stupid

sveikia: hello

Ta tiessa: It is true

tanta: aunt

tevis: father

titeni: cabbage roll

uzkod: snack

Vaika: Halt

vairia: crow

vanama: grandmother

vanamama: great-grandmother

vatruka: Litvanian pastry

yah: yes

zelty maras: golden plague (rat-bite fever)

zilzem: underground tomb

Zük: the capital city of Litvania

zurka: rat

Zurkukzen: Crazy Rat Boy

ACKNOWLEDGMENTS

In alphabetical order, the following people helped make this book what it is. Any errors or omissions are entirely their fault.

Heather Bouwman helped me to understand what homeschooling is, and can be. Katie Cunningham, my editor, waded into an awkward and lumbering first draft and explained to me what story I was trying to tell. Jennifer Flannery, my agent, made it possible to publish yet another weird, genre-fluid mélange. Mary Logue, my first reader, asked the perennial question, What do your characters *want*? Nancy St. Clair provided crucial fashion advice. Kurtis Scaletta aided and abetted the murder of some hard-to-part-with darlings.

I must also give a nod to the copyeditors, who not only had to learn to speak Litvanian but also had to educate me endlessly on the proper use of was/were, who/whom, and the dreaded hyphen.

I thank you all.